INCENDIARY

CLARKE MAYER

First Published by ROGUE STORIES LLC in 2021.

ISBN: 978-1-73554-731-2

Cover Design by J Caleb Design

Editing by JD Book Services

To my parents—all four of them.

FOREWORD

––––––

It's a quiet summer night, and I'm licking barbecue sauce from my fingers after polishing off a plate of ribs with my uncle, Glenn. I usually hate the act of "finger licking," but he just makes them so damn tasty. We're lounging on a swinging chair in the front of the house, surrounded by a symphony of crickets. You know, one of those nights of summer warmth that welcomes a good folk tale. He inhales deeply from a joint, the crackling sound of a seed alerting me that he has forgotten to clean them out, once again. I let him burn it up so he'll receive the headache, rather than me. He pinches it between his dirty, oil-stained fingers, and hands it over to me. I take a hit, grimacing at the taste of the shitty dirt he likes to smoke. Distant footsteps approach.

"Hide it for a second," Glenn says.

I tuck the smoke between my legs, keeping it in my lungs as the uneven clicking and clacking sound grows closer.

"Who the hell is this?" Glenn asks. An elderly man in a dark suit limps up the sidewalk, a briefcase in hand. The sodium vapor light above casts dark shadows under his hat. He keeps his attention forward, unaware of us as he skulks up the road. There's an air of illusion that follows him, something gloomy and suspicious in nature. An essence of noir.

"D.B. Cooper," my uncle says.

"D.B. who?" I reply.

"D.B. Cooper."

"Who is D.B Cooper?" I ask as I pass him back the roach.

"Well, that's the question," he exclaims before he sucks at it again, coughing as he spews the smoke back out. "D.B. Cooper is the guy they never caught, the skyjacker. Norjack, they called it."

"What do you mean they never caught him? How did he get away?"

"He jumped," Glenn responds.

"Out of the plane?"

"Yea, with the cash."

"Cash?" I ask.

"Yea, $200,000 or something," he says.

"And they never caught him?"

"No, and they had a ton of good suspects too."

"Bullshit," I respond. "There's no way anyone could get away with anything like that."

"*He* did. Look it up," he says, stomping on the roach with a heavy boot.

———

Look it up I did. He was right. I spent that night falling down an endless wormhole of Cooper-related crime and conspiracy, hours poring over information available on websites dedicated to Cooper-sleuthing and discussion. Was he a modern-day Robin Hood? Was he the last great criminal? Was he an airline employee? Did he serve in a war? Did he know more than the pilots about the 727-100 model aircraft involved? Was he still alive? Did he survive the fall? Was he even a *man*? All that and more can be found with a few clicks of a mouse. I was enthralled.

I was always looking for story ideas, and this was something I just could not shake. I wanted to tell a story about Cooper; however, it seemed that the real estate had already been purchased, and he had been written about *ad nauseam* in non-fiction for decades. No one had ever made a movie about Cooper, and by "movie" I mean a dramatic presentation of the events that happened— perhaps even with some Hollywood flair.

I resisted reading any other books regarding the subject and decided to stick to the information I knew could be verified and easily found. If I was going to tell the story, I would try my best to write a screenplay that presented the unique thrill of the case while adhering to as much truth as I could. This presented a problem. One of the defining characteristics of both the case and its suspects is that no one could agree on the facts. The case, it seemed, had become more about rampant speculation and the pursuit of narratives surrounding the suspects— none of whom were found guilty. Because of that, it became increasingly hard to commit to the idea that one of the many suspects was in fact Cooper, and therefore, harder to tell a story.

If I was going to tell a story about Cooper, I would

fictionalize it as best I could, assigning my own traits for the skyjacker, and my own motives surrounding his feat. I began cherry-picking the details that I enjoyed the most, or those that I could at least find people tended to agree on, while adhering to the lore and allure of the infamous event. The story would revolve around the one thing that no one could seem to get right: identity. One of the most overwhelming elements of the case is the abundance of names. Names, names, and more names. There are remarkable digital encyclopedias devoted to the search for the true identity of the man known as Dan Cooper, or misrepresented by the media as D.B. Cooper. Keeping up with both the names of the suspects, as well as researchers, is exhausting. It seemed to me that this question would never have a resolution.

Another question I constantly asked myself is "why?" Not only was Cooper never caught, but the majority of the bills—save for the small number found at Tina Bar—never entered circulation. He never *used* the money. They never found his parachute, and some claim that the parachute he chose was sealed and inoperable. He *must* have died. They never found his body in the lengthy search of the drop zone, and yet they found other bodies. But no one can even *agree* on the location of the actual drop zone. Even if they found the body, could anyone even agree what he actually looked like? Did he have thick hair, or thinning, balding hair? It depended on which person aboard the fateful flight you asked. Why would he leave a tie—the one single item that would carry a vast array of identifying information—behind on the airplane? It can make your head hurt.

I developed the story into a feature-length narrative screenplay. After getting to a place I was satisfied with, of course with some dramatic elements sprinkled in to help keep readers on the edge of their seats, I couldn't help but wonder what it would be like if the story were told in novel format. Because of that, I wrote this book. Writing the book allowed me luxuries a screenplay doesn't afford, specifically those surrounding the gears that may or may not have been turning in Cooper's head. I have fictionalized many of the elements of the story to allow for a more free speculation that wouldn't be saddled with the weight of the facts—or lack thereof.

So *why* would someone do something like this? What follows is my attempt to get inside the head of a skyjacker, maybe not Cooper *per se*, but at least the mind of a desperate man with something to prove. I also considered the authorities that hunted him. It's a story that opens itself up to conjecture. Perhaps, if you are uninitiated, this story will inspire you to begin digging yourself, or if you are a seasoned Cooper pro, you might find some Easter eggs within to keep you entertained. I deeply believe that whoever Cooper was, he did not simply carry out the crime to reward himself with unusable cash. The motive was far greater. Maybe he wanted to "stick it to the man," or maybe he was a disgruntled employee. Maybe he wanted to improve airline safety. Let's imagine for a moment he wanted to create a circus, a legacy, an act so mystifying that one couldn't help but speculate on the fact or fiction for generations. Let's imagine the *perfect* crime.

These days I've become wary of continuing to investigate and navigate "NORJAK" and the mysterious case of Dan Cooper, and yet I still do even though I've got other stories to tell. I think Cooper represents more than just a who-dun-it, or even, in my case, a why-dun-it, but more so our fundamental need for answers. The questions we ask surrounding the events and the glamour around the story are rooted in our requirement for resolution, for closure. Among life's great pursuits—meaning and identity—an understanding of just what it is we are doing here drives our craving and taste for good stories, especially the kind that inspire discussion and curiosity. For over fifty years, the polite, olive-skinned man wearing the dark sunglasses and carrying a briefcase bomb at his side has made us ask "who," and I think the answer, whether or not we ever get one, will have a better chance of revealing itself if we continue to ask "why?" For now, I, like many other amateur investigators, will continue to sift through the endless materials—new information seems to pop up every few months—and yet we are unlikely to find the answers. Like the purpose of life, we will continue to search, to speculate, and to *investigate*.

Cooper, I believe, is long gone, and with him the only true proof needed to provide a definitive end to the only unsolved skyjacking in American history. It's fun to theorize, to wonder, to think maybe, just maybe, that one clue might pop up that leads us down a new rabbit hole of information. After all, anyone could be Cooper, even that mysterious limping old man with the shadowy face, walking to who-knows-where on a hot summer night when I was smoking a spliff with my uncle. Keep sleuthing, sleuths.

1

————

"No one will ever know your name." That's what Jack Gambel's mother had always told him. "You're nothing, just like your father. You're just a bird with clipped wings desperately flapping in the wind. A name means everything. A name survives long after death. Death is permanent, but a name, an identity, is forever." She was right. He *was* nothing—or so he thought. He had never *been* anything, but today was different. Today, that would change.

His plan was drastic, and his time was limited by a diagnosis he had received earlier that month. A cancer was slowly eating at his cells from the inside out, and what had started as a simple swollen gland had developed into the unstoppable spread of a microscopic militia hell-bent on conquering his body. He had never been a smoker. He had exercised regularly. He had even made it a priority to keep a balanced diet—tossing in the occasional drink for good measure.

It had bewildered him when the doctor described what lurked in his body last month, and the terminal diagnosis had sent him into a tailspin of an existential crisis. The doctor said he was lucky if he had a couple weeks, let alone a month to live. The peculiar part was that he had felt well—up until the doctor had provided the information. It was a bit like when a child scrapes a knee. The child doesn't panic until they see the expression of fear on the parent's face. The fear provides confirmation of the severity of the injury that the child might otherwise not have understood.

Fear. He had always been plagued by an unjustifiable anxiety that limited his experiences of the world. He had learned everything he was eager to know from the comfort of the small porch in the front of his childhood home. He had devoured novels full of information until the setting sun couldn't provide any more light to the rickety wood haven. One could learn a surprising amount of information about mankind by simply reading and paying attention—information that might aid them in a quest, if they chose to partake in one.

After receiving the news, Jack had secured a bottle containing a bunch of ten-milligram tablets of amphetamine sulfate from a shifty character at the local watering hole, to keep his focus. His mental acuity had been waning recently, and that was what had prompted him to visit a medical professional in the first place. The pills certainly didn't keep his battery fully charged, but they were enough to get him out of bed and continue some semblance of a normal life. Chemotherapy was not even an option presented to him, and although it confirmed how fatal his disease was, he feared the treatments would rot his body further than the illness already had.

A funny thing happens when someone gives you a

countdown to your death. They say life flashes before your eyes when you look death in the face, but his experience during the weeks after the diagnosis had been more like flipping briskly though a scrapbook. Since then, vignettes of his life had begun to spring up from deep within his memory. His brain was constantly playing out scenes in his mind that he had buried for decades. Smaller details he had forgotten often helped to segue to the next chapter. The women he had dated, exams he had failed, events he had missed, and opportunities he *should* have taken were all on the agenda. All of these details seemed so insignificant now, and the time he had spent agonizing over which belt he should wear, or which shoes looked better with his cleanly pressed khaki pants seemed like nothing more than gargantuan wastes of precious time that he could not get back.

It was that unique thought process that had reminded him of the words his mother had spoken to him so many times when he was young. Jack imagined she meant them, too. He had tried so very hard to bury them deep into his subconscious as he limped through life. He bore a striking resemblance to his father, and Jack believed his mother had harbored a resentment toward him based on the visual similarity he and his father had shared. His father had left his mother when Jack was only an infant, and oddly enough, he did not hold any grudge against the man for walking out of their lives. If his father had been subjected to the wicked behavior that Jack had been accustomed to when in his mother's presence, then Jack honestly could not have blamed him for running. He imagined she *drove* the man out, and deep down he believed that it had nothing to do with him at his young age. Jack was just a casualty of that battle, and loss is expected in any war.

Starting with the loss of his father, Jack's life had cascaded into a vicious spiral of defeat long before he had received the news of his deteriorating condition. He had heard through a friend of the family that the man had died some years ago. Even though he never reentered his life post-exodus, Jack would have liked to attend the funeral, if only to thank his father for giving him a chance at some revolutions around the sun. Unfortunately, Jack was notified of the news weeks after his passing, but he *did* get to visit his grave.

It was a strange feeling, standing over the headstone of a man Jack only had a fleeting memory of, and although he did not feel the need to cry, he felt a sense of mourning. There was an empty space adjacent to his name which Jack assumed was for his father's current wife. At the time, he had wondered if she had taken his family name as well. Jack's mother had never chosen to revert back to her maiden name after his father left—or remarry, for that matter. Jack was sure that she had, somewhere inside her heart, hoped her husband would return. Not long after Jack had received the news that his father had moved on, his mother passed as well. Unlike his father, *she* had been stuck in the belief that they were kindred spirits.

Jack had been present by her bedside the night she had taken her last breath. He was not forlorn that she was gone, but aghast as she lay in the bed, slack-jawed and stiff. He could not reconcile the idea that someone who had spoken only days earlier was now silenced indefinitely. Mortality was at the root of all of the incarnations of fear that had manifested themselves in his adolescence.

It was the single most crippling aspect of his development. Many people experienced a mid-life crisis, but he had lived in an indefinite state of doom throughout most of his existence. What had started as a simple reluctance to venture alone to Main Street in his small town had, over time, evolved into an unwillingness to even step off his front porch. Luckily, the county library was only a stone's throw away.

Death can be a more painful process of acceptance for the mourners than the victims. Jack didn't know if he ever really loved his mother enough to cry when she passed, and he often wondered if she ever loved *him*. She had been very forthcoming about the truth of his conception and repeatedly made it very clear that he was an accident. She would always claim that scotch whiskey and bourbon were his *real* parents. He never found that saying particularly funny until he came of age to drink himself, at which point he started using it as a party joke. It always got laughs from guests.

His mother's death had isolated him and forced him into a solitary existence that preceded his prognosis. There were few other people in his life with whom he had managed to maintain relationships. Most of the friends and acquaintances he had known at a younger age had fled from the quaint community. They had kept in touch over the years for small reunions, but those had become more fleeting as time moved on. They had all met partners, built homes, started families, and constructed little picket fences in which to contain their fluffy lab retrievers. The advent of grandchildren had made their relationships all but nonexistent due to their reliance on their geographical location. Traveling was simply out of the question for him.

For the better part of his adulthood, Jack had managed an electronics research plant called Titanidyne Systems near his home. Their work existed at the cross-roads of metallurgy and electronics, specifically with regard to travel and computing systems. It was not a position to brag about, but he enjoyed the consistency and simplicity and was well-liked by the engineers the company had employed. He also picked up quite a bit of knowledge along the way. It was familiar, and comfortable, which had become adjectives he had been accustomed to for the better part of his adult life. It also haunted him to no end.

Humans often ask each other, "If you could do it all over again, would you do anything different?" To which Jack would say, "Yes." Unfortunately, he knew he *couldn't* do it all over again. But he *could* make up for lost time, even if that time was limited. He was determined to do so, no matter the wager. Once the doctor had warned Jack that death was imminent, it had liberated him from the shackles that had weighed him down for as long as he could remember. He had taken a seat at the poker table of mortality, and he was all in—and bluffing.

Jack Gambel was going to cement a legacy, but he wasn't going to do it with his name. It didn't feel appropriate to drag his family name into the story, because he never really felt like he had earned it. It did not belong to him. It was like a hand-me-down. His name was not worthy of that kind of infamy. He would give the trophy to someone else—someone who did deserve it: Al Ader.

"Who is Al Ader?" No one knew him yet, but they *would*. *Everyone* would. Whenever his name was uttered, they'd ask, "How did he do it? How did he get away with it? Why didn't they catch him?" Yet the answers would never present themselves. They'd say, "Man, was he good. He's got nerve. He's got skill and finesse." They'd be right. Up until now, Al Ader had been nobody, but today, he'd be *somebody*. It all began with a flight—the first journey Al would ever take—but first, he was going to need some coffee.

It was two o'clock in the afternoon on Thanksgiving Eve of 1971, and one of his favorite programs was going to begin, so he flicked the dial on the television set and repositioned the rabbit-ear antenna until he was satisfied with the picture. He poured the hot water into the filter, letting it flow through the grinds as the steam hit his face. The smell alone was enough to wake him up, even for mediocre motel mud. He had forgotten to get milk, so he sprinkled some non-dairy creamer into the cup to dilute the taste a bit. It occurred to him that this could very well be his last batch of coffee, and he savored what he could from the hot foam cup.

As he sat in the living room chair, a jingle chimed on the television, signifying the program had begun. He placed his cleanly pressed slacks over his legs, and the title *Men of Mystery* faded on to the screen. Jack had been waiting a while for this episode, anticipating the portrayal of one of his heroes as the titles rolled over footage of a man being secured in a straitjacket by authorities. The narrator began to fill in the blanks as the opening credits faded away.

"Harry Houdini. Notorious illusionist and entertainer, shown here getting ready to perform one of his most elaborate escapes. Of all of Houdini's impressive repertoire of tricks, his most widely known was probably his escape act, often secured by local law enforcement to add an extra layer of authenticity for the crowds that gathered to watch his performances firsthand," the narrator explained.

Harry was an eccentric-looking man, with a commanding presence and piercing eyes. He had an impeccable way of adding excitement and flair to his act that had profoundly influenced Jack. The crane had begun to hoist him high into the air after the police checked to confirm he was indeed helpless. A massive crowd of onlookers cheered him on, encouraging him to escape his canvas confinement. He was mesmerizing—a bona-fide daredevil—captivating adults and children alike. Houdini was everything Jack was not, which was what endeared the legend to him the most. Where Houdini saw fear, he also saw opportunity. It seemed that he almost courted death. Emulating Houdini, Al could elevate a complex crime to art.

"When asked what his secret was, Mr. Houdini replied, 'Never tell the audience how good you are. They will soon find out for themselves,' and indeed they did," the narrator continued.

Jack could have spent all day watching Houdini wriggle out of those straps, but he had a tight schedule to keep, and a narrow window of opportunity. He slipped a black sport coat over his white shirt, then secured a tie around his neck after tucking his feet into a pair of black loafers. The loafers might not have fit with the rest of the outfit, but Jack was a sucker for comfortable feet. After combing his hair and sucking down the last bit of coffee, he went to the small bedside desk and retrieved his only heirloom of his father's: a small mother-of-pearl tie clip. He fastened it to the tie, then checked his appearance in the mirror, confirming he looked acceptable.

He turned the dial on the television to the "off" position and grabbed the room key that would need to be returned to the front desk. He made the bed neatly, even though he knew the attendants would come rip all of the linens from the bed before the next guest came. It was a leftover habit from his childhood that had been violently enforced by his mother. "You ain't goin' nowhere until that bed is done up, Jack Gambel," she would scold. The threat of violence was always present in her voice when speaking to Jack. He retrieved his briefcase, placing a pair of dark aviator-style sunglasses over his eyes, and stopped in front of a large mirror that rested on the wall.

There were tremors in his hands, a feeling he had experienced many times in his life before he was scheduled to exit the world. Some days were better than others, but today it was easier to move forward given his newfound resolve. He inhaled deeply, counting ten deep breaths in his head, a small trick he had perfected through the help of a hypnotist. He did not believe in the hypnotic element of the process, but some techniques, including the breathing exercise, could be effective when coping with his stress and anxiety. Jack reasoned that he was already dead, which helped propel him out the door.

Jack placed the key that granted him access to the grungy hotel room on the concierge counter. Cobwebs that hung in the corners of the room signaled there was little if any recordkeeping at the establishment, which was another reason—aside from proximity to his destination—that he had chosen this place as his launching point. He rang the bell to ensure the attendant at the desk would receive the key, and a shabby old man shuffled out to the desk to tend to him.

"Ah, yes, room 2C, correct?" the old timer asked.

"It was, thank you. Are we all settled up?" Jack replied.

"We are, Mister... what did you say your name was?"

"I didn't," Jack responded without looking at him directly. The taxis would pass by outside under the canopy that shaded the entrance, and he made his way out the door, the briefcase held tightly in his hand.

2

——————

Robin Kraft didn't hear the first, second, or third time the obnoxious bells of the telephone rang. She'd been stuck somewhere between a state of deep sleep and hangover after a long month with no days off. She'd been traveling nearly every opportunity she got to collect the overtime, and most of her flights had been overnights that had sent her sleep schedule careening off the tracks. Today was her day off, and she didn't make plans for time off, especially days before both a holiday weekend and her wedding. It was the fourth ring that finally prompted her to reach for the receiver. She fiddled with it, her fingers dancing around the holes of the rotary phone before finally grasping it and bringing it to her ear.

"Hello?" she asked in a groggy, half-asleep voice.

"Hey, Robin," the peppy young voice on the other end said. "It's Connie." Robin sat up instinctively, wiping her long vibrant red hair out of her face as she yawned like an angry snake. "Listen, Prudence, the head flight attendant for the Seattle evening trip called in with the flu."

"And you want me to fill in for her," Robin replied with tempered excitement.

"That's what they're asking," Connie replied. Robin grabbed the drawer on her bedside table and rummaged around inside for a pen and paper.

"Well, yes!" she replied quickly. "I mean, I'd like to, but can I? I've never done the big job. There's got to be a list of women ahead of me."

"Well, that's the problem," Connie began. "They're all off for the holiday. We've nearly run down the whole roster, at least in LA, and you're the only one who's even picked up the phone."

Robin was getting her socks on before Connie had even finished her sentence. She'd wanted the head flight attendant job for years, and she'd been passed up many of the times she thought she might get the call. At Eagle Airlines, the job not only paid better, but also awarded some flexibility in the schedules of those who held the position. Now that she was planning to start her life with Glenn, she wanted to ditch the wonky hours of red-eyes and early evenings she'd been forced to suffer through as she tried to remain a model employee.

"They said that up top? They said that I could take the job?" Robin asked.

"Well, it'd just be for the night, but between you and me," Connie's voice dropped low, almost to a whisper, "I think they're looking to replace Prudence, and I'd say it would be a mighty good opportunity to get your name up front and center in the queue." Connie had hired Robin, and if there was anyone who could get your name up in front of the guys who placed the flight attendants, it was Connie. "You're always on time, you're good with the customers, and you're familiar with the crew flying tonight. It doesn't hurt that you're pretty."

"Do they hire any other kind of flight attendant?" Robin asked.

"I suppose not," Connie replied with a chuckle. "But the rest of them complain a lot, and I haven't heard a peep out of you."

"Just doing my job," Robin replied.

"So?" Connie asked. Robin's gaze turned to the messy head of blonde, curly hair that had been half covered under the comforter beside her. Glenn had stopped snoring, which meant she'd woken him up and she'd have some explaining to do if she said yes. She'd promised him several uninterrupted days leading up to the big day on Sunday, and she hadn't even been off for twenty-four hours before she was ready to get back in the game.

"What time is it?" Robin asked.

"It's a three p.m., and I'm confident that barring any delays it will be back in by eight p.m., just a quick back and forth." Glenn shifted in the bed, rolling over on his side as his eyes slowly opened to see her talking on the phone. She paused briefly to grab the small clock that rested on the table beside her and turned it in her direction. It was already one in the afternoon. If she was going to go, she'd have to go *now*.

"I'm in," Robin replied. There was a hint of reluctance in her voice, and Glenn's eyes squinted tightly—he knew what she was up to before he even asked.

"Great," Connie said.

"I'll be in right away." Robin hung up the phone without even saying goodbye. A mix of excitement and guilt washed over her as dueling emotions, but against her better judgement, she'd felt she *needed* to say yes. It could very well have been a test, and if it was, she believed she had passed. She ran her hand through Glenn's hair, kissing him lightly on the forehead.

"Who was it?" he asked as he fluffed his pillow.

"The airline," Robin replied. Glenn was growing more suspicious by the moment. "Prudence has the flu."

"And?" Glenn asked.

"And," Robin began before pausing for a moment. "And I'm going in for a quick flight." The words came out quickly, as if the faster she said them the less they would annoy him.

"Today?" Glenn said, his voice filled with angst. He sat up in the bed, rubbing his cheeks with balled fists. "You said we were going to sleep in."

"We did. It's one p.m.," Robin said as she leapt from the bed. Her uniform had been thrown sloppily on the floor the night before—she hadn't imagined she'd need it for nearly a week—and she brushed her hands against it to try to de-wrinkle the garment the best she could.

"Robin, it's Thanksgiving Eve. You're supposed to be off," Glenn said angrily. "We've been planning this for nearly a year."

"It's a quick flight to Seattle," Robin said. "The return flight is tonight. You won't even know I was gone."

"More importantly—" She pressed her finger to his lips to shush him before he could even finish his sentence. She knew what he was going to say. He was going to mention how ridiculous it was that an airline would call someone last minute like that on a holiday and that it wasn't her responsibility. He was going to go on about how she had promised him that she would take the time off to go over last-minute preparations for the wedding and that there was still plenty to do today before the holiday weekend.

"Glenn, I know," she said softly. "I'll be home later tonight." She didn't even bother mentioning what Connie had told her about the position. Glenn wanted her to quit the job entirely. His salary was not impressive, but they could at least *survive* on his alone, and he had kids on the brain. Robin, however, loved that she had a career, and she had never really imagined she'd quit. The topic of children had been a touchy one. She was not in a rush, and the idea that she could get promoted only encouraged her to delay. The wedding had been far more expensive than either had planned for, and she would be happy to get the overtime. If she was really lucky, she'd get cash tips.

"They ask too much of you," Glenn proclaimed. It went in one ear and out the other. She was already slipping her uniform over her body and brushing her hair. She wouldn't need to pack a bag since the trip did not require staying overnight, and with a little makeup, she'd be on her way—an impressive spring into action if there ever was one. "Besides, you promised me you'd help me with that turkey. Do you remember what happened last year?"

"Go back to sleep," Robin said to him, and she kissed him again on the cheek. She shut his eyelids with the palm of her hand as if to coerce him into just letting it go before it turned into an argument. The topic of her job had manifested itself into an ugly altercation on more than one occasion, but Robin was a hustler, and though she loved him, no man was going to stop her from doing what she needed to do.

3

"LAX," Jack told the cabbie as he climbed into the back seat.

"Terminal?" the cabbie asked.

"Eagle Airlines, whichever one that is," he requested.

"Can do."

The cabbie was looking at Jack through the rearview mirror, trying to get a read on his eyes. It was a nosy habit of cabbies that Jack imagined was likely due to the nature of their lonely occupation. He didn't want anyone to be able to identify him, so he stared out the window, hiding his face to limit how much he saw past the sunglasses. Of all of the data Jack had gathered to help him execute the plan, the terminal he would depart from was not as important as the type of plane he needed to board: a Bauering Trijet 100. It had many capabilities that few other aircraft possessed, and it was imperative that he flew on *that* specific model. They were in heavy rotation for domestic flights, and finding one via the carrier he had chosen—Eagle Airlines—would not be difficult. Where the plane intended to go initially was irrelevant since the early stages of his journey would be short.

It was Thanksgiving Eve, and procuring a ticket was unlikely to be difficult, even last minute. It was not a popular date to fly; most travelers had already arrived at their destinations prior to the festivities, and Jack did not want a full flight. Every additional passenger on board meant there was a greater risk of a "hero" being in the mix and he didn't want to be physically overpowered.

"Would you mind if I put the window down?" Jack asked the cabbie. He shrugged. Even in November, the sun was cooking the Highway 405 blacktop, and the suit he was wearing did not allow his skin to breathe well. He did not want to begin his adventure drenched in sweat. The heat, among other things, was one reason he had always hated Los Angeles—the city of broken dreams. Many hopefuls came out to the city looking to get a piece of the glitz, but the town destroyed souls far more often than it rewarded them. The movie business had "polluted the southern California area" according to Jack, and although he admired the desperate thespians attempting to make a name for themselves, most were not cut out for the work needed to cement their star on the walk of fame. *Al Ader* might find success where they had not—without even needing to do a single audition.

The neighborhoods around the airport that had been filled with homes in the past were now vacant lots. It was a rapidly expanding project, with LA being a heavily traf-ficked area, stuck in a perpetual state of construction and renovation to service travelers that had laid waste to what was now an eerie area near the runways. It was an eyesore in a community that was originally home to beautiful beaches and a fine example of runaway capitalism at its best. Although he was reluctant to enter the cesspool, of all the airports he had surveyed, LAX would aid him best in his quest.

The large white saucer arches of the Theme Building appeared through the windshield as they approached the airport. They represented the pinnacle of the Googie movement of modern architecture. Jack had always thought it was a particularly silly looking design, but it certainly was iconic, even if it resembled the home of *The Jetsons*.

"Terminal One," the cabbie said as he rolled up to the curb. The fare was two dollars, and Jack handed him an extra fifty cents for the trip. He grabbed his briefcase, stepping out onto the curb as he looked above at the signs that guided passengers to their respective airlines. Once through the doors, he found himself in a lobby where the hustle and bustle of travelers echoed throughout the room. Directly in front of him, the familiar logo of a blue eagle with red and white feathers stretched its wings above a desk. The branding of the image presented the eagle mid-flight and in strike position. Under the logo was "Eagle Airlines" in a metallic gold print. As Jack watched civilians checking their belongings, he wondered if any of the people around him would be on his flight. They had no idea how blissful their ignorance truly was.

There was no line at the desk, and Jack shuffled toward the young woman who stood behind it, feverishly banging the keys of a typewriter that sat in front of her. As he approached, she turned on the faux smile that employees were trained to display when dealing with customers like it was programmed into her. His lip had begun twitching, but he placed one foot in front of the other regardless, reminding himself that his illness could make any step his last.

The attendant was the first line of defense. He knew he had to avoid drawing attention to himself. He'd noted a couple cabs that idled outside in the queue in case he had to abandon the task.

"Hello, I'm looking to take a flight to Seattle tonight. I believe you have a three o'clock?"

"Let me check," she said cheerfully as she riffled through flight schedules. She began scanning a sheet of paper with the tip of a pencil as she searched with her eyes.

"We do," she said happily.

"Great. Listen, I'm not a great flier, and I hear that the larger aircraft are a bit easier on the nerves. What model aircraft is that?"

"Flight 197 to Seattle... " she replied as she referenced more information, "is a Bauering Trijet."

"And is that a 100 series?"

"Boy, for someone who hates flying, you sure do know your stuff," she replied, intrigued.

"A bit of a hobby. I used to paint the die-cast models as a kid," Jack explained quickly. "That will do just fine. Let's book that." A bead of sweat began to trickle down his temple. He didn't dare wipe it, lest he draw attention to his nerves.

"Excellent. Will you be checking any bags?" she questioned.

"No, I'm traveling light," he replied, displaying the small black attaché case. "Just an impromptu business trip for the company."

"Great, and who should I be listing as the passenger?"

"Al Ader," he responded. "First name A-L, last name A-

D-E-R." It was the first time he had used the name with others, and with a few small strokes of a pen, Al Ader was born. She began to fill in the rest of the information, and he dabbed at the back of his neck with a small handkerchief while she was distracted, wiping away the last remnants of sweat from the cab ride. The perspiration that had originated from the smoldering heat was now worsened by his own trepidation. Luckily, the airport was much cooler than the brutal warmth of LA, and Jack hoped it was a sign that the universe might be working toward his favor.

"Great, Mr. Ader," she said as a machine beside her punched the ticket. "That's going to be $24.50."

He reached for the cash in his pocket, fumbling for the other pair of quarters that remained after rewarding the cabbie with the first set.

"I'll be paying cash," he informed her.

"Perfect," she replied as she retrieved the exact change from his hand. She deposited the tender into a drawer and handed him the ticket displaying the relevant information.

"That flight will be boarding very soon, but you'll want to head over to gate A2 if you need to request a particular seat assignment."

"That easy, huh?" Jack asked.

"That easy," she said with a chuckle. "Be sure to remember Eagle if you haven't already booked your return flight."

"Will do," he said nervously as he deposited the ticket into the breast pocket of his jacket. "Thanks for your help." She cocked her head with an artificial smirk as he retrieved his briefcase.

"Have a safe flight, Mr. Ader."

"I'm counting on it."

The fact that Jack was traveling without luggage should have aroused her suspicions, given the rise in airplane hijacking as well as his request for a one-way flight. He supposed she thought that an ill-looking and frail man like him couldn't possibly present a threat. He was thankful she was young and probably too inexperienced to notice any of those red flags.

Now that Jack had successfully procured a ticket, he needed to make a call before he left. He searched the room, but saw nothing. After taking a small trip up an escalator, he found a group of pay phones near the hallway that led to his gate. Two were occupied, but one remained vacant. He dug in his pocket for some coins as he lifted the phone from the receiver. The voice on the other end prompted him to deposit a nickel. He dialed the number from memory, then waited as the phone began to ring.

"Hello?" an eager and high-pitched voice said.

"Hello, Emmy. This is the Count... Count Dracula," Jack announced in his best Lugosi impression.

"I know it's you, Uncle Jack!" she said without hesitation.

"Uncle Jack is on his way to Transylvania to tend to my estate," he replied, keeping up the impression. She giggled wildly, and her laugh was worth Jack's mediocre attempts. He admired the Universal horror classics to no end. One might wonder why a man who lived in a perpetual state of cowardice would enjoy such thrills, but he likened classic horror to controlled fear, like a roller coaster.

"Can you put your dad on?"

He could hear her calling for her father in the background in a muffled yelp, and a pounding penetrated his ear drum, which implied that she had carelessly dropped the phone. After waiting for a few moments, there was a scuffling noise which signaled it had been picked up off the floor.

"Jack?" a voice said.

"Yeah, Sam, it's me," Jack responded.

"Where are you calling from?" Sam asked.

"The LAX payphone."

"LAX—"

"Stop," he interrupted. "Are you going to be there or not?" There was a pause.

"Yea," Sam said reluctantly. "You're really going to do it?"

"Al is," Jack replied.

"Who is Al?"

"You'll know soon enough," he stated proudly.

"You're in bad shape, Jack."

"Midnight pick-up," he interrupted him again. "EA 197, that's the flight I'll be on. Listen, they may come looking for you if this doesn't work. You need to know that. You'll have plausible deniability, of course, but you'll need to monitor the events before you go to the pickup point we discussed. If that flight takes back off after the initial landing, you'll know what to do."

"Are you at least taking the pills?" Sam questioned.

"Yes. Amphetamine sulfate, ten milligrams," Jack said.

"Be safe, Jack."

"Al," Jack said, "you too." He hung up the phone. He had discussed his fate with his brother, and it was he who had unintentionally given Jack the idea of spending his final moments looking death directly in its cold, abyss-like eyes. After discussing some of his inadequacies at length over a beer, a small piece of advice Jack received from Sam had *clicked*. He wondered why he had never thought of it before. "Your problem, Jack, is that you let your dread dictate your life," Sam had said. "And now you're left with nothing but regret. You need to make fear your ally. Harness it."

Jack continued into the concourse, considering whether to grab a newspaper to distract him as he waited. But most of the shops were closed for the holiday. The idle mind was a playground for panic, and he didn't want a flux of failed scenarios clouding his head. The seating area to gate A2 wasn't far, and he made a detour to the men's lavatory to finish preparations.

Inside, the smell of urine was overwhelmingly foul. *At least my senses are still intact.* He scanned the floor, checking to confirm that he was alone. There was the sound of a toilet flushing. Jack nodded at a gentleman sliding the zipper up the front of his pants as he exited the stall. The man turned the faucet on as Jack approached the sink nearby and flicked his hands after just barely wetting them. If that man was going to be on his flight, Jack would be sure not to touch anything that he came in contact with. He exited, and Jack secured the bolt that would lock the door behind him as he left.

It had been a while since Jack had analyzed himself in the mirror, and the cheap overhead lighting that hung from the ceiling of the bathroom made him look even more ill than he had remembered. A sheen on his skin glistened from the hot afternoon, and he patted it with a cold, damp paper towel to keep cool. He placed his briefcase on the counter in front of him, then released both of the locks. Inside lay the tools that were instrumental to the next part of his plan. The red cylindrical sticks wrapped with wires sold the makeshift explosive device exceptionally well, and he had wedged a number six dry-cell battery next to them. It was a staple of cartoons, but pop culture had made the image recognizable. It would clue in even the uninitiated person as to its functions. Mornings spent devouring paperbacks on explosives could teach even the uninitiated how to properly construct a bomb. Jack had easily been able to construct it from memory, only briefly referencing an encyclopedia. Right now, however, it was not the reason he had entered the room.

There was a small makeup pad lying beside it, and although he had received some curious looks from the clerk when Jack had purchased the kit, he believed it would benefit his appearance. He dipped it into a small container of blush, then patted his cheeks lightly before moving to his forehead and neck. His complexion became more desirable as he surveyed himself in the mirror, and he deposited the pad into the trash along with the container of blush after finishing. He shut the case and locked it again before running a wet comb through his hair. A little water would allow the gel he had applied earlier to maintain its shine for some time—after all, he should try to look handsome for his debut, he reasoned. Jack chose an unassuming hairstyle, neatly parted at the side to the left of his scalp.

After tightening his tie once again, he stared into the mirror. It was fitting that he didn't recognize the man staring back at him. Because Jack was no longer there—*Al* was. The prosthetics that he had spent the better part of the morning applying had helped see to that. An over-whelming shiver trembled through his body, as if all of the fear he had pent up inside of him had been expelled in one purge. The identity he had adopted had a profound influence on his attitude, and he was filled with a newfound confidence.

"Goodbye, Jack," he said to the man in the mirror. His eyes were the only part that Jack recognized, and seeing that the eyes are the key to a man's soul, the sunglasses he placed back on his face locked the door. A restroom was not a fitting place for a man's funeral, and he chuckled to himself that Jack's last breath would fill his nostrils with the putrid smell of urine. Jack had been a splinter that needed to be plucked. There was no room for him in this story any longer.

"Hello, Al," he said in a deep, proud purr. He had not planned to manipulate the sounds that emanated from his vocal cords originally, but it presented itself unconsciously; he imagined it to be a byproduct of the unfamiliar man that stood before him. It was just another facet he added to the character that would mystify anyone as to who he *really* was. It was the definitive indicator that Al would be able to do what Jack *couldn't*.

4

On the concourse, Al directed his attention toward the sign that read "A2." It was from here that the flight would be departing. Now the next part of the process would require him to wait patiently, blending in like the other customers that awaited the flight. He took a seat near the desk that stood in front of the door to the boarding level.

A mousy-looking woman with blonde hair stood at the desk. The pin on her maroon uniform displayed the Eagle Airlines logo, as if it wasn't clear she was an employee from her firmly pressed blouse and skirt. Her tag said her name was Sally. A clock above her head displayed the current time, now twenty minutes to three, and Al adjusted the minute hand on his watch slightly to mirror the numbers displayed. He wanted to match the airline's clock as best he could.

Another young woman approached the desk with a quick stride. She had deep crimson hair tied neatly in a bun at the back of her head and a small piece of luggage at her side. She exuded confidence and charm. She made her way to the desk, and as she got closer, Sally's mouth fell open and hung slack.

Al wasn't fond of eavesdropping. His mother had caught him doing it as a child—and punished him with a few good smacks—and that had made him wary of the behavior ever since. He made an exception, because right now it was important to learn information about the players, and he didn't mind bending the rules. The flight attendant he chose to puppeteer would be the wide receiver of this game. As the redhead came closer, he was able to make out the word written on her nametag: Robin.

"No way," Sally yelped.

"Hey, Sal," Robin replied to her reluctantly. Al turned his head, grabbing for the newspaper nearby to keep his eyes busy as he listened.

"I'm hallucinating," Sally joked. "Why are you here? You should be getting beauty rest."

"I don't want to hear it," Robin said as she tucked her luggage behind the desk. "I need the money."

"When I saw your name on the updated list, I thought it was a clerical error," Sally said. "Did he give you shit?"

"Of course."

"How did you spin it?"

"Table centerpieces don't buy themselves. Between the band, the venue, and the cake, the money is going out faster than it's coming in, so here I am."

"And head flight attendant no less," Sally said playfully.

"That might have influenced my decision," Robin said.

"Always have to be the hero, don't you?"

"If not me, then who?" Robin said sarcastically.

"Just don't get sucked into spending your life at thirty

thousand feet," Sally warned. "You should be enjoying your new life, not struggling in it."

"How are we looking?" Robin asked as she leaned over the desk.

"Thirty-seven passengers. Thirty-one customers, six personnel—including three attendants, pilot, copilot, and flight engineer. You're with May and Norma," Sally answered. "Looks like they got sucked in too, and they didn't get a bump like you, so watch your ass."

"Quiet night."

"Those turkeys don't roast themselves."

Robin analyzed the manifest and took notes, and Sally stacked the files she had in her hand, stepping away from the desk to provide Robin with space to work.

"She's all yours," Sally stated.

"Have a good holiday, Sal. See you Saturday?" Robin asked.

"I still can't believe I'm losing my wingman. Who's going to find boys with me on those New York layovers?" Sally asked, earning a coy smile from Robin.

"Relax. It's not like it's my last flight."

As the two embraced, the gears in Al's head began turning. Robin's upcoming life event made her a viable choice for manipulation. As usual, if one simply listened, they could obtain relevant information. Now was the time to introduce himself.

"Good evening, ladies and gentlemen," Robin said through the intercom. "We will soon start the boarding process for Flight 197, non-stop to Seattle." As she finished her statement, her gaze met Al's. He hadn't realized that his attention had shifted from the newspaper to her, and he quickly sent a smile in her direction. She returned it immediately, as he was sure she was trained to do. An elderly man in a wheelchair rolled toward her and parallel to the desk. While she discussed the boarding process with him, Al folded the paper and walked toward the desk. She had signaled to an attendant outside that the elderly man would require assistance, then turned to focus her attention on Al when he arrived.

"Hello," Robin said.

"Good evening, Robin," Al said as he looked closely at her nametag. "I was told I would need to select a seat prior to boarding."

"Sure, I can help with that. Do you have any preference for your location on the plane?"

"Something in the rear... a window perhaps, and if possible, no one next to me in the adjacent seats. I have a bit of a spinal issue, and if I can, I like to stretch out a little mid-flight," he requested.

"Let me see what I can do," she responded without looking at him. "We're not very full tonight. I have a window in aisle eighteen, and it looks like that whole row is currently empty."

"That would be perfect," he responded.

"Then you're all set Mister... "

"Ader," Al said after a bit of hesitation. He'd almost used his real name, but the weight of the glasses on his cheeks had abruptly reminded him of who he *currently* was.

"Great, you'll be boarding in a moment," she said politely.

"Robin... like the bird."

"My mother predicted my hair color," she said as she pointed to her scalp, and Al laughed. "She was sure that it would be as red as a robin's breast."

"Thanks, Robin," Al said as he retrieved the newly modified ticket.

Al walked near the glass that looked out over the tarmac, watching the attendants check the aircraft. He confirmed that it was indeed the model that was promised. The plane was unique in that it featured staircases on both the rear and port sides of the fuselage. The standard load-in would be done via the port side, where the man in the wheelchair was being assisted up the stairs.

Robin, Al thought to himself. It was fitting. His mother had been an avid bird watcher during his childhood. He remembered the lessons she had given him concerning different varieties of birds, when she wasn't sleeping off a hangover. The North American Robin, identified easily by its red chest, would serenade the neighborhood with song before the sun rose, signaling the beginning of a new day, and often the coming of the new, warmer season. Al took the coincidental appearance of her name as a sign that this indeed was the end of Jack's story, and the beginning of Al's.

Another flight attendant, displaying a nametag with "May" on it, walked through the door that allowed passengers access to the exterior. She greeted Robin, then updated her on the aircraft's progress.

"We'll now begin the general boarding process for Flight 197 to Seattle," Robin stated to the rest of the waiting passengers. She left May at the desk, then trekked over toward the plane. Al looked at his fellow passengers as they hustled out of their seats. There were men and women of all colors and sizes. May glanced quickly at their tickets as they filed into a line, allowing them access one by one. One gentleman with a weathered complexion looked as if he had already had quite a few drinks while waiting, and he swayed slightly as he continued toward the gate.

Al was hesitant to join the other passengers just yet. He was going to be required to do something Jack had never done: board an airplane. He had taken a particular interest in aviation. In fact, he was confident he could fly an aircraft if he had to, but he had never worked up the courage to actually set foot on one. He would have to quickly get over that fear. The clock was ticking, and bowing out now would frustrate him far more than flying would frighten him.

The sound in the airport began to grow muffled, and Al could feel his blood pressure rising. Medical professionals often speak of strokes as if they are the "silent killer," but one can be aware of a dangerous elevation of blood pressure simply by monitoring the throbbing that occurs in the temples. *You can do this,* he said to himself. *You're already dead.* It was a statement that had worked recently to help him gather courage. A man with nothing to lose is the man that should be feared most. It wasn't just do or die, it was do *and* die.

5

As Al continued to watch the action going on outside through the window, he spotted a black plane tucked away near a warehouse in the distance. There was a white bunny painted on the tail section. It was a DC-9 airliner that could only belong to one person. He wondered for a moment what celebrity might be gracing the flying mansion. He could see the inspector was almost finished with his checks on the Trijet that awaited him. Now that the line to board had dwindled, Al grabbed his briefcase, then entered the queue.

He presented his ticket to Norma with a smile and watched as the bags were loaded onto the plane. He was quite happy that he hadn't checked any luggage, because the handlers were anything but gentle with the passengers' property. One handler tossed a bag so carelessly onto the conveyor belt that it tumbled down to the asphalt after a violent bounce. Al shuddered to think of the state of any fragile objects inside.

He finally arrived at the steps. When he began to climb them, a pang of nausea shot through his body like none he had ever experienced. He felt immediately weak in the knees by the time he hit the third step, and when he reached the fifth, he collapsed. Al was fighting, but Jack was fighting back.

A shooting pain in Al's wrist notified him that he had used it to stop his face from slamming into the steel steps, and although it stung, he was thankful his teeth hadn't suffered the consequences. The woman behind him gasped, bracing herself as if he was more of a danger to her than himself. A small misstep had almost derailed him, and his heart began to race as the first officer hustled over to him and placed his arm around Al's shoulders.

"You alright?" he asked.

"I'm okay," Al replied, a bit exasperated.

"You sure?"

"I'm sure!" Al snapped. The officer didn't deserve the aggression, but Al was more frustrated with himself for being careless. It wasn't the first time he had fallen since the diagnosis—the vertigo-like symptoms of his slow death had manifested before. Unfortunately, this was *different.* He had heard the first shots fired in a war of two identities. As Al turned to see the passengers waiting behind him, he could tell from their murmuring that they had been judging him. Perhaps they were considering whether he had abused substances before entering.

"Just lost my footing, is all," Al explained, wiping the dirt off his slacks and continuing into the aluminum tube. The badge on the man's white-collared shirt said his name was Tom, and Al could tell by the two stripes on his epaulet that he was the flight engineer.

Immediately to Al's left lay the cockpit, and he could hear the captain and copilot running checks as they analyzed their dials and gauges. Their preflight agenda was numbingly routine, and Al felt sinister knowing how quickly he would force *their* blood pressure to skyrocket. Robin was nearby, jotting down information in a small booklet. There was a brawny man in the pilot's seat and a slightly younger, handsome-looking man next to him.

The plane was quiet, and only the man in the wheelchair watched Al as he continued into the labyrinth of seats. He was following Al curiously with his eyes as if possessing some intuition about his character, and Al quickly looked away. A plump and disheveled businessman was trying unsuccessfully to jam his large bag into the tiny overhead bin, starting a bit of a traffic jam in the aisle. A flight attendant began to help him as he lost his patience. Robin stepped toward the crew in the cockpit.

"Good afternoon, gentlemen," she said with a chipper attitude.

"Good afternoon, Miss Kraft," the pilot said. "Fancy seeing you on your vacation time."

"Vacation? What's that?" Robin replied sarcastically. Her statement forced a scoff out of the copilot. Robin retrieved a document from a cabinet and handed it to the pilot.

"Here you go, Wally, final manifest," she explained as he grabbed it.

"Thanks," Wally replied as he scanned the list. Now that Al had a better look at him, it was clear he had been flying for quite some time, if age was any indicator. He had a healthy silver shine in his thick head of hair.

"Got the big job now, huh?" Wally asked Robin.

"It's only temporary," Robin replied. "Maybe if one of you gentlemen would be so kind as to put in a good word we could make this a habit."

"We'll see how good your coffee is before we make any commitments," Wally said.

"Speaking of which, can I get you boys anything before takeoff?" she asked.

"Yea, how about a martini, rocks, olives," the copilot replied.

"Very funny, Jeff," she responded. "I'm going to start safety procedures momentarily." Jeff nodded, and Robin returned to organizing the materials in the compartments near the cockpit.

"Sir!" Al heard a voice say from the back of the plane. "Please step forward." He turned his attention toward the aisle and realized that the cockpit conversation had occupied his focus, distracting him from the fact that he was holding up the line.

The old man that had boarded earlier continued to follow him with his gaze as he passed by. Al would have thanked him for his service if he hadn't been actively keeping such a low profile. The man wore a black cap on his head that announced his involvement in World War II. There was a rectangular rainbow of colors confirming his activity in the European portion of the conflict from the early forties. He had an eye for the *enemy*.

As Al continued inside the cabin, the low hum of the auxiliary power became meditative, and he breathed deeply while he searched for his seat. There was a pungent odor, and his nostrils flared. It was a cocktail of exhaust fumes, plastics, and nursing-home-quality food. A young couple tickled a small infant, and it cooed in response. They were infatuated with their newborn and didn't even notice Al as he passed.

Al noted that there was no row thirteen, which he attributed to superstition rather than function. It was probably a courtesy from the airline to potentially uneasy passengers. The process of flying was, in and of itself, nerve-wracking for most, accented by the claustrophobia he was now experiencing. Statistically, commercial flight had become a safe mode of travel, but that didn't help ease his panic. *Keep moving*, Al said to himself.

More passengers began to shuffle in behind him, loading their small pieces neatly into the overhead bin. The flight attendant with white hair met Al with a friendly demeanor near his aisle.

"Anything I can help you with, sir?" she asked.

"18C," Al replied. He noted the name on her tag, which said "Norma," and considered her as an alternate target. But he would need someone who would be in direct communication with the captain, and that seemed to be Robin. Norma gestured to the seat that waited for Al. Even though he had requested the window seat, he took his place in the "B" seat, right in the middle of the other two, and deposited the briefcase securely by his feet. He ensured it hugged his shins tightly, confirming it would not shift during takeoff. He began to consider the departure of the plane as being not unlike the Saturn V rockets NASA had been launching into space. Al knew that was farfetched, but he resolved to keep the briefcase near him at all times anyway out of fear he might lose it. He checked his watch; the flight was currently running a few minutes early, and although he had hoped they wouldn't deviate much from the schedule, early was far better than late.

A small boy was running with a model airplane through the aisle, his mother ushering him along by nudging his shoulder with her fingers. He was making buzzing sounds to simulate the motor of the plane, dipping it in and out of seats while emulating maneuvers more suited to a stunt plane than a commercial airliner. Children were ignorant of the dangers around them, and Al couldn't help but feel a tinge of jealously. The boy stopped a few rows ahead and disappeared behind the headrests.

The fuel attendant had begun to place the hose back on its spool, confirming that the plane was ready to depart. Often, planes did not fly to domestic locations with full tanks. The airlines were stingy, and a tremendous amount of pressure was put on commercial pilots to utilize the gasoline in the most cost-efficient way. The pilots were not safe from the clutches of corporate greed. It was not necessary to worry how much fuel the plane carried when it left. Refueling to capacity would be a priority later in the evening.

Al stretched out his wrist, reminded of the pain that he had caused himself when entering the plane. It was now shooting up to his shoulder. Had he broken it? He was a textbook hypochondriac, and he massaged the joint gently, reminding himself that soon enough it would be irrelevant, since a body that didn't heal needn't concern itself with a busted limb.

As he attempted to relax, Al wondered if Sam was right, and if he was not well enough to see his plan through. He was reminded of a time when he had been a small boy and his mother had commanded him to jump in a small pond near his childhood home. He had been hesitant to do so, and could only work up the courage to grace the water with his toe. He certainly hadn't known how to swim properly at that age, and he had been terrified of the murky liquid. Angered by his reluctance to go in, his mother had grabbed him by his shoulder and thrown him into the pond without warning. Water had mixed with tears as he flopped around in the muck, yet his mother had simply stood by, her arms folded, scowling at him from the beach.

"You gotta just jump in that fire, Jack Gambel. That's the only damn way to learn," she'd hissed. Jack had failed then, but Al wouldn't. Al was jumping in head-first.

Al could hear two young men in their twenties chortling near the front of the plane, disrespecting the quiet ambience. Robin was standing nearby to greet passengers entering the plane, and he saw her hand both of the young men small cups that he hoped contained non-alcoholic drinks.

An aging African-American woman with shaky hands and beady eyes approached and sat in the row slightly ahead of Al, close enough for conversation. He could tell she was nervous, as she fastened the seat belt around her waist quickly and tightly, pulling it to ensure it was snug. Al mimicked her action, concerned that the takeoff would be as intense as he had speculated. The last couple people filed onto the plane and took their seats near the front.

The *thunk* of the door closing confirmed that it was indeed sealed, and Al hoped that the air would soon start circulating through the cabin. He had felt a bit of sweat start to form in his armpits again, and the plane had not turned on the air conditioning while in the loading area. The temperature irked him to no end, but he was happy to find that no other passengers would be sitting close to him, which would surely make for less resistance during flight, if any.

"Ladies and gentleman, we'll need your full attention for this important safety demonstration," Robin said, brandishing a seatbelt without a seat. Al reached into his breast pocket, his hands shaking as he drowned out the instructions and retrieved the small pill bottle. He twisted the cap off, threw back another pill, and gulped hard to force it down. The small wonders would help him to remain alert and fit during the night. They did well to help mask the effects of haziness brought on by the sickness that ravaged him. Robin smiled around the cabin as she demonstrated the safety instructions to passengers. She displayed the oxygen mask and showed how it could be properly secured if deployed during flight. Al felt the plane switch over from auxiliary power as the lights briefly dimmed and, soon after, the jolt of the plane taxiing out near the runway.

"Evening, folks, welcome to Eagle Airlines Flight 197 non-stop to Seattle," Wally said over the intercom as various heads looked up toward the speakers in the cabin. "We're looking at an on-time arrival tonight at Seattle-Tacoma, and a relatively smooth ride once we hit cruising altitude. We've received some reports of choppy weather for our initial departure, so let me remind you that you'll want to keep your seatbelts fastened until we give the okay. I'm Captain Wally Perconte, and I'm joined by my copilot Jeff Nixon, as well as flight engineer Tom Liebgott. Let us know if there's anything we can do for you tonight, and we'll try our best to accommodate you. Flight attendants, please perform final checks to prepare for departure."

Cool air began to pour from the vent above Al's head, calming him as the crew readied for the takeoff. He could tell the woman next to him was becoming more anxious, and he shared in her dread. Robin and Norma walked about the aisles, ensuring that the passengers were properly secured in their seats. The plane stopped after a reverse ninety-degree turn, and he could hear the engines spooling loudly and the whining sound of the flaps on the wings being checked for any malfunction. The flaps rotated along the wing, both up and then down. Those flaps were another reason he had chosen that specific model of airliner.

"Flight attendants, please be seated for departure," Wally said over the PA system. Norma retreated to the front of the plane, and Robin placed herself in her jump seat in the rear. He was now sure that Robin would be instrumental. As the sound of the engines grew louder, rattling the airplane as it slowly crawled onto the runway, the sun continued along its course and fell slowly into the western side of the sky.

They paused for a moment while the pilot centered the plane on the runway. It was important to line up the nose of the plane with precision to avoid diverting off the runway. Pilots took great care to get that part right. He checked his watch one last time; it was half past four, which put them right on schedule. The plane held for a moment. Al assumed the pilot was likely speaking with the tower. He gripped the arm rest tightly, then took a deep breath. *Al* was ready. The engines kicked in, now roaring to full power.

The rattling turned into shaking, and he noticed that the woman near him had squeezed her eyes shut tight. Her knuckles whitened as if there were only bone beneath the skin. She clasped her fingers together in prayer. The plane was picking up speed now, and the satellite terminals were passing by faster though the windows. The inertia that Al felt during takeoff terrified him to no end, but he felt more alive than he had in years. The exterior of the airport began to blur. Time itself seemed to slow down. As the flaps produced lift, the nose of the plane tilted. The plane's ascent pinned his body to the seat. The feeling of butterflies flapping in his stomach was so violent, he was convinced they would begin fluttering out of his mouth at any moment.

The plane banked left, informing him they had most likely taken off in a southern direction. It would take Al a moment to get his bearings, and as they climbed higher still, the geography below started to resemble a miniature set like those used in Hollywood disaster pictures. The large grinding of the cargo doors told him that the pilot had retracted the landing gear. The thinning air provided less resistance, and he could feel the thrust increase.

The engines were working with incredible precision but all he could hear was a consistent droning. The plane dropped suddenly, replacing the seat-pinning feeling of climbing with the stomach-churning notion of weightlessness. He could hear a few cries from the passengers who didn't know otherwise, surely thinking they had dropped a thousand feet. Despite the surprise, he allowed logic to be his guide. The average displacement of turbulence was surprisingly little in terms of measurement in feet, but the feeling was far more abrasive than the actual movement. Turbulence was rarely a cause of aircraft disaster. The woman near him, on the other hand, continued to breathe deeply as the plane shifted up and down. Al was finding it quite thrilling despite his original reservations. The assurance he was trapped lent him some relief—whatever happened, he wouldn't be getting out.

"It's normal, you know," Al said in her direction.

"Pardon?" she asked.

"The turbulence. It's totally okay. These things are built like a rock, especially this model. Very efficient engines," he assured her. She nodded reluctantly in agreement, though he wasn't entirely sure he had made her feel any more comfortable.

"Thank you," she replied.

"First time flying?" he asked.

"It is."

"You're in way more danger in a car than on an aircraft like this. Look at it that way," Al reasoned.

"Right," she said while barely opening her eyes in his direction. "Except when my car stalls, I don't fall thirty thousand feet."

"Ah, that's a myth," he said, waving her off. "Even if we have total engine failure, which is highly unlikely since there's three engines in total, planes don't just fall out of the sky. This is a glider. They would coast us to the nearest airport, and then they would pay for our hotel rooms!" She chuckled at the comment, and he was pleased he had distracted her from the movement of the plane.

"Besides, we are in the tail section of the plane. In the event they were forced to ditch or anything like that, this is the safest place to be." He leaned near her, reaching his hand out toward her, and said, "Al." For a moment, he wondered if he was trying to convince her, or *himself*.

"Eileen," she responded as she shook his hand. "Thanks, Al." He felt more confident the longer he occupied the Al persona. Al was likable, approachable, and admirable—everything Jack wasn't. Little did Eileen know that only a few feet from her, a hidden threat sat waiting in an attaché case, and it was *that* which she should be fearful of.

6

Hijackings had become increasingly prevalent over domestic airspace in the last few years, but most attempts were amateur criminals seeking asylum in Cuba. The only solution to the unsolvable problem was compliance. Airlines knew that the bad press of flight disasters could kill the business, and heroism, though noble, was not an option that jived with threats. The dire situations just simply had too many dangerous variables, and since the threat could not be properly dealt with by untrained professionals, crews were trained simply to agree and accommodate. The information collected regarding common traits hijackers might possess was unreliable, making it difficult to anticipate and identify them efficiently.

Al blended in nicely in every way possible, especially since he did not possess any features that would raise any flags. Once he had boarded the plane, he was clear of any selection process which might have identified him as a threat. It had been surprisingly easy to board the airliner with the weapon discreetly hidden by his side. Who would have suspected anything unusual about a briefcase? The FAA's identification process had too many flaws. Al was just getting started.

Al's motives, however, were not expatriation, theft, or violence. His goal was to propel the identity he had created to that of a folk hero and to prove that anyone with a little nerve, expertise, and dedication could go down in history as a master of defiance. But more important than convincing the world was proving it to himself. He would elevate his identity to make up for lost time. Like Houdini, Al had a dream of mesmerizing generations with an act that would far outlive him.

"Can I get you a beverage, sir?" a voice next to him said. Al turned to find Robin hovering over him with a smile.

"Sure, how about a scotch, neat?" he asked.

"Any preference on the scotch?" she replied.

"Surprise me," he responded. She turned toward Eileen to take her order as well, and then walked to the drunken man.

"Anything I can get you to drink, sir?" Robin asked.

"About time," he said with a slight slur in his speech. "I'll have a rum and cola."

"I'll be back with that shortly," she responded before retreating to the back of the plane. Although he might have been showing signs he should be cut off, it was in a flight attendant's best interest to keep the customer happy, and Robin didn't break character as the jovial model flight attendant for one second.

Robin's calm attitude was reflected in her dealings with the customers, and Al believed this ability would aid him well. It would soon be time to acquaint her with the new flight plan. The sun was setting deeper beneath the line of clouds now, casting a light-orange hue through the windows of the dimly lit plane. The sunglasses he had been using to disguise himself were not conducive to the low-light ambience, but a man's eyes were often the most notable facet of his appearance, and he had to keep the act up as long as possible.

The plane had leveled out a bit after retracting the flaps, and its climb became more gradual as they traveled. The plane tilted on its left wing slightly, and Al could see the geography of California through the window. Judging by the direction in which Route 405 stretched below, they were now traveling north. Studying the maps of the western portion of the contiguous states was something that had required most of his attention when he had prepared, and it was already paying off. A ding that grabbed the attention of the cabin's passengers signaled new information was coming.

"Evening again, folks," Wally began. "We're just about nearing our cruising altitude, and when we do we'll remove the seat belt sign and encourage you to try some of the other seats inside and let us know which one you like best." The middle-aged man a few rows in front of Al with jet-black hair slicked toward the back of his scalp snorted. Pilots were well known for their dry senses of humor, and they took breaks during cockpit confinement to socialize over the speaker when they could.

The snorting man lit a cigarette and exhaled the smoke above his head as if to advertise his unhealthy habit. The thick stream of airborne ash started to creep back toward Al, spinning like a tiny tornado, and he wafted the stench out of his face as it danced around the light from the window.

Robin returned, and he folded his tray table down. She placed a white napkin with the Eagle Airlines logo on the tray, followed by a cup with an amber-colored liquid. Robin juggled the other drinks, and he knew he needed to get the ball rolling before she became too busy.

"Scotch, neat," she said confidently.

"Perfect. Thank you," Al replied. He was beginning to breathe rapidly again, and a small finger of booze would be just the right thing to take the edge off.

"Robin," Al said, ensuring he used her name to establish rapport. "Could I trouble you for one more favor?"

"Sure, what can I help you with?" she asked.

"I'm a bit of an aviation nut," he started, "and I'm so fascinated by the process of flight. Could you, by chance, ask the pilot what our current whereabouts are?" She squinted at him for a moment while cocking her head. She might have been warned in her training to look for comments like that, and if it did tip her off, he had to be prepared that she might warn the captain.

"Sure," she said after a brief pause. Al kept a smile pasted across his face to limit suspicion. "Let me see what I can find out." She continued on to Eileen, handing her the coffee with a couple small cups of dairy and a stirrer. She presented the rum and cola to the drunk man, who surely did not need another, and he began sucking it down loudly—to Al's dismay.

"Thank you, darlin', keep em' comin'," he said. He guided his hand along her hip as he continued slurping the drink, and she shifted slightly to inch her body away. He could become a problem, and Al peeked around the corner and attempted to survey his size. He was mostly obscured unless he was interacting with Robin, but Al could see his shoulder jutting out past the seat, which revealed that he was large. Al was not a fighter, but he had read some techniques in a self-defense book once. He worried that he might have to neutralize him if he became unruly. Jack would never dream of picking a fight, but Al wasn't going to stand for any interference. He wouldn't allow some wino to interrupt Robin when he would need her most, and he also had little respect for sexually abusive men. Al's watch now read twenty after three. The time was now fast approaching for him to strike the hot iron. He took a good swig of the scotch, finishing about half of the cup with one gulp.

Robin approached the cabin, and Al moved to the seat that was to his immediate left, then looked out the window to the northwest. The lush green crag of Burnt Peak began to give way to the tan deserts of the eastern half of California that would eventually put the plane over Death Valley. He would need to turn this plane in another direction before it went too far north. Returning to his purchased seat row, he pulled the briefcase up from beneath his shins and placed it on the seat next to him. After releasing the locks, he clicked a small button near the battery that would make it clear that the device was armed.

This was the moment. There was no going back. This tool would be Al's bargaining chip, and an effective one at that. Al was going to inform his audience of the stakes at hand. Now that the device was active, a small blinking green light would provide an added effect. He closed the case and set it down in the seat next to the window. His heart was now fluttering. *You can do this*, he urged himself. *You are in control now. You are already dead.*

Robin was now strolling down the aisle again, and Al retrieved a small piece of paper from his pocket that he had written the day before, checking over it once more for its legibility. The ink had begun to smear a bit from the sweat that had trickled down his chest, but it was still clear enough that the message would get across. He refolded the note as she stopped at his aisle.

"The captain has informed me that if you look close, you might recognize the Angeles National Forest on the right side and below us," Robin explained. Out in the distance, he could see the sandy ocean leading to what Al knew was Edwards Air Force base. It would be from there that fighter jets would likely be scrambled if the pilot did not cooperate, or if the situation evolved to disaster.

"Great," Al replied.

"Happy to help," Robin said as she left, and he gathered the courage to quickly grab her wrist, which prompted her to frown. He did not want to resort to the physical tactics of the man nearby, but he needed to ensure he had her attention. He handed her the note that had been hiding in his pocket, and smiled as she took it from his hand. She did not read it immediately, which made him uneasy. He imagined that she had been passed notes by lonely old men attempting to court her before. She returned a curt smirk to him after he released her wrist, but he noticed her roll her eyes apathetically as she walked toward the rear of the plane. *Not good.*

Al followed her, craning his neck around the corner of the seat, then unbuckled his seat belt and removed the seatback tray to make room for an exit. There were no other passengers between them, and as he stood in the aisle, he raised his voice slightly when out of earshot of the other passengers.

"Excuse me," Al called out to her. She stopped in her tracks, turning toward him. Her jaw was clenched tightly. "I think you may want to read that note." He returned to his seat, watching her as she opened the note in a huff, seemingly annoyed by his impatience. He was biting his nails—a nasty habit he had managed to keep at bay up until that point—but by the time he realized what he was doing, he had already gnawed through the free edge of his thumbnail.

As he watched her expression run through the range of emotions from confusion to shock, soon followed by fear and then panic, he recalled what he had written on the note while she followed the text with her eyes. It read: "I have a bomb. Please sit in the seat next to me, and I will provide a list of instructions that should be given to the captain immediately. No one will be hurt if the rules are followed. - Al Ader."

Her jaw began to quiver, and her hands started trembling while she read the note again. She began to fold the note back up, albeit clumsily, and braced herself against the wall for a moment panting. He had been successful in getting her attention and returned to the forward-facing position in his seat while he awaited her arrival. A moment many who worked in the industry feared had now become a reality for her, and it was important he remain calm if he was going to convince her that everyone could make it out of this escapade unscathed—if they played by the rules. Al was now officially a criminal, but ideologically he needed to become *more*.

Robin took the seat beside him that hugged the aisle, her hands trembling as she placed them in her lap. Her gaze remained locked forward, unable to look him in the eye. He twisted his body slightly to face her, attempting camaraderie. He could see a light throbbing in her neck that was surely evidence of her elevated heart rate. Al's was not far away. Judging by the speed, it had easily shot up to a hundred and sixty beats per minute.

"Stay calm," Al pleaded with her. "I don't *want* to hurt anyone."

"Where is it?" she asked with a cracking, squeaky voice.

He reached toward the seat next to him, opening the briefcase to demonstrate that he did, in fact, possess the instrument he had threatened her with. She turned slowly, and he was close enough to see her pupils widen as she became convinced it was real. He shut the case soon after, now placing it on his lap.

"I can detonate the bomb in a myriad of ways," he warned her. "So don't think that any heroics will make the situation any more manageable. Understood?" She nodded reluctantly, still hesitating to look him in the eye. He felt powerful now. He had *control*.

"Now, listen to me very carefully, Robin. It is, as you know, incredibly important that you follow my directions. Can you do that?" She nodded, and he could see her lip was now twitching. She bit down hard on it. "I'll know immediately if you don't. You're going to inform the gentlemen in the cockpit that the plane has been hijacked. You're to explain to them that I am carrying a bomb which I can detonate at will. The flight crew should make air traffic control aware that they will not be alerting the passengers to that information. This our secret for now." She continued to nod as he presented the information, but he was worried the shock was potentially forcing the information in one ear and out the other. "Are you with me, Robin? I need your help." She closed her eyes as if the problem would go away. But it wouldn't. He *knew* from experience. "Robin," he continued. "Do you understand?"

"Yes," she replied weakly.

"Good. I want the plane grounded at Phoenix Sky Harbor. I'm going to give you specific details, but first, the most important. I want two hundred thousand dollars in American currency." She turned to him, finally looking him in the eye as her face contorted with surprise.

"Is this a joke?" she scoffed.

"I assure you it is not," Al replied, tapping his fingers on the case as if to taunt her. He felt an incredible sense of power knowing that no one would dare try to call his bluff.

"I'll need two primary parachutes as well as two reserves. That's four in total. They should be examined by the officials to ensure that they are in working order. I'm experienced, so I'll know if they are ineffective. When we arrive at Sky Harbor, I want a truck standing by for refueling. The flight crew is to inform ATC that we will not be approaching the terminal gate, and that the truck is to meet us on the tarmac in a location of my choosing. Are you still with me?"

"Yes," Robin replied as her face drooped. He knew that her mind was racing, and he did not want to overload her with information too quickly. He feared that she might make an error.

"Now, go inform the captain and flight crew in the cockpit, and then return immediately. I'll be providing you with further instruction once you come back. I want you to present them with the note you received from me as well. The only information you need to bring back to me right now is the remaining fuel capacity." Robin began to breathe deeply through her nose, exhaling through her mouth. She was now feeling a fear similar to the one Al had when he received his diagnosis: a sensation as if an elephant had sat on her chest. "Thank you," he said as she regained her composure.

She turned to him, staring at him with disdain as she seemed to have an inner debate. "Robin," he said as she hesitated. "*Now*." She stood from her seat, placed the note in a small pocket near her waist, and slid her hands across her skirt and blouse to smooth them—a force of habit that manifested itself even as the sky was falling. Al had done what Jack could not: he had jumped in the fire.

He leaned back into his seat while she hustled toward the cockpit. The passengers on the plane were none the wiser, and he had made sure to keep his voice down so no one would overhear. At some point in time, most likely when the aircraft arrived at the wrong destination, the passengers would be made aware of the situation. Some might suspect something was wrong when they spotted the sandy dunes of Arizona, but Al would give the captain instructions regarding a cover story soon enough, and that would help keep people clueless until they rolled onto the tarmac. What would happen then remained to be seen, but for now, the passengers needed to be kept in the dark.

The cockpit door shut behind Robin, and now Al would have his first taste of stardom. Surely, the flight crew would not yet tell the media of his actions, but law enforcement might, and he even *hoped* they would be scrambling to deduce who he really was—with little success. It was imperative to confuse and disorient the officials as much as possible. They would have just as many people working to gather information as they'd have ready to greet the plane. The gears in the machine turned at an accelerated rate, and only *he* had the power to stop them. There truly was no turning back now, and there were only three outcomes: Al Ader would either escape, be caught and sentenced, or killed in action.

7

Robin's hands were trembling uncontrollably. As she strode toward the cockpit, all she could think of was the kiss she'd given Glenn before leaving in the morning and how he'd practically begged her not to leave for the trip. She'd hate to have to tell him he was right, as he so often was, and as she wiped the tears that had begun to well at the corners of her eyes, she couldn't help shaking the feeling that she was *not* going to earn those tips she'd hoped for on today's flight.

"Miss?" the woman with the small child called out as Robin made her way toward the flight crew. She didn't answer for fear that she couldn't hide her expression currently and dismissed the woman's request without even looking at her. She'd get to her, of course. She had to. She was good at her job, and more importantly, Mr. Ader had made it clear that the last thing she was supposed to be doing was tipping the passengers off to the danger behind the scenes.

She slid the cockpit door open, and Wally, Tom, and Jeff were mid-conversation, Jeff holding court as he normally did. Robin slammed the door quickly, the loud crack halting the otherwise playful conversation. Jeff turned to her, the smile spread across his mouth slowly drooping at the corners when he noticed the look of utter panic on Robin's face.

"Hey, Robin," Jeff said, concerned, "What's wrong?" Robin didn't speak, the words unable to exit her lips as her eyes darted between the three of them. She reached into her skirt, fumbling clumsily for the note that Al had handed her. She handed it to Jeff without speaking a word.

The color left Jeff's face as he retrieved the note, unfolding it carefully and scanning it from top to bottom as he breathed deeply. His face now transformed like Robin's upon reading the demands and instructions on the note. Tom was the first to interrupt the quiet of the cabin.

"What does it say, Jeff?" Tom asked, nearly yelling. Jeff's eyes immediately moved back to Robin, and now his jaw hung low. He turned to Wally, but Wally's eyes were already forlorn and defeated. Wally was the oldest one on the team, and certainly had the most experience, and yet despite all the time he'd spent in the war, he'd never dealt with anything like this. He knew *exactly* what was happening without evening looking at the note.

"Are we being hijacked?" Tom cried, searching frantically around the faces of the rest of the present crew. The only answer he received was complete silence and the doom in the eyes of the others in the cabin.

"Squawk 7500," Wally said sternly to Tom. He hesitated for a moment. He knew exactly what the code meant, and his eyes wandered out to the cloudy sky that lay ahead of them as the realization set in. "Tom!" Wally cried again. There was no time to waste. Tom grabbed for the transponder without a further moment of hesitation and pressed it to his mouth.

"This... this is EA 197," Tom said, stumbling over his words. "We, uh... we've been hijacked. Transponder seven, five, zero, zero. Repeat, transponder seven, five, zero, zero, EA 197 requesting assistance. We have been hijacked."

The radio crackled for a moment. Robin's head felt light and woozy, and she braced herself against the interior wall of the cabin for fear of collapsing. Jeff shot up out of his seat and grabbed her to prevent the fall.

"You're all right," he said to her. "Come on now, stay with me, Robin."

"I'm okay," Robin replied, breathing heavily as she gasped for air. "It just feels so tight in here. How the hell do you guys stay in here so long?" she asked. Jeff laughed for a moment, interrupting the tension and forcing a smile out of Robin.

The radio hissed again. "We hear you, 197," the en route controller said. "This is Phoenix ATC. Please confirm the number of souls on board."

Tom quickly flipped through the manifest. "Thirty-seven, including flight crew."

"197, are you currently planning on maintaining course?" Tom turned to Jeff. He hadn't seen the note himself, and was now flying blind. Jeff nodded.

"Yes, Phoenix," Tom said. "We, uh... we weren't originally scheduled to see you guys. We're scheduled for Seattle."

"Phoenix," Robin said. "He wants to go to Phoenix."

"But it looks like we need to come pay you a visit," Tom said into the transponder. He snapped his fingers quickly in Jeff's direction, and Jeff handed him the note that Al had given Robin. Tom began to read from the note into the transponder, "Here's what I've got for you: the hijacker is claiming to have a bomb, given name Al, Ader. That's Alpha, Lima, Alpha, Delta, Echo, Romeo, and he's requesting a landing in Sky Harbor." Tom scanned the note quickly before clicking the button to talk, a mixture of confusion and astonishment in his eyes, "Among other things."

"Thank you, 197," the en route controller replied. "Is he with you in the cockpit right now?"

"No," Tom replied.

"Copy that. You guys just maintain a course for Phoenix. We're going clear the air for you and get you down here. In the meantime, we're going to call this in. Keep the line open."

"Will do," Tom replied.

No one spoke. Wally clicked a few buttons on the control panel to alter their course toward Phoenix, and Jeff grabbed for a manual from a shelf inside the cabinet nearby that contained information on proper procedures.

"Does anyone know?" Wally asked Robin.

"No, I don't think so," Robin said. "Just us."

"Good, keep it that way," he replied. "We can't have a panic." He turned to her, locking eyes with her sympathetically. "How are you?"

"Wishing I didn't come to work today," Robin said with a faint smirk, "but otherwise okay."

"Is he a big guy?" Jeff asked angrily. His chest was heaving up and down, the vein in his neck throbbing and his fist balled up at his side.

"Are you out of your mind?" Tom barked. "The guy's got a *bomb*."

"Do we know that for sure?" Jeff snapped. He turned to Robin, seeking an answer. She nodded.

"Certainly looked like one," Robin said. "Dynamite, I think."

"Christ," Tom replied. He massaged his temples between his thumb and forefingers, and his face fell into his palm.

"What's he look like?" Jeff asked.

"Well," Robin said, "he doesn't look like anything in particular. He's relatively handsome, I guess, but he's got dark sunglasses on. His hair's parted at the side, he's trim, about your size, I guess."

"Robin," Wally said. "You've got to get back out there." Robin nodded, wiping the sweat from her temple and the hair that had had matted itself against her forehead.

"Right now you're the only one who can keep this train on the tracks," Wally said. "Keep him happy. Whatever he needs, give it to him."

"The note said he's going to let everyone off the plane if he gets the cash," Jeff chimed in.

"Yeah, that's what they all say," Tom said defiantly. "Didn't they give Flight 85 the cash? That booty wound up spread across the Atlantic, along with the crew and passengers."

"Well we have to assume that's the truth," Wally said in a harsh growl. He was the captain, and he reminded Tom with the furrow of his brow that *he* was still in charge, no matter what Ader had going on in the cabin of the plane.

"What if I took a walk back there and made like I was taking a leak? Maybe get an eye on it?" Tom asked.

"If he suspects something, then we could endanger everyone," Jeff replied. "How we do know he doesn't have his finger on the detonator? What's it look like anyway, Robin?"

"Well, he's got a briefcase. There's all these sticks in there, you know? It's got blinking lights."

"Well, I could wrestle it from him," Tom said. "You heard her, he doesn't sound so mean."

"He doesn't need to be," Tom replied. "Any guy who boards a commercial airliner claiming he's got a bomb has balls in my book, and neither you nor I should be the ones to call his bluff."

"What if I took my uniform off?" Jeff began. "You know, look like a civilian and just try to size him up?"

"Don't be stupid," Wally said. "If he's telling the truth and he's going to let everyone walk, then why even risk it?"

"I'd like to get out there and take him out myself," Tom said. "Grab his neck with my hands and show him whose plane this is."

"But that's not the way we do things," Wally replied. "That's not the way the company wants it, and that's not the way I want it. So you just sit in that seat and keep your hand on that damn transponder until I tell you otherwise, understood?"

"Sir," Tom said sheepishly.

"He wants to know how much fuel is remaining," Robin said.

Wally eyed the gauge before saying, "About 4500 gallons."

"Maybe he does want to land. Maybe he's going to get his dough and make off with it, but let me just ask this," Tom started again. "What the hell would he need four parachutes for?"

8

Rex Schulz twirled a cigarette in one hand and a lighter in the other. It had been weeks since he'd had one, and he was proud of himself for making it nearly a month without a smoke. He'd been hearing the reports about the dangers, but he still felt good despite picking the habit up in his teens. His wife, Sandy, had made him quit after reading a report in the *The Heat*, a Phoenix, Arizona-based newspaper, about the correlation between cigarette smoking and lung cancer, but most of the guys in his atmosphere still did, and that made it that much harder to quit.

A no-nonsense, gruff man with sandy blonde hair and a shave so close it could only belong to a federal agent, Rex had relocated to the Phoenix area after getting kicked down the ladder. He loathed the Phoenix heat, and he felt he'd been shafted, but he was thankful to have the job. Nothing mattered so much as the job. Earlier in the year, a hostage negotiation in Richmond had gone terribly wrong, leaving three hostages injured and the criminals who'd stuck up a bank still on the loose. He'd handled the situation to the best of his ability, actively trying to protect the innocent people who'd been trapped inside the facility. When the teller had rung for the authorities, a good Samaritan with a gun had signaled to Rex through a window that he was going to participate, but the men he was dealing with were not playing games, and Rex wound up with egg on his face when they blew their way through the garrison that had been formed outside the building. The exchange of gunfire had taken two agents out in the process.

Though he maintained he'd won the fight because anybody who didn't ask to be there had come out alive save for the heroic gunman, the top brass didn't see it that way. The Bauer brothers—as Jackie, Jody, and Jasper Bauer were known—were old-school heist kind of guys, and rather than plan and plot, they were known for popping up at banks around the country and sticking guns in tellers' faces to get the job done. They'd thought they were still cowboys, only instead of rolling in on horses, they chose stolen cars that they'd commandeer the morning of the hit and ditch when things got hot. They'd already knocked off seven banks across the east coast with no pattern whatsoever before they'd even crossed paths with Rex. Unfortunately, Rex, though being the only one to corner them, had let them not only slip through the bureau's fingers, but also injure two of his own in the process.

Never mind the fact that the injured parties who'd lived to see another day thought of Rex as a hero, he'd lost the bandits during the firefight, and to him, there was no greater failure. When dealing with criminals, casualties might be expected—he was prepared for that—but nothing drove Rex more nuts than just barely catching his man only to see him live to rob again. He'd been given command of a small group of men in the greater Phoenix area—what he considered babysitting since they were young guys—and most of the work they'd been doing since he had arrived consisted of tracking financial crimes in the state of Arizona.

He'd been fed up with the case he was currently working on—a check forger known as Slim Kenny—whom he'd been very close to catching leading up to the holiday. There weren't likely to be any developments on the Wednesday night before Thanksgiving, so when the phone rang and his wife halted the prepping of her famous cranberry sauce (Rex's favorite dish) to hand it to him, the bewildered look on her face made him leap from his chair with great anticipation.

"This is Agent Schulz," Rex said into the phone.

"Hi, Rex," a cautious voice said from the other end. He knew who it was right away: Agent Kerry Ahern. His wife watched anxiously, wiping her hands nervously on her apron as Rex's face wrinkled. Ahern had been a partner of Rex's during several cases in which he worked closely with the Maryland Bureau; after Rex got the boot from Virginia, Ahern had taken his job and, to make matters worse, quickly moved up the ladder. Rex hadn't particularly felt animosity toward him, but it was hard to be excited to hear his voice.

"Hello, Kerry," Rex replied. He was spinning the cigarette between his fingers, now awaiting a response. It drove Sandy nuts, but she'd got him to quit, so she didn't have much room to complain if he still felt some attachment to it. He'd been clutching the same cigarette for weeks, and she'd been just as astonished as him that he hadn't smoked it yet. "I'm hoping you're calling me because my friend Slim Kenny has decided to come your way?"

"No," Kerry replied. "How fast can you get to the office?"

Rex made it to the office in record time. He'd had his wife call all of his men to save time and be the first one in the door after getting the news. Though she was anything but thrilled to see him walk out on Thanksgiving preparation—she'd invited fourteen members of her family, after all—she saw a pep in his step that she hadn't seen in months. For a moment, she even thought it might be okay to let him have the cigarette that had been dangling from his mouth as he put his suit on hastily.

She pulled the cigarette from his hand when he went to kiss her goodbye, and after crumpling it between her fingers, handed him a pack of gum instead. The gum helped to an extent—at least he said it did. "Freud would have a field day with you," she'd often tell him. She told him to be safe, and that she loved him. She never asked much about his cases, because ever since the Bauer Brothers fiasco, he didn't much like talking about them. Judging by the speed at which he rushed out the door though, she knew it was something *big*.

———

The Phoenix office was the pits as far as Rex was concerned. It had been converted into an FBI field office only a couple years earlier and not only did it smell of rust and mold, but it had a mouse problem that had forced the men to stop eating in the place entirely. Luckily for them, smoking was still on that table, and though it only made Rex more anxious to be around it so much, he kept busy out in the field to reduce the temptation. The walls had once been white, but the amount of smoke that filled the structure on a daily basis had turned the walls a yellow cream color.

When Rex entered the conference room, his men were all eager and ready, buried in a sea of paperwork that made him proud he had at least been given a good team to command. All of their shoes were as cleanly polished as his, casting glossy black reflections whenever they entered a room, and they all wore the same black sport coat, slacks, and tie that Rex wore. He made it very clear when they'd come aboard that no matter what the situation was, they would always look like they should be feared. He took the job seriously, and he demanded his men did as well. Never mind the fact that they'd take his job given the opportunity; for now they were eager to please.

Rex reached into the breast pocket of his jacket, removing the pack of gum Sandy had placed inside earlier. He shook it, and found there was only one stick left. A hazy cloud of cigarette smoke hung thick in the air, but Rex removed the stick from its foil wrapper and tossed it into his mouth. He was relieved to find it revealed a refreshing wintergreen flavor that permeated his mouth with an icy cool chill that mimicked the menthol cigarettes he'd become fond of right before he'd quit.

"Talk to me," Rex said, not looking at anyone in particular, but addressing all of his team in unison. All of the men briefly looked at each other, wondering who might be the first to open his mouth. Mitch O'Hallaron, a muscular, handsome man who looked like he couldn't have been more than a few years out of the military with his squared-off buzz cut, leaned forward and cleared his throat as he opened a small manilla envelope. For all intents and purposes, he was the second-in-command.

"EA Flight 197 heading from LA to Seattle receives the threat from a man at seat 15B—though that's debatable since we got two different reports already from the cockpit —via handwritten note," Mitch said as he scanned his notes with the tip of his pen. "The hijacker gives the name Al Ader." Mitch glanced around the room to confirm everyone was still listening. "That's Alpha, Lima, Alpha, Delta, Echo, Romeo for the spelling-challenged." The room rumbled with a chorus of laughter, but Rex's face remained stoic. "Flight attendant, a Miss... uh-" Mitch said as he continued down the page, "Robin Kraft, confirms the explosive."

"What do we have on Ader?" Rex asked, the gum now slapping inside his jaw like he'd been taught to chew by cows.

"Nothing," Mitch said in a semi-defeated tone. "No criminal record, no history, deeds, banking information, driver's license. The guy's a ghost."

"Maybe he's got a library card," Ken Hammer said, and the room responded again with a chuckle. He was a plump man whose horn-rimmed glasses hung at the bridge of his nose and obscured his eyes slightly with forearms covered in a thick fur coat of black hair. Rex turned to him, his eyes accusing and punishing as he made it clear without words that *he* wasn't laughing. "We're looking into the possibility it's an alias, sir," Ken quickly course-corrected as he sat up in his chair. These guys didn't yet know that when Rex Schulz meant business, he didn't have time for jokes. They hadn't yet been in a situation like this in his company. The current case at their desk concerning the mysterious whereabouts of

Slim Kenny was small potatoes compared to a skyjacking.

Rex began to pace, massaging his jaw with his hand as he turned away from the team and toward the plethora of documents that had been laid across the desk. "And the requests?"

"Two hundred thousand in negotiable American currency," Mitch began. "Four parachutes—that's two full and two reserve—and a tanker waiting at Phoenix."

Rex continued his trip around the room, the men watching him as the gears in his brain turned. "Do we know if he's armed?"

"The man ain't revealed no weapon yet other than the explosive," a man with a thick Texas twang said. Otto Byrne, an older gentleman who had a thick head of white hair that made him look younger than he truly was and still wore a bolo tie with his suit, had taken the lead on researching the bomb. He'd been a demolitions expert in the Second World War and he knew a thing or two about things that went "boom."

After scrutinizing the papers on the large desk briefly and walking a full circle around the room, Rex stopped again at the head to address his team. He paused, breathed deeply, and everyone waited patiently while they witnessed the calm before every piston in his head started firing on all cylinders. He exhaled and chewed the gum rapidly before opening his mouth to speak.

"All right, I want schematics of the aircraft," Rex said. He turned to Mitch. "What did you say it was?"

Mitch looked down at his paper. "A Bauering Trijet, 100 series, sir."

"Good, get those," Rex replied. "I want a map of Sky Harbor. I want a unit at ATC." Rex turned to Ken and Dale

Bledsoe. The first he wanted out of his face, and the second he knew had experience as a pilot. "That'll be you two." He turned back to Mitch and Otto. "You two are on the ground. Mitch, get the Phoenix Sheriff's Department on the line and send them over too. Then, call LAPD and see if they've got anything on that name in their database. Check in with the airline reps at EA and see if they got a visual or any record of his check-in."

"Roger," Mitch replied attentively.

"Ken, when you get up to ATC, tell them to prep a tanker, but do not—and I can't stress this enough—dispatch any personnel near the aircraft—theirs or ours. Tell them to halt all incoming and outgoing flights immediately unless it's our bird. Make sure that information makes it way to our friends at Phoenix PD as well." He turned now to Otto, who'd been eagerly awaiting the next instruction, admiring Rex for his ability to spring into action. "Otto, I want a three-hundred-foot perimeter around that taxi zone. No one goes in our out unless it gets my okay."

"Will do," Otto replied.

"It's a holiday weekend," Rex said. "Our time is short, and our resources are limited. Mitch, after you make those calls, pinpoint every diving school and military base in the Arizona area. Find us some parachutes."

"Ten-four," Mitch replied.

Rex turned to the group, giving no one in particular the next set of instructions, but making them all responsible to work as a team as he believed they should. "I want a flight manifest, too. How many people on board?"

"It was thirty-seven, sir," Mitch replied quickly. "Including flight crew."

"Do we want to call UAF?" Ken asked.

"No," Rex replied swiftly. "Not until we learn more. We don't want to scare him just yet. I want him on the *ground*. When we get ATC on the line, tell them to ensure that the pilots do not alert the passengers." Rex paused for a moment, mulling over the plan in his head, and harkening back to the Bauer Brothers disaster earlier in the year. "We can't afford any heroics."

"With all due respect, Schulz, are you planning on bargaining with this man?" Ken asked with a hint of defiance in his voice.

"Right now we're going to play Mr. Ader's game," Rex answered. "Anyone who's got a problem with that, the door's right there." Rex pointed with a strong finger toward the exit, "Take it up with DC. I'll be en route momentarily."

Rex grabbed the briefcase he'd entered with off the desk and made for the door in one quick motion. The gum in his mouth was already losing its flavor, and the waft of smoke that followed him as he made his exit was as tempting as an apple in Eden. He could have bummed a cigarette from any of them with the snap of his fingers, but when he was out of the room it would be that much easier.

"Sir, where are you going?" Mitch called out.

"To call Van Cortland," Rex replied.

When Rex had left, Mitch glanced around the room as the other men stared with glassy eyes. "You heard the man." The group quickly gathered their belongings, and the sound of a thousand shuffling papers filled the room.

"Yeehaw," Otto said energetically as he fixed his tie.

9

The pilot, Al was sure, had now squawked 7500 on his transponder, which was code for "hijacking in progress." He had familiarized himself with the codes of communication in addition to what he already knew about aviation. His mother had had little to no money to her name, and she'd spent most of her sober hours working double shifts as a waitress at a local truck stop. Al spent one summer reading extensively about air travel while she had been gone.

ATC would take the threat seriously, and soon they would be playing by Al's rules. The captain and flight crew have full authority over a vessel in a flight situation that has turned dangerous, but the actions Al had taken had effectively transformed *him* into the captain—no matter what the protocol was. Although he was not physically flying the plane, he would soon have control over its actions.

By now, the FBI had received the information and would most likely contact the owner of the airline to inform them of the situation. The owner of Eagle Airlines was a successful entrepreneur named JG Van Cortland. Van Cortland had dealt with threats like this before, and Al was counting on the fact that previous scenarios had ended poorly for the wealthy old man. After a recent—and certainly personal—snafu over the Atlantic, Al was confident Van Cortland would at least *attempt* to play by the rules. Airlines did not want the bad press of playing hardball, and if the Bureau allowed it, soon old JG would be a player in this game as well.

At this point, Al imagined that they were running the fake name, trying desperately to develop a psychological profile based on the little information they received. It would yield no results. The name itself would only function as a yarn ball of misinformation. He was hoping to run them in circles, providing them with few clues as to his motives, which would make their dealings with him work in his favor. At least that was what he hoped, for a simple bit of misdirection that would tangle them up in that yarn like distracted cats.

The door to the cockpit opened again, and Al could see even from a distance that Robin's perfectly applied makeup had become a bit messy. She shut the door behind her, applying the phony persona that she presented to the passengers yet again, and made her way toward him to continue their dialogue. She took the seat beside him, and although it blocked his exit when she did so, he believed it unlikely that she would attempt to overpower him. Still, he would have to keep his wits about him in his current state. Al was not at the top of his game in terms of focus, and if anyone attempted to subdue him, it was possible that he could be detained by the passengers themselves.

"How did it go?" Al asked nicely. He wanted to assure

her that he wasn't some dangerous maniac, even though he was sure she thought he was. Robin surveyed the other passengers nervously, but most were just sleeping, reading their periodicals, or otherwise distracted.

"Roughly 4500 gallons. Now what?" she asked nervously.

"I want to make sure we don't alert the other passengers," he warned, "so our communication from this point forward will be through myself and the captain, with you acting as an intermediary. I'll tell you what I need, and you will repeat that back to the flight deck. Understood?"

"Understood," she replied with a trembling voice.

"Relax, Robin," he assured her. "Are any other attendants aware of the situation?"

"Just the cockpit crew," she responded.

"Good," he said. Keeping control of this orchestra would require all the instruments to stay in their rightful sections, only to be called upon when the music commanded it. He had to think of all of the variables like a maestro. Right now, Robin was performing a solo.

"What's next?" she asked.

"I'll need to know our elevation, heading, and current location, as well as flight speed. Repeat that back to me."

"Elevation, location, and heading."

"And flight speed," he added.

"And flight speed," she responded quickly.

"Robin, it's very important that you bring me back accurate information." He let his glasses fall a bit to the bridge of his nose and looked her directly in the eyes. "If you're lying, I'll know," he said gravely. Al then returned the glasses to their rightful place over his eyes. He didn't want to give away too much of his appearance, but he had ensured that he would be unrecognizable, and he wanted to be positive that she took his words seriously. "Don't make me clip your wings." She wrinkled her nose at him, clearly offended.

"Miss?" a voice called out from in front of them. Robin looked to Al, wondering whether she should tend to the passenger, and he nodded to grant her approval. She would have to maintain the illusion that everything was still normal inside the plane to keep up the charade.

The drunk man was requesting another drink. But when he handed her the empty cup, Robin dropped it, spilling shards of ice all over the floor. He grumbled in response, and she apologized to the man profusely. Al couldn't fault her for her clumsiness given the circumstances. He had to keep a closer eye on him. He was becoming more of an unnecessary distraction.

The plane began to turn right, and Al took that as a clear sign that they were now moving in an easterly direction that would take them to Phoenix. Seattle was still far north, and he knew that the personnel corresponding on the ground had given them the okay to comply with him at least until the plane sat safely on a runway. At this point, Al was sure Van Cortland was aware of the pirate that had gained control of his plane, though whether he cared more about the property or the passengers was irrelevant. They had taken the bait.

The plane would soon be crossing over the Mojave, and it was during this time that the officials would be rapidly gathering the items that he had requested. Although Al had made large demands, the government agents were capable of acquiring nearly all of what he needed with relative ease, especially when lives were at stake. The cash and fuel would be easy to obtain. Additionally, the money was readily available for an event like a hijacking or hostage situation—which he had easily discovered with just a bit of research—and the gasoline resided at the airport. The parachutes, on the other hand, were of the greatest concern. He was sure they would love nothing more than to see him plummet thousands of feet to his death, effectively closing the case. He wouldn't put it past the feds to consider giving him a defective parachute, but the request for four would make them second guess that idea. They would consider the notion that he might force someone to jump with him—and maybe he would. If they did not provide him with an adequate method of escape, the situation could become more dire.

Robin passed by him briskly and handed the slurring man yet another beverage. His retrieval was both sloppy and ferocious, which made Al more anxious of his actions by the second. She continued toward the cockpit to issue the next set of instructions, and the bell inside the cabin dinged once again.

"Evening, folks, this is the captain once again. I hope you are all having a comfortable flight so far. I hate to be the bearer of bad news, but unfortunately we're going to have a slight change of plans this evening," Wally explained through the intercom. Eileen became uneasy as her eyes opened. She had been sleeping throughout most of his interactions with Robin, unaware of what had transpired. A slight deviation in the plan was a nightmare to someone like her, and she briskly rose in her seat as Wally continued.

"I assure you it's nothing to worry about, but we've been directed by the guys on the ground to head to Phoenix to put the aircraft down." There were groans and complaints throughout the cabin. Al was counting on the flight staff to keep them calm.

"We apologize for any inconvenience, but when we land, we'll make sure you get your flight rescheduled and back on your way to Seattle. Although we're delayed, we here at AE prefer to arrive late in this world, rather than early in the other one." Al chuckled at Wally's comment, but an audible gasp inside the aircraft confirmed others did not find it as funny. "Just a little joke, folks," Wally said. "We'll have you back on your way in no time." There was that dry pilot wit in action. It was a clever line, but Al didn't think it would help to calm the nerves of the surely annoyed passengers. He admired his tranquility under pressure. After all, Wally knew what was going on behind the scenes in the back of his plane. Al didn't have that coolness down yet, though he was learning. *Nothing left to lose.*

"Minor mechanical difficulty?" Eileen asked as she leaned in Al's direction.

"It's nothing to worry about," he replied.

"You think?" she said. He could see the worry in her face setting in yet again.

"Sure. You think if it was *that* bad they wouldn't tell us?" he reasoned.

"I suppose not," she said with a smirk. She was wrong, dreadfully wrong. That was *exactly* what the crew would do, but she didn't know any better, and he certainly wasn't going to be the one to tell her. Flight crews were trained to alert their passengers to updates purely on a need-to-know basis. If the plane were going down, you wouldn't know until it was absolutely unavoidable.

Robin walked past him once again, not making eye contact, and he followed—briefcase in hand—and diverted to the bathroom for a moment. He could see Norma approaching the rear of the plane before he shut the door. May had been too busy tending to passengers and preparing items in the front galley to be privy to what was going on, and he hadn't had to worry about her—yet. Now Robin was about to come face-to-face with Norma, and Al was worried that Norma could recognize Robin's rare form.

He patted his face with a tissue, trying to rid himself of sweat. He worried that his complexion had become worse during the time he had spent on the plane, but hoped the cosmetics he had applied would continue to keep up the disguise. He felt a bit shaky, but invigorated. Who was this man that stood in front of him? The flight had probably taken its toll on his already weakened body, and he was glad they would soon get a reprieve in Phoenix. Even though the Phoenix runway would make less physical demands on his body, his brain would need to be firing on all cylinders.

10

James Grady Van Cortland sat quietly in the long shadows that stretched across his office. The late afternoon sun cut sharp swaths of light through the large picture windows, leaving him in a gloomy, hollow corner. The only life besides his own that could be found in the room resided in the color of his plaid print sport coat. Though he was proud of the 16,000-square-foot-property he called home in Scottsdale, Arizona the only other current resident was Norman Krüger, his attendant and butler who'd been around since before JG had even been born. Norman had grown up in service to the Van Cortland family, much like his father Berit Krüger before him, and Van Cortland had thought of him more as an older brother, and at times even as a sort of consigliere when concerning certain matters for which he was unequipped.

JG twirled a small black and white photograph in his hand—a picture of both himself and his younger brother, Jacob, taken mere months before his tragic death. JG had been mourning him more than a year now, and the loss coupled with his rapid aging had sent him into an almost agoraphobic state. Despite the morbid event—a hijacking and extortion attempt that had gone completely wrong and in which his brother had met his death—Eagle Airlines, the company which he had parlayed his family's fortune into, had continued to grow. JG had not inherited his father Abe's ability to always be ahead of the curve—that was Jacob's doing—but he did have the knowledge and, of course, resources to both grow his fleet of airliners and offer the most competitive prices, which had aided the two brothers successfully when turning Eagle Airlines into *the* commercial air carrier.

Despite the wealth it had brought him, nothing was going to bring Jacob back, and it was then that JG, who'd otherwise spent frivolously in the tradition of his rich family, realized that money could not buy *anything*. It was a harsh reality that had forced JG to question many of the actions he'd taken in his life, and now that he had realized his own mortality, he was at a standstill with what to do next with Van Cortland Industries. Though he was prepared to move into the next decade and once again turn the company into something his father could have never dreamed of—even without the help of Jacob—he was not prepared for the knock at the door that would change the company's fate forever.

"Mr. Van Cortland," Norman's muffled German voice said through the thick wooden door. Regardless of their kinship, Norman always kept up with proper tradition and wouldn't dream of calling his boss "JG" Or "Jim," as some of his close associates would.

"Come in," JG answered. He quickly discarded the picture into the drawer of his desk, as Norman had already caught him staring off into it in a melancholic state before, and though he hadn't pushed JG to stop with his sobbing, he'd made some subtle remarks about wallowing. Norman entered, a balding man wearing a black tuxedo that he'd never taken off when on the job, and JG noticed the dire expression on his face immediately.

"Ahem," Norman said, clearing his throat. "Line one, sir. Very urgent."

JG placed the phone to his ear, mumbling only the letters "JG," as if he couldn't be bothered.

"Jim," the voice on the other end of the line said, "it's Rex." JG'S chest puffed up instantaneously. A call from a federal agent was never a good thing, especially one he knew personally. He wasn't up to anything suspicious, since he'd always kept the books clean and hadn't dared commit a financial crime.

Rex and JG had spent some time together when investigating a fraud case at one of his New Jersey locations—Van Cortland Park—in which some criminals had been funneling money through one of his businesses. Rex had been in need of his assistance to weed through the paperwork. They had become quite friendly, not that JG often spent time with guys like Rex, but the time spent together had eventually put them on a first-name basis.

"It's happening again," Rex simply said, and JG knew everything that he implied with the statement. JG buried his head in his hand, massaging the thick white line where his hair—which had remained very healthy despite his age—met his forehead. "Phoenix," Rex said. "He wants cash."

"It's like déjà vu," JG said softly. It had been just over a year since the last time he'd dealt with a situation like this, and it had ended so poorly he'd almost considered selling the airline outright. The FAA hadn't helped with the matter, and there was so little airport security that it might as well have been the wild west. JG's hadn't been the only company dealing with the problem, but it certainly didn't need the press of another disaster like EA Flight 85.

JG looked down at the watch on his wrist—a small piece of jewelry that did nothing but tell the time and cost more than the average sucker made in a year. "Contact America Bank on East Van Buren Street," JG said. "Tell them what you need. I'll see you there."

JG slammed the phone on the receiver so forcefully he nearly cracked it. He'd barely gotten over the last debacle and here he was looking another one in the face. This one, however, was local, and as JG stood from his desk, he couldn't help but think that it was *not* pure coincidence that it would be taking place so close to his home. EA Flight 85 had required him to travel to bargain with the terrorists, and that flight had wound up scattered—along with Jacob's remains—across the Atlantic Ocean. He was determined not to see that happen again. JG opened the drawer in front of him, grabbed a small .38 revolver, and tucked it into the back of his waistband.

———

The America Bank on East Van Buren Street in Phoenix was not open on the Wednesday night before Thanksgiving, but when you're the FBI, or better yet, JG Van Cortland, you can make anything happen. JG arrived with Norman at his side just as the sun began to sneak behind the White Tank Mountains. Norman would always offer input if asked, and JG had been bringing him along more frequently now that Jacob had left his side.

Rex stood beside the front glass doors, his arms folded and his mouth chewing rapidly on a piece of gum. Two agents stood by at the front door, both dressed in black suits and wearing no other defining articles other than the guns that rested on their hips. When JG finally arrived at Rex's position, they shared a handshake like old friends, but there were no smiles to follow.

"How are you, Jim?" Rex asked.

"Unnerved," JG answered. Rex noticed how dark the bags under his eyes had gotten. The billionaire had already looked old when he'd first met him years ago, but he'd suspected that the fallout from his brother's death had done a number on him, and he also sympathized with how painful this repeat performance might be. "I thought you were heading to Richmond."

Rex paused for a moment. He was too embarrassed to tell the man with whom he was about to walk into a hostage situation that the guys up top had thought he was unfit for a situation like this. This particular one had fallen into his lap, and the last thing he wanted to do was make JG feel like he wasn't in good company. "The wife likes the desert," Rex replied. The bank manager appeared with a key ring from behind the glass door and opened it to allow entry, then directed Rex, JG, Norman, and the agents into the bank.

"Follow me, gentlemen," the bank manager said to the team. He knew exactly who JG was, as he'd dealt with him during the purchase of his estate, and considering the rest of the men had badges, there wasn't much more to prove.

"Have you given the flight crew compliance orders?" JG asked Rex as they strode into the dimly lit bank. The manager hadn't even turned the lights on since he'd arrived hastily, and an orange hue was cast throughout the entrance.

"Immediately," Rex replied. "So far so good."

"And the amount?"

"Two hundred thousand," Rex replied sheepishly through the wad of gum slapping against his teeth.

"Fucking madman," JG replied. The manager opened the vault deep inside the bank, and a large metal door swung open to reveal a stainless-steel table in the center of the room.

"The transaction will be deducted from your account, but the bills will be monitored on our end," Rex reassured him. The bank manager began to pile neatly stacked bills onto the table, and the agents accompanying Rex opened two large canvas bags.

"L series," the manager said. "All linear, and registered into the system via microfilm. If anyone uses them, you'll know.

As the agents began to pack the bills in the bags, JG became visibly nervous and began pacing around the interior of the vault. Rex walked over, speaking in a low tone.

"Jim," Rex began. He wanted to tell him it was going to be okay, that they were going make sure this one didn't go south and that they'd learned from past mistakes—or at least, *he* had—but JG knew better.

"A man walks onto a plane and threatens the crew, scrambles the department, and extorts me for cash—and we reward him," JG said somberly.

"Hey," Rex said reassuringly, "this ain't no 'fly me to Cuba,' and we're already close to getting that plane on the ground." Rex's efforts to convince JG otherwise were failing, and it wasn't helping his own confidence where he'd already been lacking. "We bargain with him. We give him what he wants in exchange for the safe release of the passengers. Then, we take it from there."

"I've heard that before," JG said, looking at Rex with a hollowness in his eyes that stretched infinitely into a black void.

"Except this time *I'm* in charge of the operation," Rex responded.

"And if you're vetoed? If the order comes from the top down and you're left with no choice. Then what?"

"I'm not going to let that happen. *Nothing* is going to happen to those people. They're all going to be home stuffing their faces with turkey tomorrow."

"That's what we thought last time," JG replied. His eyes wandered toward Norman, who'd been standing quietly at attention while the big boys talked. Though JG hadn't spoken a word, Norman knew his opinion was being summoned, and he gathered his thoughts for a moment before speaking.

"Unfortunately, sir," Norman said, "he's left you no choice. A grounded plane gives you options. I'd imagine it's best to deliver his requests and reevaluate the scenario as needed."

"He's got a bomb, Jim," Rex said to JG. "We're going to play nice." JG wasn't biting, even with Norman's reassurance added, and as the agents packed up the last couple piles of cash from the table, JG nodded reluctantly to signal he had no choice but to play the game.

"I'm coming with you," JG said. "I want to be on the ground with your men—every step of the way."

"Can do," Rex replied. There may have been a protocol that dictated whether or not he was allowed to be there for the process, but since they'd be forming a perimeter around the airliner, Rex doubted JG could cause any real trouble or stop his men from doing their jobs effectively, and more importantly, he felt bad for the guy. He'd known people thought of JG as one of those out-of-touch billion-aire philanthropists that you'd read about in the paper or see in the movies, but he'd known Jim, and that was good enough for him. Besides, if there was anything they needed to know about the plane or the flight crew, JG might have the answers.

The agents walked out of the vault with the money bags slung over their shoulders, and both Norman and JG followed along toward the two black cruisers that had been parked out front. Rex trailed behind as the manger resealed the vault. A situation had been dropped in his lap that was more dire than the last he'd failed to resolve, and it made him uneasy. He didn't have JG's confidence, and he didn't have any flavor left in the damn gum, but he was determined to get his man.

11

A crash outside the lavatory prompted Al to open the door slightly to search for the source of the commotion. He gathered by the ruckus that Norma had bumped into Robin and surprised her. He placed his ear near the crack of the door, listening intently.

"Sorry, hun," Norma giggled.

"That's... that's alright," Robin said tremulously.

"Hey, you alright?" Norma asked.

"Yea, just some asshole in 14A."

"There's always one," Norma joked. "Can't believe you got the big job tonight. I've got nearly ten years on you and they just passed me right up."

"Oh," Robin replied awkwardly. "Well, I guess because I've been through the training, I could pick up the slack."

"Don't be silly, little bird," Norma said, leaning in and dropping to a whisper. "My hips ain't as cute as yours and you and I both know it." Robin didn't reply. Al imagined if he could see her face she would look offended. Norma probably *could* do the job, but the airline surely believed that a car that ran well wasn't as desirable as one with a flashy coat of paint. "What's the malfunction?"

"Malfunction?" Robin replied, confused.

"Yeah, I heard we had difficulty over the intercom," Norma answered.

"Oh. Right. Faulty oil gauge," Robin replied quickly. "ATC couldn't solve the problem using the manual. They'd rather be safe than sorry. I'm sure it will be quick." Al was impressed by Robin's ability to think quickly, and he was reassured that he had made the right choice when selecting her to help him. He could hear the clinking glass signaling Norma had retrieved a fresh pot of coffee from the galley, and then opened the refrigerator to get some milk. Al couldn't see the interaction well through the sliver of open door, but he could hear it clearly.

"Let's hope so," Norma said. "Don got a new color TV for the living room, and we're going to watch the parade together. See you in a bit." Al waited for Norma to leave, then exited the bathroom as Norma glided down the aisle with a cart. He closed the bathroom door, and Robin nearly leaped out of her skin.

"Hi, Robin," Al said, with a cat-like purr. He could tell she was uneasy when she searched around his sunglasses, his eyes lost behind the dark circular lenses.

She breathed deeply, regaining her composure before saying, "Elevation is thirty thousand feet," in a soft whisper. "Flight speed is four hundred fifty-two miles per hour, heading of three-fifty—"

"And it looks like were leaving the Death Valley area," Al interrupted.

"What do you need me for if you know so much?" Robin asked impatiently.

"Simple," he replied. "If I go into the cockpit, it's

possible I could be overpowered. I'll be staying back here where it's nice and safe and I can see everything that goes on. Great work, Robin. I'm going to return to my seat now. I'll give you more instructions when the time comes."

When Al returned to his seat, he fastened his seatbelt. He still had a small amount of scotch on the adjacent tray table, and he threw it down his throat while enjoying the familiar sting of hard liquor. He could not afford to be drunk, but the perfect amount of liquor could put a person into a laser-like focus. It was a fine line he thought of as the alcoholic Goldilocks zone. Robin returned to his seat, to his surprise, and she was gritting her teeth.

"You don't have to do this," she said.

"I do," Al replied.

"Why?"

"There's many reasons, a few of which are infamy, legend, and legacy. *Legacy*, Robin," he proclaimed.

"Why like this?" she asked, shaking her head in frustration.

"It's not the escape audiences remember. It's the danger," Al explained. She stood there waiting, her eyes wide and moving rapidly. He now saw in her what so many others must have seen in him: true fear.

"Don't look at me like that, Robin. If all of the directions are followed properly, this will end well for all of us. That's a promise. Promises aren't meant to be broken, are they?"

"You're a criminal. You're a terrorist. *That's* your legacy," she replied with disdain.

"Not if no one gets hurt," he assured her. "Besides, I don't believe that's how they trained you in flight school to manage an emergency situation, is it? Provoking the suspect, that is." Robin buried her head in her hands, covering her face and rubbing her eyes aggressively as if trying to force herself out of a nightmare. He was concerned that he was losing her. It wouldn't be long before the men on the ground heard more information about his requests. Soon enough, she would be free, but he had to keep her—as well as the rest of the plane—in line to keep the train on the tracks. "That ring on your finger," Al began, hoping to distract her with conversation. "Are you married?" Al had already suspected how the bit of small talk was going to play out, but he wanted to continue to keep the unholy alliance.

"I'm supposed to be," she replied with disdain.

"When?" he queried.

"Saturday," she said after scoffing.

"Who gets married on Thanksgiving weekend?"

"People who can't afford to get married on a normal weekend," she retorted.

Al smiled, excited, and began again, "That's wonderful news!" He was trying to maintain his low whisper, but he got a little loud for a moment and peeked above the seats, wary he had attracted unwanted attention.

"Glenn was right," Robin said to herself. "I should have never left the house. I'm not even supposed to be here today."

"Dare I say that it's your lucky day?" he asked in an encouraging tone. She was clenching her jaw tightly again, and for a moment Al suspected she might lash out at him as her fingers curled into a fist. He pulled out a small map of the Phoenix airport to defuse the tension, and spread it out neatly on the top of the seat tray. After looking at the layout of the runway, he turned again to Robin, whose face began to sink into a pout.

"Robin, what did I say? If you cooperate, you're going

to have your wedding. You're going to have kids—if you want them—and the silly white fence, and the Labrador Retriever. You'll grow old together as you watch your children start their own families. You'll forget this ever happened, and one day someone will remind you and you'll have a laugh about it."

"A laugh? This is funny to you?" she asked, bewildered.

"In a way," Al replied.

"You think you're going to be famous? You think you're going to be some kind of celebrity? When they catch you, they're going to lock you up and throw away the key," she replied defiantly. "They'll laugh at you and your assumption that you could pull it off. I hate to break it you, Einstein, but your plan is foolish."

"If at first the idea is not absurd, then there is no hope for it."

"What?"

"Einstein said that."

"What do you want? Money? You want to take the easy way out? Are you running from the law?" Al let her air out her grievances. He understood the state of panic he had put her in all too well, and he had to have some sympathy in order to continue to make the relationship work.

"It's not about the money," he explained. "Those bills will be marked, so I'll never be able to use them. This is bigger than that. I'm not an expat, and I don't want to go to Cuba." She stared at him blankly, not comprehending his intentions. His new persona was already doing well at causing confusion.

"You're a coward," she said contemptuously. The words *hurt*. She was right. *Jack* was a coward, but that was the past. *Al* had nothing to fear anymore, other than failing. Failure was an option. Fear, however, was not.

"Listen, Robin—" Al started.

"No, *you* listen," she interrupted. "You're no one. You're nothing." The tone of voice she used was eerily similar to the shrill sound of his mother's, a triggering tone if there ever was one. He tried desperately to keep his temper under control, but if he couldn't keep her working with him, the mission would be severely jeopardized. He started to feel faint.

That familiar nausea he'd experienced set in alongside the lightheadedness, and Al fumbled in his pocket for the pills. He didn't want her to see him take one, but he was worried he might collapse entirely. He dug one out of the bottle through shaky fingers and threw it back, and then sipped the last few droplets of scotch left in an attempt to chase the dry pill down his throat. He had no idea if the amphetamine was really helping, but the placebo effect had become effective, much like Al's personality. "And if I don't succeed," he said, panting as he struggled to keep it together, "it will be just as much your fault as mine. I may have dragged you into this, Robin, but it does no good to blame and point the finger. It doesn't matter who's responsible for the problem, all that matters is how you are going to fix it."

"What is that?" she asked, intrigued by the pill bottle in Al's hand. She was attempting to read the label, but he quickly obscured it with his fingers.

"Vitamins," he lied. "Right now, this situation is in your hands. You're responsible for the passengers on this plane."

"You swear you'll let the passengers go when it's over?" she asked somberly.

"I swear."

Al could tell she only half believed him, but it was enough for him to keep the conversation moving forward, and the wooziness was already beginning to wear off as her defensive tone subsided.

"You're going to go give the pilots a bit more information," Al started again. "This information is *very* important." She rolled her eyes, shaking her head back and forth. "When we arrive in the Phoenix area, the pilot is to circle the runway at 10,000 feet, at a rate of 100 knots. I need him to continue circling until there is confirmation that my demands have been met. I want the pilot to communicate to ATC that the passengers will be allowed off the plane *if* that happens. It's very important that this message gets back to the people who will be in charge, for all of our safety."

"What else?" Robin questioned.

"He is absolutely not, under any circumstances, to land until I have given him the okay. Tell the agents on the ground to inform the en-route controller when the items have been procured; they will then inform the captain, who will report the information to you. At that point, you will notify me, understood?"

"Yes," Robin said, her voice breathy. She was now in a perpetual state of frustration, and that was exactly where Al wanted her to be. Frustration would keep her compliant and ensure that everything was being done to accommodate him.

"Good. Don't come back here until we begin circling Sky Harbor. We don't want a panic," he reminded her.

"You'd better keep your word," she said. "Don't lie to me."

"I'm not, but if I were, would you be the one to put me

in check?" She stared intensely at him, scrutinizing his face as best she could, but he knew the glasses helped keep his expression unreadable.

"Always the hero," he teased.

"Excuse me?"

"Sally, the woman at the desk. She said that to you. She said you always have to be the hero. What did she mean by that?"

"It means the airline always relies on me to save the day," she explained.

"Interesting. Let's hope that is true today as well."

12

JG stared through the window of the vehicle in which he'd joined Rex as the agents poured over schematics of the plane. He'd given Norman the okay to go home and decided to go it alone. Surely there would be calls to the field and inquiries by the press at his estate, and if anyone was capable of putting out those types of fires it was Norman.

Above, the plane that Mr. Al Ader had stolen circled at roughly 10,000 feet. It was easy to spot not just because it remained at a low altitude, but also because it was the only plane in the sky. Rex had directed Phoenix Air Traffic Control to divert any other flights that were schedule to arrive in Phoenix to other nearby airports, and the rest of the facility had been evacuated entirely in record time. JG knew that when the feds wanted to get things done, they could. But clearing the runway was the least of their concerns.

"Rex, it's Ken." Ken's voice came in crackling over the radio. One of the agents handed the radio over to his superior, and Rex clicked the button to talk.

"I'm here," Rex replied.

"That's our man up there," Ken replied. "Otto's got binoculars on it, and it is indeed a Bauering Trijet 100 series, not to mention there isn't anything else in the sky. ATC cleared a one-hundred-mile-radius as no-go."

"Copy that," Rex replied. "We're rolling in now with the cash. Does ATC have that fuel truck standing by?"

"They sure do," Ken replied.

"Good, I'll contact you when I land."

"Ten-four," Ken replied.

"Hey, Mitch," Rex said again into the radio. "You there?"

"I'm here, Captain," Mitch replied.

"You at the perimeter line?"

"Yes, sir."

"How did you do on those parachutes?"

"We've got all four up here at the line, two primary, and two reserve. We were able to grab two NB-8 models from a local military flight school and two sport-style numbers called "Drop Zones" from a skydiver that the good folks at ATC recommended. They seem to be in working order, but I wouldn't know. The guy who donated them said they'd been inspected recently, though. The NB-8 models were packed by the chaps over at the flight school, and they were sure on those two."

"Good," Rex replied.

"Parachutes?" JG asked, petrified by the notion. "You didn't say anything about parachutes!"

"Sorry, Jim," Rex replied. "We're flying by the seat of our pants here. You're the money man."

"Bull shit I am!" JG growled. "That's *my* plane up there. *My* customers, and *my* crew."

"That's not entirely true," Rex said. "Now that Mr.

Ader's branded himself a criminal, he's our responsibility, and 10,000 feet in the air is our jurisdiction. You know that."

The tires screeched as the car passed through an entry point in a chain link fence, and JG eyed a few local news trucks that had been setting up shop just outside the perimeter. The entire runway flanking the airport had been cluttered with Phoenix Sheriff's Department cruisers, black sedans that could only belong to federal agents, and a sea of personnel that had formed a line along the tarmac. "This is a god damn circus," JG said as his eyes darted nervously around the plethora of people that had gathered to meet the arriving plane.

"Why does he want parachutes?" JG said to Rex, his mind still trying to angle its way around the request.

"Why does he need two hundred thousand dollars?" Rex retorted.

"Because he's trying to extort my god damn company for money, but what the hell does that have to do with parachutes?"

"Relax, Jim," Rex said. "We don't know anything yet. We don't even know what the guy looks like. Once we have him on the ground, we'll get more information. Until then, I'm just as much in the dark as you. And wondering what the hell his plans are isn't going to do us any good, right? We've got to get him on a line, get in his head, and figure out just what the hell he wants and what he plans to do."

"I can give you a couple guesses," JG cried, losing patience. "The maniac wants money, a fuel truck, and parachutes. Now I'm no federal agent, but I can come up with a few good guesses, and I didn't need to come from Langley to figure them out."

Rex paused, trying to find the words to make JG understand that he was on his team. He was looking into the eyes of a man who'd already seen what the worst-case scenario looked like up close and personal. Still, he had people to answer to up at the top, and he was getting a second chance here to make this right—another at bat—and if he managed to bring all his runners home, it would be a *grand slam*.

The car came to a halt at a barricade of black cruisers that had been set up on the tarmac. The agents, along with Rex and JG, hopped out of the car and made their way to the wall that had been formed. On the hood of one of the cars, schematics of the plane and the airport runways had been laid about and held down with clips of ammunition doubling as paper weights. The men on the ground had enough weapons to overthrow a small country. Mitch approached Rex and handed him a radio unlike the one that was standard issue.

"This'll get you the tower," Mitch said.

"Thanks, what do we have in the way of eyes on the building?" Rex asked.

Mitch pointed toward the top of the airport terminal, "We've got eyes there," and then to the top of the ATC tower, "there," and then pointed to a grassy patch that hugged the runway where the plane would be arriving, "and there." Mitch sized JG up for a moment, his eyes wandering up and down his frame suspiciously. JG's plaid jacket was contrasted in vibrant color against the black-and-white garb of the law enforcement agents swarming around him."

"He's alright," Rex said to Mitch. "Mitch, JG Van Cortland." Mitch stuck his hand out toward JG, and the two shook firmly.

"Sorry to hear," Mitch replied. "We're gonna get him." JG shot him a cold stare that lacked any confidence whatsoever, and Rex responded by shaking his head toward Mitch, ensuring he didn't try to push the conversation any further.

"We've got everything in place," Rex said into the radio. "Let the flight crew know so they can inform him."

"Copy," Ken said over the radio.

JG continued to stare up into the sky as the plane circled. The whine of the engines was almost hypnotizing, and JG almost, Rex thought, seemed lost in a daydream as it soared above. His lips were pursed, and his forehead was wrinkled into deep folds that could not hide his distress.

"Listen, I know what happened last year," Rex said to him. "Shit, who doesn't? I read the papers. Hell, I wish it'd been me that had been there with you. If I had it my way, nothing would have gone down the way it did, but this is here, *now*, and there's a way we do these things. Let's concentrate on getting him on the ground, and then we'll see what can be done. Until then, we've got to give him what he wants. Everyone here wants nothing more than to see those people get off that plane and this man in cuffs, but he hasn't indicated that he doesn't intend to just take his money and run, and most of these guys are stupid. They're *dangerous*, but they're stupid. Until we can get a better idea of what he's going to do, we play ball. Now, do you trust me?"

JG's brow furrowed. He didn't trust anyone, but right now he knew Rex was right and there was probably no one out there that cared more than him. Rex had always done things by the book, and JG knew from the last go at it that Rex Schulz loved nothing more than to get his man.

"Just concentrate on getting all those people off the plane," JG said somberly. "I don't care about him, I just want my people safe."

"I'm not going to let that plane leave, Jim," Rex said. "It's the last thing I plan to do."

13

The sun had started to sink beneath the clouds, and the interior of the cabin had become a gloomy shade of blue. Al was sure they had made considerable progress in their trip toward Phoenix, and judging by the pitching of the plane, they were probably even above it. He was mesmerized by how magnificent the colors of the atmosphere became. Under the right conditions, spectacular hues of magenta, amber, and fuchsia could paint the kind of twilight sky he had only ever seen in photographs. It was a majestic sight—especially for a man so close to death. He found the hum of the turbines to be incredibly soothing, and his theory that airline crews used to put anesthesia into the oxygen tanks to keep travelers complacent for long trips was quickly eliminated. Even if he wanted to rest his eyes, that would be far too careless.

"How long?" Al heard a young, high-pitched voice up front question.

"As long as it takes," a woman replied. Al craned his neck to get a look at the commotion, and the small boy had been tugging on his mother's blouse.

"Play airplanes with me," the boy cried.

"Not now," the woman replied sharply. Judging by the tone of her voice, she couldn't be bothered.

"You said we would play airplanes!" the boy yelped.

"You're on an airplane!" the woman screeched. "What more do you need?" Al finally caught a glimpse of her, and her eyes never left the newspaper her face had been buried in.

The boy hopped out of his seat, guiding the toy plane down the aisle and mimicking a flight through the rows as he continued toward Al.

He caught Al's sunglasses through the crack between the seats and froze in his tracks, bobbing his head around the edge and staring. Al could make out his tiny eyes and messy hair as the child surveyed him curiously through the narrow opening. When he realized Al was looking at him, he retreated behind the seat again.

"Pssst," Al whispered as he peeked his head between the seats. His face retreated around the seat again, and Al shifted out of his sight to initiate an impromptu game of hide and seek. Al slowly moved into his view, and then hid abruptly once again, covering his face with his hands as the child mirrored his actions. When he opened them, Al made a silly face, sticking out his tongue before he hid once more. The boy giggled a bit, and after Al met his gaze once more, he retrieved a deck of cards from the breast pocket of his sport coat.

"Do you want to see a card trick?" Al asked him. The boy nodded, so Al removed the cards from the package, shuffling them in his hands as the boy came closer. He climbed into the seat directly in front of Al, and Eileen smiled as he passed by her. He leaned his head and hands above the head rest, peering over the seat with eager curiosity at the cards flipping through Al's hands. He performed some simple shuffles, flinging the cards from hand to hand and fanning them out. Al had always been flashy with a deck of cards. Years of practice keeping himself busy could have easily netted him a career as a casino dealer if he had ever worked up the temerity to go to Vegas. He was gambling now, of that he was sure. The gentle breeze of the blackjack shuffle method made a few hairs in front of the boy's face move, which prompted him to giggle.

Al removed a card from the deck: the only face card that featured a weapon attacking its wielder—and his favorite card—the suicide king, more commonly identified as the king of hearts. He had always had a fascination with this particular card since it was so unlike any other in the standard deck. It had characteristics he did not, like passion and identity.

"Do you think I can make this card disappear?" he asked the boy. He shook his head no, staring at the card as Al twirled it in his fingers. It was easy to hypnotize people with card-based illusions. They were actually incredibly simple to perform with minor practice, but appeared far more difficult to execute.

"No? Well I think I *can*," Al assured him. The boy's eyes scrutinized Al's fingers while he wiggled the card around in his hand. After holding it out for him to see, Al flipped it out of sight instantaneously in front of the boy's face, leaving his mouth gaping as his eyes widened. It was a technique known as "back palming." One could hide the card behind their knuckles with relative quickness and a little determination.

Al quickly presented the card again, and the boy smiled, jumped up in the seat, and leaned in closer. He reminded Al of a younger version of himself when he had been mesmerized by Houdini's illusions. With a wave of his hand, Al made the card disappear once more, revealing his palms to help sell the trick.

"You try," Al said. He handed the card to the boy, and he fiddled with it clumsily as he attempted to mimic Al's technique. Al glanced out the window, immediately noticing a sea of beige. The plane had now dipped beneath the ceiling of clouds above, and they were getting closer to their destination. He hoped Robin would be providing him with an update. "Like this," Al explained to the boy, taking the card from his hand after he struggled with the attempt. "Between the fingers, and swung around the back. Make sure you say 'abracadabra' for added effect."

He plucked the card from Al's hand again, and after watching him demonstrate it one more time, had become quickly more adept at executing the trick. The sound of heels clicking against carpet grabbed Al's attention. "Okay, time to go back to your seat," Al told him as he glanced around the corner. Robin was returning, and he couldn't have the distraction of the child any longer. He handed the card back to Al, and before the boy sprinted off, Al messed his hair up a bit as if he were petting a puppy. The plane banked again as Robin neared, and Al felt the familiar feeling of the butterflies in his stomach. They were descending.

"Here's your drink, sir," Robin said contemptuously.

"I didn't ask for another drink," Al responded.

"Well I'm running out of reasons to stand around here."

"You're right, good thinking."

"They've secured your requests."

"Great, tell the pilot he's free to land. He can notify the controllers that he'll come in with a heading of 340 to runway L1. They'll have cleared the entire airport at this point, and they won't be grounding any other planes here while we're present. Make sure the people in charge know that I don't want anyone near the plane until I give the go-ahead. I want all the window shades down for the landing," Al requested. "*All* of them. Go inform the pilot of the next set of instructions."

Robin strode off yet again. She had finally calmed down a bit, and the next part of the plan was going to present another turning point in how the events played out. Al would need eyes in the back of his head—which he didn't have—so he could continue to use her to interact with the officials on the ground. Even if none of the passengers on board the aircraft had realized yet what was going on, it was only a matter of time until they discovered the teams ready to engage the plane. At that point, all bets were off. In the event that he had to manage the panic, he hoped the tools in the briefcase would help him keep order. This was now a sky prison, and he was the warden. He shuffled the cards in his hand as they drew closer to their destination.

"Folks, we're going to be making our initial approach to Phoenix Sky Harbor," Wally said after the intercom system sounded. "Once we are back on the ground, we will do everything we can to get you on your way, and we do apologize for the inconvenience, but we take pride in keeping you safe." He was laying the safety angle on really thick—Al imagined corporate had hammered that in during training in an effort to make sure they could still keep customers subconsciously loyal. They didn't care about safety—they cared about numbers. It wasn't their fault, after all, that someone had decided to put the customers in danger.

The plane was sinking quickly now as it circled the area to line up with the appropriate runway. Al could see the team had moved its flaps down to maintain some lift as they throttled the engines back. The cards were a welcome distraction while he waited out the final descent and had been far more efficient helping him keep his cool than any of his other nervous habits. Robin appeared again from the cockpit as May and Norma continued to make their final rounds collecting trash from the other civilians. It seemed silly to Al that trash was still a priority, but he reasoned that it was all a part of the illusion of normalcy.

Al could see the airport now. Even from this distance, he could see a barricade of cars had been formed around the tarmac. They were easily identifiable, since a tarmac was not often a home for automobiles. Landing at L1 would put the western setting sun in the eyes of the people who would handle the negotiations when they taxied in, obscuring their vision of the interior of the plane in his favor. He was quite proud of himself that he'd left no detail to chance.

"The captain has requested that all of the sun shades be brought down for landing to ensure we keep the plane cool," Robin requested loudly. "It's very hot in the Phoenix area." It was a reasonable cover. Phoenix could still get pretty sweltering in November if the conditions were right. She moved in and out of the aisles, adjusting the windows herself in rows without occupants, and May followed suit.

As she passed the drunken man a few aisles ahead of Al, he put his hand on her arm, stopping her again. He could see her face growing redder by the second, and it was clear she was in no mood to continue to deal with this man's antics.

"Hey, darlin', what kind of compensation do we get for an inconvenience like this?" the drunk asked. She grabbed his hand reflexively, removing it from her arm.

"Sir, I need you to place your seat in the upright position," she requested. He was sloppy now, and he attempted to touch her yet again.

"Okay, relax. We're just talking here," he assured her as he guided his hand down her hip.

"Sir," she pleaded as he slumped over his arm rest into her personal space. Al could see how frustrated she had become with him when he lifted his head above the seat to watch, and as if on autopilot, he unbuckled his seat belt and stepped up and into the aisle. When Al arrived at the man's seat, he grabbed his hand, removing it from Robin's body, and bent his arm backwards, applying pressure to the elbow. The drunkard winced before even realizing what Al had done. Al had counted on his delayed reaction, sure that he would be pliable from the booze.

"Hey relax, buddy!" he shouted at Al. Robin retreated, surprised by his intervention.

"She told you to put your seat back," Al growled. He applied a little more pressure to his elbow, and even though he didn't have much muscle on his body anymore —if any—very little weight was needed to cause immense pain.

"Alright, alright. Relax, guy!" he cried. Al applied a bit more pressure before releasing his arm, just to let him have a taste of the pain. He caressed his arm, then cowered in his seat. Al held the button down on the arm rest that would allow his seat to move and slammed it from the back with his free hand, sending the man tumbling forward in a panic.

"You're lucky we're in the air, pal," the drunk man said angrily. He was right, and as Al walked away, he reconsidered his actions. At his current weight, this guy could squash him like an ant on the street, but he had caught him off-guard, and the man had no choice but to back down. An altercation during flight wouldn't work in anyone's favor, but Al felt it had seemed necessary to help Robin de-escalate it. She had enough to worry about.

Al felt a surge of adrenaline at how effectively he had handled the situation. Jack had never picked a fight in his life, and here Al was, swooping in valiantly. It was a technique that a punk named Gus had used on him in grade school. Gus's family had also been poor, and he'd seen fit to steal Jack's lunch to compensate for the fact that he didn't have any. Jack being the bony child he was could do little to defend himself, and if he complained, Gus was fond of attacking pressure points and bending limbs in an effort to get his point across. The elbow trick was one Jack had found especially abhorrent. *Look what you can accomplish without fear,* Al thought to himself. He was beginning to see how his phobias had governed his life, and he was *truly* beginning to feel like someone else.

"May I take my jump seat?" Robin asked.

"Of course," Al replied, and she moved toward the rear of the plane. The plane continued to glide closer and closer to the ground. Al waited patiently as they drew nearer to Phoenix, doing his best to calm his pulsating heart down with a series of deep breaths. He was still seething from the altercation with the drunk man.

"We'll now be making our final approach to Phoenix Sky Harbor," Wally advised. "Flight attendants, please be seated for arrival."

14

The sound of wind hitting the cavities of the hull howled through the plane as its landing gear was extended—the dull roar of that beast that was soon to roll in. Al could see the blockade that had been formed even better now as he pressed his face against the glass to get a better view. He had opened his sun shade to monitor the situation, but he was confident no one was aware up front. There was a sea of blue-and-red flashing lights all around the airport, and he assumed it had been locked down at every possible entry and exit point. No matter how hectic things might get, Al had to remember that everyone would remain fearful of the bomb, which had worked well thus far.

The aircraft whined as the flaps were further adjusted, and the plane rocked from side to side as Wally did his best to keep it steady. The sky had evolved into an incredible rose color now, and Al prayed the remaining light would be useful for the short time they would be grounded. Thankfully, the skies had been consistently unremarkable and clear over the course of the early evening. He couldn't have asked for a better hand had he dealt it himself. Inclement weather could have presented disastrous consequences, and there was none to be found. But if that plane wasn't back in the air before dark, it opened up a slew of possibilities—none of which were in Al's favor.

The rocky desert gave way to businesses and homes when they drew close. Al saw the asphalt of the runway as they drifted over it. He barely felt the shock of the wheels hitting the ground, which he imagined was a cushy landing compared to horror stories he had read about in periodicals. He might not have noticed had the flaps not raised up from the wings to slow the plane down. The brakes hugged the wheels as he felt his torso being pulled forward against its will, and the application of reverse thrust emanating from the engines screamed like a banshee before the plane finally came to a slow crawl. He was *grounded* again.

Now that Al could see the airport terminals clearly from this angle, he realized he had underestimated the response of the officials. The sheer amount of bodies waiting made him worried that he could be easily over-powered. It was far more than he'd expected. He'd hoped that the explosive would be enough to keep the party going, because he did *not* have an ace in the hole. The bomb was his trump card.

"Hey, what's going on out there?" Al heard someone say. Judging by the distance, it might have been the mother of the boy he had demonstrated the card tricks to earlier. Al peeked over the seat to find that she had opened her sun shade. The interior became slightly brighter as other passengers joined in to witness the commotion, lifting their shades up one after the other and filling the inside of the plane with a rosy glow that fore-shadowed the hell they'd just been introduced to. The noise in the plane grew to a low rumble, and concerned voices began to crowd each other. They all clamored toward the left side of the plane in a panic. He walked over to get a look himself, attempting to blend in with the rest of the crowd. There were even *more* units on the other side of the plane ready to respond to the threat. The agents had set up a perimeter. He couldn't see much detail, but he could tell by their garb that they were most likely federal agents up front, with local PD not far behind.

"They're aiming at us," Eileen said, clearly confused as she turned to Al. Chaos could soon break out if he wasn't careful. He walked back toward his aisle and grabbed the briefcase before turning to address everyone before him. *Okay, Al, time to introduce everyone to the new sheriff in town.*

"Hello, everyone," Al said loudly. "I've hijacked this aircraft, and this a bomb." He pointed to it to ensure everyone understood what hid in the briefcase. An instantaneous fear overcame everyone in the plane, as if he had told them they were *already* dead.

The mother of the boy grabbed him, hugging him tightly as if shielding him. Eileen leapt backwards into the aisle to separate herself from the bomb, and the drunk man's lips wrinkled as he scowled at Al. May and Norma walked up to the front of the aisle cautiously after exiting their seats, and Al looked behind himself to find Robin partially obscured by the wall that housed the lavatories. She was the only person that currently flanked him, but now that they were grounded, the chances of her doing something stupid were unlikely.

"I don't plan on using it," Al assured everyone politely.

"*If* you all do as I say." He had their attention now. One might even say they were *captivated*. He could not detect a single movement among the group. The passengers were frozen solid like ice sculptures. "You're going to get off this plane momentarily," Al continued. "Please, do not attempt to disarm or disable me, because I assure you, the bomb will detonate."

Al could tell the small boy was confused as he looked at him. The young couple who had been tending to their infant were both crying, and he felt a twinge of guilt for involving them in this scenario, but he could not allow his emotions to cloud his judgment. He was center stage now, hoisted up above a crowd in a straitjacket and locked up in chains for which there was no key. So far he had done well.

"I plan on letting every passenger off of this plane safely, because my intent is not to put any of you in danger. That is a *promise*. All I require is that you sit patiently while I negotiate with the agents on the ground. If I don't have your cooperation, I will not hesitate to use the bomb. It's that simple. Miss Kraft," Al said as he looked toward Robin.

She approached, and he could hear her whispering, "It's going to be fine," to the passengers as she came nearer.

"Can you begin to organize the refueling of the aircraft please?" Al requested.

"Yes," she responded. It seemed her resolve was as strong as Al's now. Her compliance confirmed she was aware of how close she was to safety.

"And Robin," Al started again before she left, "no funny business. Just the truck, and the attendant."

"Right," she said before walking away.

"Please follow the flight attendant's instructions and shut all of the sun shades. She made that request earlier, and it was not followed. It's for your safety, as well as mine," Al said after turning to the passengers again. They all responded hastily, and he was reminded of how effective a bargaining chip the explosive could be. They were aware that there would be no chance to escape inside the claustrophobic tube. Everyone could be silenced in the blink of an eye. "That means you too," Al said sternly to the drunk man as he stood staring at him defiantly. The drunk man spat on the ground in front of him, but he complied nonetheless.

In addition to the explosive's devastating impact, the amount of gasoline on the plane would undoubtedly ensure that it erupted into a fireball. Phoenix would be an ironic location for that type of outcome. The clever newspaper headlines wordsmiths wrote to capitalize on the tragedy flashed across his mind's eye.

"Contact ATC," Al could hear Robin saying as she spoke through the phone on the wall. "He wants the plane refueled, no one but the fueling attendant."

Al scanned the crowd of faces as he waited. He couldn't afford to look away while he held them hostage, and he finally had a chance to see all the people who had boarded the flight with him. The veteran that had arrived in the wheelchair was watching Al disapprovingly through squinted eyes. Even though he was at the other end of the plane, Al realized he might have to keep an eye on him. He was, after all, a trained serviceman.

"Cute kid," Al said to the woman with the small boy. She was unamused by his comment and didn't return any word or gesture.

The pilot had now cut the engines, and soon after Al

could hear the approaching sound of a motor shifting gears. The fuel truck was approaching. Another reason he had selected this plane specifically was for its single-point fueling feature. This meant that the fuel would be replenished through only one location on the plane's exterior, allowing Al to keep an eye on its progress. He had predicted rightly that it would be too demanding of his attention to monitor multiple attendants. The bureau could easily slip an agent undercover if given an opportunity. He had to keep an air of mystery between himself and the federal officials. The less they knew, the better.

Al would have to hold off on the money and the parachutes. The first priority was to get the plane refueled. He was going to need as much fuel as possible for the next task, and it was just as important, if not more so, as the parachutes and cash. Without fuel, his range would be limited, and he still had another trip to make before the night was over.

Al searched the sea of officials through a tiny crack in the window shade now that he could see faces and bodies more clearly. They would be attempting to make contact with him very soon—there was no stopping that—and he looked around eagerly to see if he could find the point man. He noted some snipers trying desperately to blend in on the roofs of the structures that housed the terminals and gates, but he'd expected them, and although about the size of ants from his point of view, visible nonetheless. Their guns, like many of the others present at the scene, were aimed directly at the windows of the plane. They wouldn't dare fire blindly—at least Al was counting on that—which was why it was so important to keep the shades managed around the plane.

If a description of Al had been provided, or his seat

location given, it was possible they could snipe him where he stood. A bullet from a high-caliber rifle like they were wielding would tear through the window with ease, and packed such force it might continue to rip an exit wound from his body and leave through the other side of the plane. He also could not afford to endanger anyone else in the crossfire. One of the most important pacts Al had made with himself was that no innocent soul would be hurt in the process. If someone were injured or killed, the entire operation would be a failure in his eyes, and it would tarnish Al's identity. All the players were on the field now—game on.

15

Al's request for parachutes was a dead giveaway that he would jump, but if he released the passengers safely, he predicted they would allow him to leave again unhindered. With all of the hostages returned, they would deal with him later. Where they would find the parachutes on such short notice, he was not sure, but he was confident that if the military could not supply them, the agents would surely strong-arm them from a nearby flight school. They were good at things like that. Whether or not they were good at catching crafty hijackers still remained to be seen.

Al had designed the heist to be innovative and dazzling to disorganize and confuse the federal agents. It would take them a long time to begin to work together and figure out how he had duped them—or so he hoped —if all went well. The truth was, he was relying on the knowledge that the bureau did not know how to quickly handle a crisis—though the media might say otherwise— and he was counting on his opinion that they wouldn't be very good at it.

A *thump* in the hull of the fuselage confirmed the refueling process had begun. They would surely take this opportunity to initiate the negotiation. It was also a chance to learn as much as they could about Al and his intent. At this point, he imagined they were huddled over a schematic of the Bauering Trijet 100, scrutinizing and hypothesizing about every entry point and weak spot on the plane. He worried that they might send a team to break the door down, but once again the bomb had proved to be the perfect tool. Surely they would fear he might detonate the explosive if he anticipated a coup. Al was confident that the bomb would continue to act as the ultimate disadvantage to anyone but himself. Once again, it invigorated him to no end to discover just how much command he had in this situation.

The passengers were now watching Al's every move as he waited patiently for the refueling. This part of the process would probably take around fifteen minutes, judging by the last notification he'd received about the fuel left on board. He took another look outside of the aircraft. The sea of navy, khaki, and charcoal-colored garb that belonged to the teams standing by made most of the men indistinguishable. There was, however, a tall older gentleman with an atrocious plaid jacket standing at the head of the garrison. That was JG Van Cortland, the owner of the airline.

Anybody who'd ever picked up so much as a newspaper new who Van Cortland was. His family had accrued their wealth from a smattering of businesses including construction, engineering, and drilling, but the family's company had been failing until the boom in commercial flight. Their air-based branch capitalized on the market, reawakened their former glory, and made JG a fortune. He was descended from tycoons that had capitalized on the rapid western expansion of America, making billions in steel and engineering contracts as the country inched toward the golden coast. They were the epitome of the vulgar display of runaway capitalism.

As the eldest of two sons, JG had received control of the company when all of the remaining members of his family had died, and he and his brother were at the helm of a massive corporation that had suffered a great deal during the late thirties. While the country continued to grow its economy during the war boom, Van Cortland Industries had not been awarded any contracts that directly corresponded to the manufacture of weapons or supplies and had changed their focus to automobile engineering to compensate for a shift in their business model.

When the military and commercial airline industries had merged closer and closer, JG had all but closed the automobile sector of the business, a move that had shocked the press during the fifties. A family that was a knighthood short of royalty had squandered much of their fortune via decadence. JG and his brother had grown up in a fractured family that had seen its share of well-publicized suicides and scandals—and his brother had recently suffered a great misfortune that was characteristic of Van Cortland-style headlines. JG was different than the unsavory characters that had populated his blood relations, and had chosen to reinvest the money toward the future.

When the last living shareholder, his advisor and faux mother Edna Van Cortland had died, JG used the liquidity he had left over and parlayed it into a relationship with airline manufacturers, birthing Wilville Airlines. The company's title was a mediocre play on the names of both

Wilbur and Orville Wright. Its initial launch had put JG's finances in the red, but a simple name change coupled with the frequency with which its airlines were used at a multitude of airports had ensured that the company quickly rocketed into the financial stratosphere.

JG had reinvested the money year after year, and continued to purchase assets to keep up with the demand. It was his brother that was the seer, though, and JG had the check book. Other carriers had been unable to keep up with its competitive prices, and Eagle became *the* airline in America with lightning speed. The recent hijacking aboard Eagle Airlines Flight 85 had ended not only with the fiery deaths of passengers when it had crashed near Florida in the Atlantic, but also the well-publicized loss of his brother. The tragedy was largely due to botched negotiations with a crazed criminal on board. Al believed that the death of his brother drew sympathy for the tycoon, and therefore the incident had not hurt his pockets. Al had expected that JG would show his face. In fact, he'd *planned* it that way.

"They want to talk to you," Robin said to Al as he lowered the shade a bit.

"Absolutely not," he replied. He checked his watch again, making a mental note of the time the refueling had started. It was a quarter to five. The sun was clutching the tops of the mountains now, hanging on for dear life as it dipped quickly in the western sky.

"Is it possible to speak through that phone in the aft section?" Al asked, pointing to a small phone that sat on the wall in the rear of the plane.

"No, you would have to go to the cockpit to speak with the controller," she responded.

"No good. If I go to the cockpit, it's likely they'll try to spot me through the windshield, which is just as much a danger to everyone else as it is me."

Robin deflated. "So what do you want me to tell them?"

"You're going to tell them that, right now, we communicate through you, and only you. Warn them again that I will not tolerate any agents or personnel near the plane unless I myself approve it. Call them back and get an ETA on fueling, and let's do the parachute exchange."

"Why are you bringing me into this again?" Robin asked.

"Because I can *trust* you," Al assured her. She shuddered at the comment, but it was true. He was sure Robin would not deviate from the plan for fear she might be responsible for an error.

"And tell them I want the plaid man to do the exchange." Al pointed to JG through the crack in the shade he had left open to monitor their movement.

Robin peaked through the window, squinting to get a look at the man. "That's JG Van Cortland," she said, surprised.

"You know him?" Al asked.

"Who doesn't?" Robin replied. "He's my boss. Then again, you don't have to work for Van Cortland to know who he is."

"Have you ever met him?"

"No," Robin answered.

"You will."

Al had selected JG specifically because he knew the airlines would be more willing to work with him. The FBI played hardball, and JG would prefer a scene for the media that did not feature a bullet-riddled plane. He already had one to show and would be far less threatening than a trained federal agent.

A clanging sound against the hull of the aircraft drew attention, and Al hustled over to the window—briefcase clutched tightly in hand—to see what it was. The fuel attendant was spooling up the hose back onto the reel. Al didn't need to check his watch to know that the process had not yet finished, and as the attendant hopped into his truck and took off, Al grew wary.

"What's going on?" Al snapped at Robin.

"I left my crystal ball back in LA," Robin replied. "I think I still have some tarot cards in my luggage case. Would you like me to check—"

"Get on the line with them," Al barked. "That wasn't enough fuel."

16

The diesel engine of the fuel truck growled a guttural roar as it approached the barricade. Mitch waved it through, thinking he had completed the process, but the man stopped abruptly in front of Rex. Rex knew something was up. He'd never fueled a plane before, but he was certain it wouldn't be quicker than filling his cruiser.

"What happened?" Rex asked the man. He was a heavy, burly man with an unshaved face and a hairy, meaty arm that hung out the window gripping the door.

"Faulty vapor lock," the attendant replied. "I could barely get anything in there. I'm gonna have to replace the truck."

"Damn it," Rex replied. He hated any deviation in the plan. He wasn't scared to think on his toes, but there was a man inside the plane with a bomb that was more than likely impatient, and who now would be wondering why the first request had not been met in a timely manner. "Do you know what the fuck you're doing?"

"You don't believe me, then get someone else, pal," the attendant replied guffawing.

"Alright," Rex called out. "Get another—double time." The man saluted Rex with a snide smirk, and Rex half-thought he was mocking him.

"Kraft's on the line, sir," Mitch said to Rex, pointing to the hood of one of the cars. "You can take it over there." JG had been following Rex like a hungry dog looking for scraps, and he skipped forward to catch up with the agent.

"What happened?" JG asked.

"He says the hose is bad," Rex replied. "He's going to get another truck."

"That's great!" JG cried like a child.

"And why is that?" Rex asked, his stride unbroken as he made his way to the phone.

"We should slip one of our men in his place!" JG said. "He'll never know."

"One, they're not our men, they're *my* men," Rex replied. "And two, that's a dumb idea. If he already got a look at the attendant, then he's going to know it's a different guy. His antennae are probably already up because he didn't get his fuel." Rex stopped mid-step and turned on his heel to look JG in the eye. "Listen, Jim, would you just leave this part to me? How many times do I have to tell you I'm on your team? I know what I'm doing."

"Just hear me out, Rex," JG said. "Would you just think about this?" Rex continued to walk toward the row of cars, half listening out of respect, but not attentively. "The son of a bitch plans to jump."

"Jump?" Rex replied. "Who the hell would be stupid enough to jump out of an airliner? It's a diversionary tactic. He wants to confuse us."

"He knows exactly what he's doing," JG replied. "He

chose this plane *purposely*—single-point fueling, aft stair-case, low flight capability. Christ, he's probably one of *mine*." Rex's mind wandered as he and JG arrived at the cars. He hadn't thought of that, and he had begun chewing his gum extra aggressively as more possibilities swirled around in his head like a whirlpool. He was wondering how the gum had any elasticity left at all. At this point, it was like chewing on a condom.

"Sir," Mitch said, holding the radio out toward Rex. "Suspect won't communicate directly. He's only willing to transfer messages through the flight attendant, Kraft."

"What's your plan, Rex?" JG asked as Rex placed the walkie against his face.

"To try to have a civil conversation with Mr. Ader." Rex pressed the button on the walkie, and a clicking static sound emanated from the speaker. "This is Agent Rex Schulz with the FBI, with whom am I speaking?"

"This is Robin. Robin Kraft," Robin said through the speaker. "I'm the head flight attendant... or I am today, at least."

"Great to meet you, Robin," Rex replied, the gum slapping between his teeth as he paced in circles. "How is everyone on board?"

"We're great," Robin replied unconvincingly. "Just another day at the office." Rex chuckled briefly during the pause in the conversation. "We're terrified, Agent Schulz." JG listened intently, hanging on every word coming from Robin's mouth.

"Listen," Rex said, "you've done great so far. You need to keep complying with his orders. We are doing everything we can to get everyone off the plane safely."

"He wants to know what happened with the refuel," Robin asked.

"You can tell Mr. Ader that the truck carrying the fuel had a faulty vapor lock, at least that's what the attendant said, and that another one is on its way to you right now." Rex wasn't lying, Mitch was waving the new truck back through the barricade as the words exited his mouth. "How are *you* holding up, Robin?"

"I feel like a ping-pong ball right now."

"That's understandable," Rex said, "but we're going to need you to stay sharp. That's the way the chips fell and that's unfortunate, but we need your help as much as everyone else on that plane does."

"What is it you'd like me to do?" Robin asked.

"For now, just answer some questions." The agents began to gather around the conversation, some with notepads and pens, eager to record any valuable information they might gain from the conversation. One agent was recording the conversation with a microphone and a reel-to-reel tape machine in case it needed to be played back, perhaps for official records. JG leaned against the hood of the car, snagging the best seat in the house, but keeping his mouth shut against his urges. "Is he armed?"

"Not that I know of," Robin said. Her voice cut out for a moment, and Rex tapped the radio with the back of his hand until it became clear again. "He hasn't shown us a firearm. He won't go in the cockpit because he knows he could be cornered or overpowered, maybe even sniped through the window—his words, not mine."

"Smart man," Rex replied.

"He's threatening to detonate the bomb if that happens."

"Okay, well, the good news is we're not looking for any heroes right now—not like that, anyway. Leave that part to us. You need to do your best to ensure that everyone on that flight follows the order precisely. I'm sure the passengers know by now, am I correct?"

"They're well aware," Robin replied. "You've got a small army pointed at us."

"That's true," Rex replied. "You don't worry, that's just to let him know we mean business."

"Okay," Robin said, but her voice wasn't confident.

"Did he show you the explosive?"

"Yes."

"Can you describe it?"

"There were a lot of wires," Robin said. "Multicolored, I'm not sure what types though, maybe blue and yellow, or red. I'm not so sure."

"What else? How did you know it was a bomb?"

"Well, there were eight red cylindrical sticks, dynamite, I guess."

"And how did he show it to you?" Rex asked.

"It's concealed in a briefcase." Mitch sniffed in the air, miming someone getting a whiff of something. Rex nodded, catching his drift.

"You notice any smells?"

"No," Robin replied.

One of the other agents tapped his watch with his index finger repeatedly in Rex's direction. "How about a timer or a clock or anything like that?" Rex asked. "Did you see one of those?"

"I didn't," Robin replied.

"Did he ever say there was a time *limit*?"

"No," Robin said. "But now that you mention it, he checks his watch a lot." That comment made JG's ears perk up. It was another piece of evidence that favored his theory. Al had an agenda, and JG was *sure* of it.

"What's he look like?" Otto called out in his thick,

twangy Texas accent. Rex nodded to signal he received the note.

"Can you describe him, Mrs. Kraft?"

"Oh, it's Miss," she corrected.

"Right, sorry," Rex answered.

"Well, he's a bit handsome, I guess," Robin said. "Not like in a celebrity sort of way, but you know, he's well-groomed, well-kept. He's wearing a nice suit, but I can't seem to get a look at his eyes. He's got these dark sunglasses on, and he doesn't really take them off. He's thin, and about average height."

"Is he drinking, smoking?" Rex asked.

"He did have one drink. Oh!" Robin cried excitedly. "He was taking some pills."

Rex's interest spiked yet again. "What kind of pills?"

"Vitamins, he said they were," Robin replied. "But they didn't look like vitamins to me, and they were in a prescription bottle, only there was no label."

"The training," JG called out. Rex hesitated to press the button and listened to JG as he moved closer.

"The what?"

"The training!" JG called out again. "All of the flight attendants go through training to prepare for things like this. There's a section in there on terrorists, bomb-threats —that sort of thing. Ask her if it *feels* real. Does she think he's bluffing?"

"Alright," Rex said to Robin, "to the best of your training and experience, did you feel that the bomb was a legitimate threat?"

"I suppose so," Robin replied. "I mean, it hasn't left his side, it looks the part, and he claims he can detonate it at will. That's the best I can do. I think he might have some sort of fail-safe if it leaves his possession."

"Is there such a thing?" Rex asked Otto.

"Radio frequency," Otto replied. "Like blasting."

"Okay," Rex began. "Well, Miss Kraft, we're certainly not suggesting anyone try to remove it from his possession. You let Mr. Ader know that right now we want to give him what he wants, and that everything he asked for is here." Rex peeked toward the plane, and the attendant was once again mid-fuel. "It looks like his fueling is back on track. You let him know we're willing to comply with his demands to ensure everyone's safety."

"I think he plans to let everyone off," Robin said with a hint of confidence. "He seems, well, he actually seems like a nice guy."

"Well, be that as it may, nice guys don't threaten airliners with bombs, do they Miss Kraft?"

"I suppose not," she said.

"One more question, Robin," Rex said. "What's he wearing?"

"A black suit, white shirt, and a black tie."

"And his shoes?"

"Loafers." There was a look of confusion among all the agents present. No one said a word, but everyone was in silent agreement that it was a strange choice for a dangerous man on a mission. Mitch shrugged in Rex's direction. It was certainly not what they expected to hear.

"What kinda' damn fool hijacks a plane in loafers?" Otto said. The tension was a broken with a chuckle amongst the group, but JG wasn't laughing, and Rex took note.

"Come on, now," Rex said to the group, a smirk pursed across his lips. "Look sharp."

"He has a question for *you*," Robin said as the chuckles died down.

"What's that?"

"He wants to know if Van Cortland will do the exchange." Every face turned on JG, and an awkward, grim silence hung heavy on the tarmac. JG was thrilled to know he was going to be a player in this game, whether Rex liked it or not.

17

"I don't like it," Al said, one eye keeping the passengers in his peripheral, the other tracking the attendant who was yet again fixing the nozzle of the hose to the plane's wing.

"It's common," Robin explained. "They're old trucks and they don't service them until they break."

"It's procrastination," Al said. "And don't tell me otherwise." He was becoming more enraged by the second. This was the first time a step in the plan had not happened as he anticipated, and he was starting to feel weak in the knees.

Al craned his neck to get a better look at the attendant. *Is he a different man than arrived the first time?* Al couldn't be sure. He hadn't gotten a good look at him in the first place. He could be an officer in disguise. They might attempt to muscle their way in if they felt confident they could call Al's bluff. Luckily, there was a bomb standing between the door and the aft staircase of the plane.

"They said it'll only be another few minutes," Robin said.

"That sounds like a load of bull," Al snapped. "Do I have to remind you what I'm capable of doing?" Robin didn't reply. He didn't need to remind her. The bomb would deter the feds from trying anything stupid—that was why he'd come up with the plan in the first place. One wrong move and *kapooey*!

"Relax, Al," she pleaded. "We've been playing by the rules this whole time. I don't want anyone to get hurt, and I wouldn't do anything to jeopardize that, and I don't believe *they* would either." Although he knew she was probably telling the truth, it was a miraculously coincidental problem that would help buy them some time, and it was time he didn't have. Al didn't want to be on the ground any longer than twenty minutes total. The inconvenience would add some unwanted length to their time on the ground. The more light they lost, the more danger Al opened himself up to, on the ground or *otherwise*. It was fading fast.

Either way, he *had* to believe her. He couldn't risk making his way toward the cockpit to check the gauge himself. If they were bluffing, and they took off with too little fuel, that might cause the plane to crash. His mind was racing with possibilities. Minor deviations in the plan made waves. *Keep it together*, Al said to himself. *Fear is your ally.*

Al finally got a glimpse of the attendant. He was an overweight man who looked like a grunt that worked for the airliner. *Great, one more person capable of overpowering me.*

Robin's hovering was making Al nervous. She had become accustomed to standing by and waiting for orders, and her proximity was becoming a nuisance when she didn't have a task. "Go watch the gauge," Al said. "Report back when it's full. I *expect* it shouldn't be quick," Al said, with an ominous tone in his voice.

Robin strode off yet again, leaving Al in the rear of the plane with a crowd of eyes still fixed on him. The passengers on the plane were stirring a bit now. The immediate shock had worn off, and although the mood inside the cabin was tense, they wouldn't have to wait much longer if all went according to plan.

"Where are you headed?" Al asked a young man in a polo and khaki pants who couldn't have been very far removed from college.

"Me?" he asked, confused.

"Yeah, you got family in Seattle or something?"

"That was a layover. I'm heading to Pittsburgh," he said nervously.

"Pittsburgh, huh?" Al continued. "Steelers fan?" Al could tell that some of the other passengers, Eileen especially, were miffed at his attempt at small talk, but the quiet was starting to unnerve him a bit.

"Not this season," he replied with a small laugh. "I don't think Bradshaw is capable of getting it done."

"You're out of your mind!" Al said to him.

"He's garbage," the young guy replied.

"No way, Bradshaw is one of the single greatest quarterbacks to play the game," Al reasoned.

"*You're* out of your mind," he said timidly. There was irony in the notion that Al would accuse *him* of being unhinged.

"Look out for the rookie, Harris. I think he's going to surprise us this season."

"Only divine intervention could help Pittsburgh," he chortled.

"When are you going to let us go, asshole?" the drunk

man slurred. Every eye in the room shifted in his direction. Whether it was due to the welcome distraction of something other than the bomb holding court, or the raw nerve it would take to make a statement like that, Al didn't know, but it caused a thick layer of unease to hang in the air.

"In time," Al replied.

"Heh," the man replied defiantly. "Well you didn't get me to my destination *in time*. What gives anyway? Who the hell do you think you are?"

"Well, I'm Al Ader," Al replied. "You don't know me, but you will. *Everyone* will."

"He's a magician," the young boy called out gleefully from the front of the plane.

"Quiet, Dennis," his mother said, cupping his mouth instinctively and pulling him in tighter. He broke her grip and stepped forward again.

"He's a great magician, and he makes things disappear. He's good at it too," little Dennis said. "Show them, Al. Show them how you make things disappear."

"I will," Al replied. "You might have to tune in to the tube later to see it, but I'll show you one of the greatest escape acts you've ever seen."

"Better than Houdini?" Dennis asked.

"I'm going to make what Houdini did look like a parlor trick," Al said confidently.

"Having fun?" Robin interrupted when she returned. She had been using the phone in the rear of the plane, and he hadn't even heard her appear behind him. He was *slipping*, and it was too early to be making mistakes or losing his awareness. This part of the plan was becoming far less like a magician's act and more like juggling.

"Just making conversation," Al replied defensively.

"They're going to send Van Cortland with the parachutes," she informed him. "The plane is full." Al turned to the window and witnessed the attendant winding up the hose one last time.

"Great, open the aft staircase and meet him outside the plane. Don't go to him, let him come to you. See that corner right there where the grass meets the asphalt?" Al asked, pointing to the location. "That's where you meet. I want to be able to see the transaction clearly."

Al could see the agents clamoring around JG. Even obscured by the large group of men standing by, Al was catching glimpses of his plaid attire. It was rare that they would send a civilian in to do a trained hostage negotiator's job, but Al wasn't interested in letting them get any leverage on him, and his idea had worked.

Robin hit the button at the back of the tail section, and a gust of hot air rushed through the plane as the Phoenix warmth intruded. A wave of nausea accompanied it, and Al touched his face lightly to ensure that he had not been sweating too profusely. Once again, a debilitating heat was licking the back of his neck. The grounded plane was becoming unbearably warm, and he was beginning to worry it could tarnish his appearance.

"Okay," Al told Robin, "let's go. Remember, just take them from him and walk away. No talking, no handshakes. Nothing. Just make the exchange." Robin stepped down the stairs as Al continued to monitor the perimeter through the window. Robin arrived at that small patch of grass roughly forty yards from the tail end of the plane and waited patiently for the agents to finish prepping JG.

18

———

"I am not okay with this," Rex replied, gnawing on the now rubber-like gum. It was beginning to feel like chewing on a small tire, and his teeth might have been shaved down to the root if he didn't have it. What he wanted more than anything right now was a smoke, but he'd made it this far, and he decided against it. "My men do the trades."

"I'm not a threat, and he knows it," JG said to Rex. "Do you want to be the one to tell him no?"

Rex hated the idea of sending a civilian in to do a trade like this, especially a high-profile one like JG, but the truth was, JG *had* him. Rex didn't dare deviate from Al's request, even if it meant one of his men couldn't do the job. They were bargaining with a terrorist, and Rex feared what would happen if he told Al "no."

"It's my company," JG began. "I'll be the one who has to answer to those families if something goes wrong, not you."

"Arms out," one of the agents said to JG. He complied,

and the young guy started placing a bullet-proof vest around JG's arms.

"Is this necessary?" JG yelled over the shrill scratching sound of the velcro being strapped to his body. He immediately felt the heavy weight of the kevlar vest in his knee. Though it was only seven or eight pounds, he was no spring chicken. "He's got a bomb, not an assault rifle."

"Yea, but you'll be in our men's crosshairs as well," Rex replied. "Trust me, it's as much for *our* protection as it is yours."

"That doesn't exactly give me confidence, Rex," JG said with disdain.

"Yea, well I don't like the thought of sending *you* out there either, but I'm playing the game," Rex replied. "You want to play ball, you respect the umpire."

Mitch rolled the four vests—two pairs of each style—in an aluminum cart and left it in front of JG. The thought that they were handing Al an escape plan continued to make JG uneasy. But now he was going to be able to tango too, and though he hadn't yet considered his dance steps, the feet were moving. One of the agents handed JG a walkie that was tuned so he could hear the conversation with Robin—if any—as it happened.

"What if he's bluffing, Rex?" JG asked.

"Jim, we went through this," Rex answered. "All threats are considered legitimate. *You* of all people should understand that."

"Something's smells of bullshit. This whole thing reeks of phoniness. What if it's a fake?" JG asked. "You heard the way she phrased it. 'Red sticks.'" JG turned to Otto, who was standing by listening intently, a half-chewed and saliva-soaked cigar hanging from his lips.

"You're the bomb man, right? When's the last time you've seen dynamite wrapped in red paper?"

"True," Otto responded. "They's usually wrapped in a tan paper. The blastin' kind, at least—"

"I've considered that," Rex interrupted. "They could be soda cans. He could be Wile E. Coyote. They could be road flares, for all we know, but road flares are flammable, and that still poses a risk on that flight if they're ignited."

"I'm begging you, Rex," JG said, "call his bluff. Send a team in there. He's unarmed!"

Rex grabbed JG by his bicep forcefully, guiding him out of ear shot of the rest of the agents and facing the empty concourse. He was getting sick of answering to JG in front of his team, and his annoyance had hit a fever-pitch witnessing JG wrapped in the vest. "Who's wearing the fucking badge here, Jim?" Rex growled. "You want my men to think you're in charge? You're a civilian. You want this to go the right way, then you need to shut the fuck up and let us work. My higher-ups might have my head if they even knew I let you in here, and here you are sewing the fucking seeds of insubordination in front of these guys. How many times I gotta tell you? We do this *by the book*. You want this to go like *eighty-five*?"

"Eighty-five never would have gone the way it did if they didn't let it off the ground again," JG replied.

"Be that as it may, that's not my goal. I'm trying to gather as much information as I can before the clock runs out. How many times do I have to tell you that we want the same thing?"

"Aft staircase is lowering," the sniper who'd set up shop behind one of the cars called out. His eye was pressed tightly to his scope, and he adjusted the lens slightly as a form came into focus. Rex hustled toward him, eager to get a view of what he was seeing. "Heels," the sniper said as the body moved down the staircase. "Definitely the flight attendant."

"Alright," Rex said to the sniper. "Hold your fire." Rex turned to Mitch. "Relay that command to everyone who's got eyes on the target. We're just doing an exchange." Rex placed the walkie to his mouth. "Owl 2, can you get a look in the tail section?"

"Negative," the sniper in the distance replied. Rex couldn't see him; he was lying low in a patch of grass that he had planted himself in well before the plane's arrival. "It's dark."

Robin made her way toward the grassy patch at the corner of the runway, and Rex placed the binoculars in front of his eyes to get a look. He then scanned the fuselage of the plane, stopping at each window in an attempt to gather what little information he could, but every shade save for one was shut tightly. And he imagined that was the one that Al would be monitoring from. He would have liked to fire a bullet right through it, but there was simply no guarantee the target would be behind it, and it was useless to make a snap judgement like that, anyway.

While Rex was busy tending to the men keeping watch, JG took the opportunity to grab Otto's ear. The old Texan's face was buried in a schematic of the plane, searching for any weak spot he might find that could aid them in their quest to take Ader out. JG knew the plane well, and that made him privy to the fact that Otto wouldn't find one.

"Can I ask you a question?" JG asked the old-timer as Rex's attention was diverted.

"Sure can," Otto replied.

"Dynamite," JG began, "how much does it weigh?"

"Well that'd all depend on just how much ya' had."

"Right," JG replied. "Well, Ms. Kraft said eight sticks. How much would you wager each stick weighs?"

"S'pose about half a pound each," Otto said curiously. His eyes hung on JG's for a moment, analyzing his facial expression like he was trying to spot a liar. Otto knew damn well JG was up to no good asking that question, but he didn't think the man bold enough to try anything stupid in front of the authorities. Otto would rather be truthful than give him the wrong idea and have him do something unwise after being ill-informed and further jeopardize the mission. They were sending him over the top, after all. "'Course, you'd want to take into account the weight of any of the other components involved," Otto said, "like a battery, or a clock, or a briefcase."

JG hung on his words for a moment. "Yeah, I suppose you would."

"You ready?" Rex asked JG. The withering old man breathed deeply for a moment, then nodded. "Mitch," Rex said to his subordinate, "get me a walkie." Mitch unclipped one from his belt and handed it to Rex. He handed it to JG. "Give this to her. I want to talk to him."

"All right," JG replied, placing the walkie on the aluminum cart.

"Sniper team," Rex said into the walkie, "be advised, we're sending our man in for the first exchange."

"Copy that," the snipers responded in unison.

"Don't do anything stupid, Jim. Don't make me regret this." Rex looked him sternly in the eye, man to man, his gaze unbroken. "If you do, my hands are tied. You know these things can change real fast. I'm in charge right now, but if this goes off the rails, I can be usurped, understand?"

"Just the exchange," JG replied.

"Well, let's not keep the man waiting," Rex said, and JG gripped the cart and made his way through the gap in the wall of cars that had barricaded them from the tarmac.

19

The cart rattled against the asphalt as JG began the short journey to Robin. Even at this hour, it was a particularly hot night in Phoenix, and soon sweat started to gather near his hairline. The energy he exerted pushing the cart combined with the weight of the vest on his body was more labor than JG had done in most of his adult life. He had people to do everything for him; the most strenuous work he often did was lift a pen.

Robin stood patiently on a small patch of grass that separated the plane and the barricade almost evenly. The sky behind her glowed a bright rose color that made her uniform and hair blend almost seamlessly against the background. The low whistle of the plane running on one engine to keep cool drowned out the noise of the men watching closely behind him as JG drew nearer to her.

Even from this far, JG could see Robin was objectively beautiful. Eagle Airlines had a habit of hiring good-looking people—men or women, though far more of their staff were women if they weren't behind the controls for the plane. JG's brother, Jacob, believed that aesthetics were an important part of what made their brand so powerful, and hiring gorgeous people wasn't about being shallow, it was simply, to him, a fact of life: the people traveling—mostly men—wanted to be catered to by good-looking women, and Robin was no exception. He'd never met her before, but he'd never met many of the employees that weren't in managerial or upper tier positions within the company.

The black silhouette of the plane against the faint Phoenix skyline triggered a memory in JG's mind that was far more vivid than any he'd experienced within the last year, and soon Robin disappeared and was replaced with scenery that did not in any way resemble Phoenix. Now, the tan-soaked sand stretching out in every direction was replaced by lush green lawns and palm trees. Though the sun was still setting, it was a harsh orange hue that made the sky resemble a canopy of fire. Where Robin had been standing, a man clad entirely in black stood, a mask covering everything on his face but his eyes, and an automatic rifle slung over his shoulder. He was wearing combat boots and a bullet-proof vest not so dissimilar from JG's. In the distance, one more obscured dark silhouette just like the other waited beside the plane, his firearm aimed directly at JG and providing cover fire in case the man he was going to meet needed it.

As JG got closer, he could see the number "85" in bold red letters painted on the wing of the plane. JG felt the weight of the bags of cash in his hand, though he didn't physically have them present, as if this fever-dream he was now living in had manifested itself into a reality. Though he knew it wasn't real, everything about the vision had seemed so authentic not just because he was experiencing it so clearly, but because he had actually *lived* it. The colors were as vivid as the day he had experienced them, and so too were the armed threats that stood before him. He was nearly face to face with the man, caught in a delusional nightmare that he worried he might relive all over again if he didn't end it as soon as he could. He scanned the windows of the plane, and for a brief moment, he thought he might have even caught a glimpse of his brother Jacob's face.

"Mr. Van Cortland," the voice of a woman said, and with it JG was snapped back to reality with a thunder-like crack that seemed to reverberate through his ears. He was in Phoenix again, and standing in front of him was the woman he'd come to meet, dressed not in the garb of the evil men who had taken his brother from him, but in the traditional uniform assigned to the employees working in his company.

JG paused for a moment, his knees weak and his mouth dry, and he licked his lips as he regained his composure before saying, "Miss Kraft?"

"Yes, sir," Robin replied.

"No need for the 'sir,'" JG replied emphatically. "Right now we're in this together. There is no boss-employee relationship, we're just two people trying our best to get out of this mess, right?"

"Right, sir—" Robin said before correcting herself. "I mean, right. Thank you."

"I'm sorry this is happening to you," JG said. "To all of you. How is everyone on board?"

"They're managing," Robin said. "They're frightened, though. That's for sure. We *all* are."

"Of course. Well, we're going to get through it, aren't we?"

"Let's hope so," Robin said with consternation.

"Robin, I want to ask you a favor. I want to you to help me get a better idea of what's in that case. You're the only one we've got in there that we can count on right now, and the men back there," JG said, throwing a thumb toward the agents behind him, "well, they only know so much. Now, it would obviously be incredibly difficult to get any type of chemical test, but what we *can* get is an idea of the weight of that case, and I think that would help us greatly."

"R-right," Robin mumbled, trying to follow along with his request. "So what do I do?" Her nerves were nearly shot, and if he was asking her to do what she thought he was, it would mean she'd actually have to acquire the case from the madman on the plane. He had been guarding it so closely, she thought that was damn near impossible.

"You said there were eight sticks in the case," JG began. "At half a pound each, that's about four pounds of dry weight without the briefcase. Do you think you could approximate that?"

"The coffee pot weighs about four pounds," Robin replied.

JG chuckled. "It does, doesn't it?"

"Give or take," Robin said with a light smile. "Maybe five."

"That's perfect," JG said. "You'll want to take into account anything that's inside the briefcase, and the weight of the case itself. I believe you know what to do. Can you do it?"

"Yes, sir—" she replied before pausing again, "I mean, yes, I'll try."

"Just do your best," JG said. "If you sense any danger, or if you believe that in any way it's impossible, don't risk it."

"But," Robin said, her eyes falling in defeat, "how am I supposed to get a chance to grab the case? How can I distract him?"

JG grabbed one of the parachute packs from the cart and lifted it up slightly. "I believe this is what was requested?" When he gestured with his free hand, Robin saw not just the parachutes, but a walkie-talkie wedged between two of the packs.

She glanced toward the window of the plane, and there she saw the faint silhouette of Al's face staring back at her. She prayed he hadn't seen the walkie. She'd already been conversing with Mr. Van Cortland for far too long, and she was very worried about the people still stranded on the plane.

For a moment, she thought of sprinting away from the plane and running straight back to Los Angeles as fast as she could. *How long would it take?* She was in pretty good shape, and she could run for a long period of time at a pace of ten minutes a mile. If she kept that pace, it would take three days or so. The silliness of the idea became apparent when she glimpsed the wall of authorities blocking her from the airport exit, and more importantly, she had friends that were still on that plane.

The walkie made Robin nervous, but she caught his drift. What would Al say when he saw it? She'd begun to start to resent the requests. So far her day had been comprised of men telling her what to *do* or *not to do*, and she was getting sick of it. Still, she wanted nothing more than to get everyone out of there safely. A feat like that might even get her the big job. If she was being honest with herself though, did she even want it after today?

20

Why is she taking so long? Al wondered to himself. He was beginning to become impatient. At least the parachutes were on their way. If things went south after Al retrieved them, he could still try for an escape without the money. But where was the flair in that?

Al could see the old-timer's mouth moving as Robin took the parachutes from him, but he wasn't a lip reader. He'd known she would speak with him briefly—even though he had warned her not to. It was inevitable that he would attempt to either gather some relevant information from her, or present it, but this was becoming unbearable. She finally rolled the cart back toward the aft staircase, and Al breathed a sigh of relief. Al met her at the top of the stairs, careful not to expose himself too much in the cavity. The sun was almost entirely gone, and he was confident anyone peeking into the hole—and surely he was in the crosshairs of someone's scope—wouldn't be able to make him out quickly enough to get a shot off. Robin climbed the stairs with a pack in each hand. She was struggling with the cumbersome parcels and quickly deposited them into the two seats in the rear of the plane.

"Took you long enough," Al said to her. "Did you and James Grady get to know each other?"

"There's two more," Robin replied with contempt, and he resolved not to push her too hard as she ran his errands. He began to inspect the two packs she'd just dropped. Hooked to one of the parachutes was an item he had *not* expected to see: a walkie-talkie.

"Why did you accept that?" Al asked her.

"They want to talk to you."

"But I didn't tell you to retrieve it," Al replied. "What did I say about following the rules?" Robin said nothing. The light was catching the lenses of his sunglasses at just the right angle so that she could finally see his eyes, and there was fire behind them. She looked for the words, but they wouldn't come. Robin feared that her retrieval of the unwanted item might have just jeopardized everyone's safety. He was waiting for an answer, and there simply wasn't a good one. Robin had shown a glimpse of defiance, and Al was *not* happy.

"Mr. Ader?" a static-distorted voice sounded over the radio. "Mr. Ader?" The tension between Robin and Al was palpable, and with no rebuttal to provide, she breathed a sigh of relief when he broke his gaze with her and his attention shifted to the walkie. He was angry that she had taken the initiative, but Al quickly reasoned it was an unplanned opportunity to let him have a moment with the authorities.

He wanted to be able to put a voice to the name, because they would surely record it. A moment of celebrity wasn't necessarily part of the immediate plan, but Al would entertain the communication to keep the wheels in motion. He unhooked the walkie from the small clip on the harness.

"Who am I speaking with?" Al asked as he twisted the knob that controlled the frequency.

"This is Rex Schulz of the FBI," a gruff voice responded. His tone had the commanding presence and intimidation that Al had expected it should. The radio was much clearer now that Al had adjusted it, and he laughed internally. If these guys couldn't even tune a radio, they had little hope of thwarting *him*.

"Good evening, Rex," Al replied with the polite and calculated voice that he had developed.

"It's Agent Schulz," he corrected, "but if you'd like to speak on a first-name basis, that's fine with me. What should I call you?"

"Al," he replied, "but we won't be talking for very long, so why don't you tell me what you'd like to know, Rex?"

"Just hang on, Al," Rex said quickly. "I just want to know some more information. You owe me that much, wouldn't you agree?"

"I understand your position, but there's really not much to say," Al replied. "You've been given a specific set of instructions, and as long as you follow them, I'm going to allow people off of this plane. There isn't much more we need to discuss."

Al motioned for Robin to gather the remaining parachutes. The rear of the plane was still open, and he had to keep his eyes trained on the window, the door, and the passengers now. The juggling act was becoming overwhelming, and the radio was just another unwanted distraction. *Keep it together.*

"You seem like a smart guy, Al," Rex said encouragingly. "And if I had to wager, I'd guess you plan to jump from that plane, don't you?" Robin piled the final two parachutes up on the seat near him. Al moved toward the window to continue to monitor the situation outside—to make sure Rex hadn't begun to scramble agents toward the plane.

He could see Rex in the distance standing next to Van Cortland at the front of the barricade. He was the only one holding the radio up to his face. He had sandy blonde hair and a thin frame, and he was dressed very similarly to Al with a black suit and tie against a white-collared shirt.

As Al continued to entertain Rex, Robin's eyes darted to the briefcase resting in Al's seat. The radio diversion had *worked*. Whether it was because Al trusted Robin, or because he was slipping, it didn't matter. He had walked away from the case, and she was the only thing between it and the exit staircase of the plane. Al's face was fixed firmly on the window, and Robin shuffled slowly toward the briefcase.

"I haven't decided yet," Al replied. "I can tell you that you need not worry about the passengers in the event that I do decide to jump."

"Well *that's* why I'm worried," Rex said. "I'm wondering who is going to fly the plane when you do?"

"I'm fully capable of flying it," Al responded. He didn't want to give too much information away at this point, but he'd be lying if he said he wasn't enjoying the game. He wanted to confuse the agents as much as possible.

"I assumed you were," Rex said. "I think you know a lot about the plane you're on, don't you? I bet you picked that specific plane for a reason."

"I did," Al replied. "Be sure to tell Mr. Van Cortland that he owns some very fine machinery. This 100 series has unique functions that make it very helpful to me." Al could hear him laugh on the other side of the radio. The tone of their conversation was almost like strangers enjoying a beer together at the pub. Rex was just the liaison that had been appointed to the case.

"But I'm worried you *don't* intend on flying it yourself," Rex said.

"And why is that?"

"Well, if we let you take back off, and you do leap off that plane, I'm concerned it's going to wind up scattered across a civilian neighborhood."

"Or an ocean," Al replied. Al could hear Van Cortland barking in the background as soon as the words left his mouth, and Rex cut the transmission when Van Cortland lost it. Al glanced out the window, and at the front of the barricade. Van Cortland was waving his hands in Rex's face like some kind of loon. Rex cupped the radio with his hand, scolding the old man before placing back near his mouth.

Robin reached for the briefcase, her hands trembling. Al turned toward the front of the plane to monitor his surroundings, and she quickly returned to her prior position when he turned to her. He hadn't seen her, but it had been close.

"That's a low blow, Al," Rex replied. "And I hope you aren't thinking about doing anything like that."

"Let's talk about that after I've got everything I asked for," Al told him.

"How is everyone on board?" he asked.

"They're well, Rex," Al said as he turned to the passengers. They'd been able to hear the entire conversation, and Al thought for a moment that it was probably the greatest theatre they could have ever seen—interactive theatre, *in-flight entertainment*. "I think they're a little shaken up, but nobody has been hurt."

"Are you armed?"

"Now why would I tell you that, Rex? You're smarter than that. I may have a firearm, I may not. What I *do* have is enough explosives in the case beside me to ensure this plane never flies again."

When Al returned his gaze to the barricade, Robin reached again for the briefcase. The small boy up front, Dennis, eyed her curiously for a moment. She pressed her index finger to her lips, miming to be silent, and her fingers clasped around the handle. Al began to pace, and she lost the opportunity yet again. If he caught her, who knew what could happen?

"I heard," Rex responded. "What are you wearing?"

"Mr. Schulz," Al replied, giggling, "I'm blushing. We just met." He laughed again over the radio. "Besides, I'm sure you know exactly what I'm wearing. That information surely would have been given to you when you received the notification regarding the hijacking. I imagine you're just trying to keep me on the line, and this conversation is becoming very unentertaining."

"Wait," he said quickly. "Now we've done everything you've asked of us so far—"

"That's not true," Al snapped. "I didn't ask to have this conversation with you, and here I am. I don't think it would be wise of you to make a habit of breaking the rules, Agent Schulz."

"Can you blame me?" Rex asked.

"I suppose not," Al replied.

"I've got a lot of money sitting here, and you've got the

parachutes you requested and a plane full of gas. I need to know I have your word that when we bring the money, you'll safely release the passengers from the plane."

"You do," Al explained. "I don't want to hurt any of these people—although I will if I have to," he said in a grave voice.

Robin mustered up all the courage she could find to make one final attempt at grabbing the briefcase. Her fingers closed around the handle, and it was finally in her hand firmly.

"I believe you," he said. "But you understand the position I'm in, and I had to hear it from you. Because if you don't, then the situation might change."

"In what way?"

"Let's just say if you endanger them any further, then I'm willing to take some risks to put you down."

"Understood," Al said. "But I assure you that won't be necessary."

Robin lifted the case ever so slightly from the seat. She just needed one good lift to gauge its weight, just one moment of reveal and she'd be in the clear.

She felt the weight and was surprised to feel how *light* it was. There was no way that anything inside the case weighed close to the four pounds. She could feel the weight of the briefcase clearly, and that was all she could feel. Whatever was inside the case was certainly not even close to how heavy she'd imagined it should feel.

"Is it possible that I could speak with some of the passengers?" Rex asked.

"You're going to have hang on for a moment, Rex," Al told him, his eyes turning to the parachutes. The conversation was beginning to do exactly what Rex had wanted it to do: distract Al. "I want to make sure the parachutes you found for me don't have any issues, or else we might be back to square one. Although, I'm sure you wouldn't have tried anything silly. After all, the bomb could be on a timer."

Robin let the briefcase fall from her hand, and maneuvered away from the seat just before Al could see her. He looked at her curiously for a moment. Her heart raced, and she worried that he might suspect what she was doing. But he was none the wiser, and now *she* had information.

"Go right ahead," he said. "I assure you they are all fit for duty."

"No talking," Al warned as he handed the radio to Robin. She breathed a sigh of relief. She had *done* it.

The olive-colored packs were NB-8 containers. Al was familiar with them, and for the workload they were going to be required to handle, they would do just fine. The packing card revealed that a C-9 canopy was contained inside. It was a circular, twenty—eight-foot nylon parachute, and although not highly steerable, from what Al had read, it would withstand the demands of the dangerous departure. Some of the models had been modified to allow for the pulling of suspension lines to help with direction, but unfortunately he would have no way of knowing whether or not the one in his possession *did*. It also featured "D" rings to secure a secondary chute near the abdomen as a backup and would be suitable for the high speed at which the plane would be moving.

The other two models featured small stitching on the bottom corner of the tan bag that read "Drop Zone." They were far lighter, and although Al was confident in the activation of the rip cord, he had never actually operated one. To the best of his knowledge, they were meant for sports and acrobatics. He knew they featured vents to allow for better mobility and directional control, unlike the military-style models. Al finessed a small piece of the white nylon fabric from the parachute between his fingers. He had to decide whether he wanted to sacrifice navigational capabilities for reliability—and soon.

Al was confident the authorities wouldn't dare attempt to sabotage the gear. His request for four parachutes was an ingenious touch that had come to him during the early planning phase, but also required he play into the idea that he might not be departing alone—and that's where things got sticky. After checking all four, Al was sure the officials would make good on his other request, especially since the parachutes were the hardest items to obtain. It was time now to receive the ransom money, and Al was one step closer to letting the nervous people that were beginning to stir go.

"Can I ask you a question, Al?" Rex said over the walkie. Al waved Robin over and she handed the walkie back to him.

"I'm here, Rex," Al replied after clicking the talk button.

"Why are you doing this?"

"Isn't it your job to figure that out?" Al responded.

"You're right, and I'm still scratching my head wondering what kind of man would attempt to jump out of a plane wearing loafers."

"One with nothing to lose," Al explained. Rex was trying desperately to make conversation with him, trying to establish rapport to get into his head and cause him to slip up. That was the way the agents worked, and Al could tell that Rex was certainly no stranger to negotiations with dangerous people.

The sun had finally completely slipped away, and the sky was beginning to give way to an indigo twilight. Al *had* to finish this leg of the trip before it got dark. A lack of light would only add another unwanted layer of complication.

"Good work with the parachutes, Rex," Al started again. "I would like for Mr. Van Cortland to go to the same spot to meet Robin he previously did, and this time I want him to bring the cash. I hope you have made it convenient to transport."

"We've consolidated it into a duffel bag," he assured Al.

"That will work," Al said. "Wait a moment, Rex." Al turned to Robin and asked, "Are you hungry?"

"What?" she responded, clearly bewildered.

"For food? Are you hungry? I'll be glad to accommodate you and the flight team with food as well."

"How could I possibly eat now?"

"Well I'm hungry. Do we have any of those pretzels on board?"

"We don't," she responded contemptuously. Al was sure that his blood sugar might be low, considering he hadn't eaten in a while, and a little sustenance might go a long way in keeping his energy up. The excitement of the situation had brought about the debilitating effects of the homicidal cells inside him again, and some food might have helped to offset that. Instead, he'd have to chomp down some more drugs.

"And Agent Schulz," Al said, "no surprises. Christmas isn't for another four weeks or so, and I don't want Mr. Van Cortland giving Robin any more gifts."

"I'll be sure to relay that message," Rex replied.

Al gestured for Robin to move toward the door. "Same

rules, Robin," he warned her as she exited. She rolled her eyes, and Al could sense she was becoming increasingly irritated with him again. Her patience was running short. He didn't have much time left, and he needed to get the next phase of the plan in motion to keep on schedule.

21

"**Y**ou just keep us updated on the situation inside the plane, and let us know that you're satisfied with the cash," Rex said into the walkie. "We're sending it over to you momentarily."

"You're up again," Rex said to JG as he turned the walkie off and placed it on the hood of one of the cruisers. Mitch opened the front passenger door and retrieved a large black duffel bag.

"So that's it?" J.G asked. "You just hand over the cash?"

"You can afford it," Rex replied.

"I don't care about the money, what I care about is the fact that the baby wants his bottle and you just keep handing it over."

"Nobody wants to listen to a crying baby," Rex rebutted. "Especially one with a bomb."

"*If* it's even a bomb," JG replied. "I gave her a task, you know?"

Rex's ears automatically perked up. "You what?"

"I told her to get a handle on the briefcase," J.G began,

"to try to gauge the weight." Otto sauntered over, the gnawed cigar wafting a trail of smoke that seemed to follow him everywhere he went. He'd known JG had been meddling, but he was surprised he'd actually got the flight attendant to bite, and now he was curious what—if anything—she had discovered. Rex began to chomp so rapidly on the gum—it had now become like chewing clay—that JG thought he might be at risk of dislodging his jaw.

"Why the fuck would you do that?" Rex snarled. "You don't give the orders, I do. If you're so concerned about everyone's safety—and that's what you've been bitching and moaning about since we walked on the goddamn tarmac—then why in the hell would you risk endangering their lives?"

"Because I think he's bluffing, Rex," JG said. "And if she did manage to get the job done, then I'm sure she'll get me some more information as soon as she gets the cash."

"And then he'll be releasing the passengers," Rex retorted. "So what's your point?"

JG and Rex were face to face, now nearly nose to nose, and the men around them watched intently as if a new threat had just manifested itself—and it wasn't on the runway. "You know damn well he's not going to release everyone off that plane," JG said through gritted teeth. "He couldn't give you a straight answer. He's fucking with you. I don't care if he can fly a god damn zeppelin or a cruise ship, he's going to keep the flight crew to get him to his next destination, and what then?"

"Then at least we'll have gotten the civilians off," Rex said. "They didn't ask for this. The rest of the people on that plane," Rex said, pointing an extended finger toward the plane, "they know the risks when they sign up for the job. This ain't nothing new!" Rex yelled. "This has been happening nearly once a fucking a month—you of all people should know that. Now you're going to go give the man his damn money," Rex said as he returned the finger to Rex's chest and poked it. "And when those people get off that runway and past this wall, that's thirty-some-odd people that ain't in the scopes of rifles or the blast radius of a bomb."

JG had no response. There was no reasoning with Rex at this point, and he didn't have a badge. He was at the mercy of the bureau and their tactics, and if he was wrong, it would be just as much on him as it was Rex. He knew Rex wanted the same outcome as him, but JG knew what it looked like when it went bad first-hand, and he wanted nothing more than to prevent that. Rex turned to the grassy patch at the corner of the runway, and Robin had been waiting there yet again to retrieve the last of the demands.

"Sir," Mitch said, cupping the walkie in his hand. "It's Ahern. He wants an update."

"Get her the money," Rex said before storming off toward Mitch. JG grabbed the money from the agent and slung the strap over his shoulder.

"Don't mind him," Otto replied. "He's just tryin'a settle up and get outta' Phoenix."

"Pardon?" JG asked.

"The boss," Otto replied. "He got a lot to prove, ya know? Went south for him out in Richmond and he's been tryin' to get back in good with the boys up top since he came out to the desert."

"What happened in Richmond?" JG Asked.

"You ain't heard?" Otto mumbled through the soggy cigar nursed between his lips.

"No," JG replied.

"Man botched the job n' they gave him the boot," Otto said watching Rex through squinted, cataract-scarred eyes. His best years were behind him, and he was just along for the ride to keep a roof over his head. His years had also made him wise, and he had the sort of slow, calculated speech of a man who knew more than many of the young guys in the room but kept his mouth shut most of the time. "He let the Bauer brothers walk—three pricks knocking off banks—and some of ours got hurt in the process," Otto mused. "What a mess. They shoulda' had 'em in Richmond, ya' ask me. From what I heard, Agent Cowboy was tryin' to make sure that his people got out alright too, and in the process he let them boys fall through the cracks. The top brass kicked him back down the ladder and put him out here with us. Now he wants to grab the trophy and get back to where he was. Tha's all. He don't want anything bad ta' happen no more n' you do. He's jus' got an iron fist is all. Little much if ya' ask me. He means right, though."

JG suddenly realized that this case was as much about Rex proving himself as it was getting those people to safety. What Rex wanted, though—what he *really* wanted—was to get his man. Sure, he cared about the civilians, but Rex wanted Al, and JG wondered what he might do to silence him—and who could get hurt in the process. The bureau had a way of polishing those turds, but JG's soul couldn't take much more weight. Luckily, it was exactly the variable that JG had considered as the gears in his head turned.

"Let's say she managed to get a gauge on that briefcase," JG began. "If it didn't weigh much of anything, then what are the chances it's got any explosive at all?"

Otto puffed on the cigar. The bright cherry reflected orange circles in his eyes and gave them a devil-like glow in the twilight atmosphere of the darkening tarmac. "I'd say the man's got a talent for arts and crafts." The light died down, leaving Otto with only dark, hollow circles in his eyes. "Well," Otto said as the cigar smoke curled from his lip, "get on out there, Mr. Van Cortland."

JG didn't have any idea about explosives or bombs. He also didn't have much of a plan. What he did have was a .38 tucked in the back belt loop of his slacks, and a strong feeling that it was time that someone on that plane had a weapon of their own.

He passed one final time through no man's land, the bag slung over his shoulder and Robin within sight. The weight of the bag was surprisingly light—yet another reason he knew that, in all likelihood, Mr. Al Ader planned to jump out of that plane with the money. The light had been almost completely extinguished, giving way to a darkening sky to which the sand could not reflect any of the sun's rays, and he knew that he was confident he could get away with handing that .38 to Robin sight unseen.

As he approached, he took one last look at the fuse-lage of the aircraft, and this time he was sure he saw his brother Jacob's forlorn face in the window—a ghostly image that reminded him what was at stake, and that if anyone had the opportunity to change it, it was *him*. The armed terrorists had once again appeared—more specter-like images that kept JG caught somewhere in between the real world and a fever dream. His mind was playing out scenes that he had never seen firsthand, but had imagined, like a projector with an unruly roll of film spinning wildly through its gate.

Next, he was hugging the wing off the aircraft, the numbers "85" printed in bold on its tail, and a concussion rocked the fuselage and engulfed the plane in flames. It was dark, and the surroundings could not be gauged other than the starlit night sky, but what was clear was the plane was falling fast, a gaping hole torn into its side from the blast. The engine spewed a trail of fire where the blast had caught one of the gas lines and would burn endlessly until either it ran out of fuel or was extinguished.

The plane was spiraling now, caught in a death roll as it plummeted back to Earth. Though he had never witnessed it happen, he had been debriefed extensively— at his request—after the crash. He knew it was falling, and falling *fast*, because planes did not fall upwards. There was a haunting howl where the air met the cavity left in the wake of the plane's injury. It was the plane's one last gasp—or scream—as JG relived the final moments of EA Flight 85.

He could finally make out something in the distance, and it was approaching fast. It wasn't clear at first, but when he saw the waves reflecting off of the plane's exterior lights crashing upon each other, he knew that it was the ocean. It was growing closer and closer, the plane nosediving towards it. The engine dismounted, tearing the wing to shreds as it ripped through it, and there was little hope left that the plane would ever regain control. The plane was about to make impact on the black sea.

"I did it," Robin said. JG was immediately sucked from the daydream before EA Flight 85 hit the water. He didn't need see the how it ended—he'd already seen that movie.

"And?" JG asked.

"There's no way that briefcase has four pounds of weight in it. It barely weighs two," Robin said.

"Did he see you?"

"No," Robin replied confidently.

"I see," JG replied. "Miss Kraft, are you familiar with EA Flight 85?"

"Sure," Robin said somberly. "Happened during my first week at EA."

"And you stayed?" JG said with a smile.

"I needed a job," Robin replied. The corners of her lips curled, and if she hadn't had such a rough day, she might have even laughed. The tension decreased for a moment. Here, on the tarmac, were two people who were only casualties of either side of the battle, just having a quick respite from the madness on both ends.

"How would you like a *career*?" JG asked. "Robin, we let them take off after we played along. We had those men in our hands and we acquiesced. Do you remember how that turned out?"

The newspaper headlines ran through Robin's head, a mental image of bold lettering on the front page that read "**Airliner Owner's Brother Dead in Tragic Hijacking**." She knew better than to give him the nitty gritty, and she simply said, "People died."

"They did," JG replied, his eyes wandering toward the plane sitting before him. His face became grave and distant. Robin wasn't sure what—if anything—to say, so she didn't speak.

"I heard you're getting married this weekend," JG said to her.

"We'll see how that goes," Robin replied. "After this, I think he might leave me."

"What's his name?"

"Glenn," she replied.

"I never married," JG said. "Never had the time. I suppose if I could go back and do it all over again, I would have done things differently."

"You've done alright for yourself," Robin joked.

"That depends on who you ask," JG said. JG felt the hard metal of the gun pressing between his back and his pants, and he took the opportunity to move it under the bag he was holding. "Robin, he's going to need someone to fly that plane again after he lets the passengers off."

"He said he was going to let everyone walk," Robin said.

"Do you believe that?" JG asked. "Do you believe that a man who's boarded a plane with a bomb to be a truthful man?" Robin hung on his words. She thought that if she brought Al the money, that he'd let everyone walk and figure the rest out on his own. Something about JG's insinuation was right, though. *Who would fly the plane?*

"Do what you can, Miss Kraft," JG started, handing her the bag. "I assure you when you return back to us there will be a large bonus and plenty of vacation time. Perhaps you'd like to get off the planes and get into the office?" His eyes were piercing in the moment, as if he was looking right through her.

There was a sternness to his words that she didn't quite understand until she had actually grabbed the bag from him and felt the gun underneath pass between his hand and hers. Her eyes grew wide with fear, and his gaze did not break from hers until he made sure she had it. Robin quickly tucked the gun into her skirt. She was terrified that Al might see the bulge. She had always asked for the responsibility—had always been confident she could do anything and handle any situation—and now she had it, and she didn't *want* it.

"Godspeed, Miss Kraft," JG said, and he turned and headed back to the agents. But now they were on the sidelines, and Robin and JG had two minutes to go in the fourth.

22

Robin materialized at the top of the staircase again carrying a duffel bag, a dark silhouette only separated from the blackening sky by her red garb. Al's eyes had adjusted to the dim glow inside of the plane, and it was very hard to see what was going on outside save for the lights that had been activated on all of the authorities' vehicles. They'd also set up bright spotlights facing the plane to deter Al from getting a look at was going on at the base of operations, which was precisely why he hadn't allowed Robin to venture much further than the junction in the asphalt.

Al had watched her with owl-like eyes, and now he was sure she hadn't taken so much as a stick of gum from JG. He'd done a poor job managing the exchange of the parachutes, and Robin had been brave enough to bring a walkie-talkie on to the plane. He was determined not to make that mistake again, and now he had his final demand in his proximity.

"Open it," Al commanded her, pointing to the duffel bag. She unzipped the bag to display small stacks of crisp cash. They were banded neatly in twenty-dollar denominations.

Al grabbed a stack, removed a bill, and rubbed the paper between his fingers, holding it up to the light to get a good look at it. It was real. He would have been insulted to find they were counterfeit, but he wouldn't have put it past them. Al grabbed the walkie and said, "Well done, Rex."

"What do you plan to do with the cash if you get away, Al?" he asked.

"I can't use this cash," Al said with a laugh. "We both know these bills are marked and traceable. I would be an idiot even to buy an ice cream cone with any of them."

"Of course they are," Rex replied. "Two hundred thousand dollars is an oddly specific number, Al. I bet you knew we had that amount on standby."

"I did, and I'm impressed you managed to make sure they were crisp new bills," Al told him.

"We're good at what we do," Rex said.

"That remains to be seen," Al replied.

It seemed Robin had become nervous again. Al could see her hands trembling, and the color had nearly left her face. Her skin had become a pasty white, nearly translucent against the bright rose uniform. *What had changed?* She was almost home free. "We're almost done," Al assured her. Her head bobbed a bit, and Al became increasingly unsettled by this new Robin that had manifested before him.

"What kind of bomb is it, Al?" Rex asked.

"Now why would I give you that much information?" Al responded coyly.

"Well, rumor has it you've got some cartoon-style package close by. I don't know of any dynamite that comes in red sticks other than the kind you see in those animated shows with all those silly animals. They sound more like road flares."

"Would you like to find out?" Al asked impatiently. "I already told you, Rex, this conversation has become increasingly dull. You're wasting your time, and you and I both know it. Now, if you let me get back to it, I can speed up this process."

"Calm down," Rex said. "I believe you. I'm just intrigued that you're such a capable individual. Not only do you know about aeronautics, but also explosives."

"As you said before, I'm a smart guy," Al responded.

"Is the cash suitable for you?" he asked. "Because I would really like to see those folks get off the plane."

Wally, Tom, and Jeff had appeared at the far end of the cabin now. Their arrival signaled that they must have been kept in the loop through the cockpit's intercom system. Norma and May had surfaced as well; Al had barely seen them since the plane landed because he had kept his dealings strictly between him and Robin, and mostly to the rear of the plane. They seemed as eager as the others to finally see an end to this.

Al decided it was time to put a parachute on in case things started moving fast after takeoff. He selected the NB-8 pack and secured the straps tightly around his shoulders. He reasoned that due to familiarity and trust-worthiness, it would be his best option. He had never leapt out of a plane, but today held many firsts.

The plane was really sweltering now, and even though the bomb was their major antagonist, Al was sure the heat wasn't helping the passengers' nerves. It was no longer necessary to involve them—they had served their purpose. Al would make good on his guarantee.

"Okay," Al said to Rex. "Have your men stand down. I'm going to begin releasing people from the aircraft."

"I'm glad to hear that, Al," said Rex. Al tucked himself in the row he'd been calling home, putting ample space between himself and the passengers.

"Go head for the cockpit while I evacuate the plane," Al instructed Robin. He couldn't have her wandering about as people moved freely past him. He needed a controlled funnel. "The copilot and other flight attendants may leave as well."

"What about me?" she asked, concerned.

"Soon," he assured her. "Go." The rest of the passengers stared at Al eagerly. They'd heard the chatter, and they knew the end was close. Al took one last look at them —people he'd involved in his grand plan who hadn't otherwise asked to be there. But they were the witnesses he'd craved nonetheless.

"Thank you so much for your cooperation, folks," Al said to the crowd. "I am now going to allow you to safely evacuate the plane. Please walk, don't run. We don't want anyone getting hurt. We've made it this far." Al motioned to the aft staircase, which was still wide open. He knew the agents wouldn't risk storming up it, and he maintained a safe distance from the cavity so he wouldn't end up looking like Swiss cheese. "Line up toward the rear of the cabin. Feel free to recover your belongings from the overhead bins if you have any." They began to file into the aisle, and Eileen presented herself in front of him with disdain in her eyes. Al had briefly made a friend, but he had quickly ruined that trust.

"Sorry, Eileen," Al said. She shook her head at him. "I hope this doesn't affect your desire to fly in the future. After all, this was my first flight too."

"Just let me off the damn plane," she said.

Al stepped deeper into the aisle and gestured toward the exit as she continued out into the tail section. He still had to keep aware of the blockade that remained active nearby, but now that he was letting people off the plane, he was confident Rex wouldn't make any drastic calls so close to safety.

"I would recommend placing your hands behind your head as you exit," Al warned the passengers. "Interlock your fingers so that they're sure you're not a threat." The drunk man was retrieving his briefcase as he grumbled. "You, sir, need to drink less," Al gathered the courage to tell him as he passed by. He paused for a moment, his free hand clenched into a fist at his side. Al second-guessed his comment, but the man turned and walked out, taking his opportunity for a safe exit. Al was getting a bit cocky, if he was honest with himself. "Enjoy your time in Phoenix," he said to a muscular man with European features he hadn't noticed until now.

"*Arschloch,*" he mumbled. Al didn't know what it meant, but he could tell by the man's tone it wasn't intended to be friendly.

"Have a good night," Al told the Pittsburgh-bound college kid. Whether or not these people liked him, they had developed a bond similar to people who go into war together. Although they had spoken little, it was a shared experience of trauma. They would never see him again, or he them, but they would never forget it. Al was counting on it.

"Safe travels," he told the young couple with the newborn. Considering the horrible reputations infants had garnered during commercial flight travel, the child had been incredibly well-behaved and quiet, especially in a dangerous situation. Al hadn't heard the child so much as coo. The baby's mother approached, unable to place her hands behind her head because she was gripping him tightly as he hung from her shoulder like a monkey.

"Abracadabra," Dennis said as he passed by.

"Indeed," Al said with a smile.

After a few more passengers shuffled out, the old man in the wheelchair appeared. Al had forgotten about him as well, because he'd probably never got much of an opportunity to stand during all of the commotion.

He would need help descending the stairs, and Norma and May obliged. Al would have loved to give him a hand, but it would have been dangerous, especially given the action that surely had been happening outside. Al watched through the window as the passengers' steps evolved from walking, to jogging, to sprinting as they neared the ocean of authorities. Al had promised these people they wouldn't get hurt, and he had made good on that promise.

"You've got some balls," the old man said to Al.

"Thanks for your service," Al said, saluting him as he did so.

"Did you serve?" he asked.

"What makes you ask?"

"Stunt like this? I thought you might have seen some action. Takes that kind of gall."

Al was sure they would speculate that he had served in the armed forces at some point in his life. Only *he* knew that he hadn't, but it would only help his cause to confuse them when they interrogated the crew, which they certainly would.

"Flew a B-17 in '43," Al lied.

"Even been to Hamburg?" he asked curiously.

"Yeah," Al responded, "but I didn't land." He laughed for a moment before Norma and May whisked him away, then the copilot, Jeff, followed them out. Al heaved a sigh of relief that the myriad of people he needed to keep an eye on were finally off of the plane. Not everyone on the plane would be so lucky.

23

R obin had been keeping a watchful eye through a crack left open in the door to the cockpit. As May and Norma assisted the elderly gentleman in the wheel-chair out from the rear of the plane, she reached for the bulging metal grip tucked in to her skirt—perhaps to be sure it wasn't showing, or maybe to reconcile the fact that she might just need to use it. Her father had taught her to fire a gun, but shooting bales of hay was far easier than putting a bullet in a man.

"That's it," Robin said to Wally and Tom. "The old war veteran sitting up front was the last of them."

"And our people?" Wally asked.

"They're off, too," Robin replied.

"Thank God," Tom said. "Well, what are we waiting for?" Robin continued to monitor Al through the crack, her eyes following his every move as she blocked Wally and Tom from the exit. She wasn't moving, and Wally and Tom were waiting impatiently, trying to understand why she hadn't exited the cockpit just yet.

"Robin?" Tom said. "Is there a reason you're so keen

on sticking around?" Robin didn't even hear his words. Her attention was still glued to the dangerous man in the rear of the plane. She made her way to the window of the cockpit and took one last look at the group of authorities watching the situation unfold. A handful of agents had hustled out to meet the evacuating passengers, and Robin was happy to see that they had been received safely. She'd done well.

"Hello?" Wally said to Robin. She was caught in another world entirely, inattentive to the conversation and clearly distracted by all the action outside. "I don't know about you, but I'd like get home to my family."

"Listen to me," Robin said as she turned to the two of them. Her expression was grave, and considering the pilot and flight engineer thought they were on the up and up, she looked as if the situation had not improved, but deteriorated. "He's not letting you off this plane."

"You heard the man," Tom said. "We're free to go."

"Do you really believe that?" Robin asked. "How is he going to fly the plane?"

"That's his business," Tom rebutted. "And I don't give a damn what he decides to do—I want off this plane."

"Do you really think that's true? If he lets the two of you off the plane, what's stopping the authorities from storming in and taking him out? He's not that stupid."

"Well, he's dumb enough to hold a plane hostage," Tom said. "Maybe he didn't think his plan through. I don't want to call his bluff."

"An hour ago you were ready to storm the bastard," Robin argued, "and now you're so sure he's willing to just let you walk?"

"An hour ago I was thirty thousand feet above sea level," Tom replied defiantly. He pointed a finger toward the exit. "And solid ground is only a few short steps away."

"Bullshit," Robin said.

"What the hell's gotten into you, Robin?" Wally asked. "The man got what he wanted, and that's it for us. Now what the hell are we standing around here for?"

"What if that's not it?" Robin asked. "He's going to let me walk, but the two of you aren't leaving. Don't be stupid. Just because he can fly this plane doesn't mean he wants to, or is *going* to."

"Fine," Tom began. "Maybe that's the truth, but just what the hell do you plan to do about it? I've had enough of this whole fucking scenario and I want off this plane. If you want to stick around, that's your business, so just get the hell out of my way so we can be finished with it."

"Stick close to me," Robin said. "Stay behind. Don't do anything stupid and just let me do the talking."

"What the hell does that mean?" Wally asked, confused. "What do you know, Robin?" She swung the cockpit door open and took a step out into the aisle, and Wally noticed a curious imprint tucked behind her blouse. He knew exactly what it was. He'd spent enough time in the armed forces to tell when someone was packing.

The plane was quiet now that the majority of people had left the aircraft. It was just Al and the remaining flight crew, and Al stood in the aisle now that everyone else had gotten off safely. Wally and Tom were trailing behind Robin as she approached. She stopped a few feet away, hesitating for a moment.

"Alright, Robin, you're free to go," Al said. "Captain, Flight Engineer, I'll still need the two of you. I apologize, but soon you'll be on your way home too." Robin was shaking again. It felt as if the request Al had made might cause her to jump him, and he kept his distance even though he still blocked the aisle.

"Listen, buddy, you said we were going to be able to go!" Tom shouted.

"No, I said that the passengers would be free to go. I never said anything about the rest of the flight crew. I'll still need the two of you for a short while."

"We made a deal!" Robin screamed. "We did everything you asked for!"

She was caught in a moment of indecisiveness—walk or protect her friends. She'd had about enough of it all, and though she could taste freedom, something inside her was telling her to put her foot down. She was sick of being told what to do by men who treated her as some proxy by which to conduct their business—nefarious or otherwise. Now she had a real chance to take control, and it was dangling between her blouse and her skirt, nearly screaming for her to just grab it and put a stop to all the madness.

It had been quite some time since she'd fired a pistol, but you just needed to squeeze the trigger, right? It was a single action. She knew that much. Just one squeeze of the trigger and the gun goes boom—the rest was in the aim.

"Robin, get off the plane. Don't you want this all to be over?" Al responded. He grabbed the case instinctively, predicting he might need it in these final moments. He had carelessly left it on the seat while dealing with Rex and confirming that the requested items had been delivered. As soon as he lifted it from the seat, Robin reached behind her back.

"Robin, don't," Wally said softly. Robin produced a small revolver that she aimed directly toward Al's chest.

24

"What are you doing?" Al asked. He was surprised Robin had worked up the nerve to pull a stunt like this. He even admired it. She'd become as daring as him.

"Clipping your wings," Robin growled. There was a burning, searing look in her eyes he had never seen before. Who'd put her up to this? Surely not Rex, and through quick process of elimination, Al deduced that only Van Cortland could have pulled a stunt like that—an ace in the hole in case he tried to leave with innocent bystanders again. Did Rex even know? It was unlikely.

The nausea rushed through his body once again, and Al became increasingly aware of how hot the plane was now getting. The aircraft had been choking to keep cool, relying on only one engine to filter air, and the air was becoming heavy. Al began to feel light-headed, and was instantaneously overcome with an immense fear—a fear he had managed to quell up until this point. Al's head was spinning, and the tremors were running through his body like a locomotive. He had not concocted a plan to deal with someone like Robin pointing a gun in his direction.

"Don't do this, Robin," Al pleaded. His voice had gone weak—a whimpering, cracking sound that was anything but intimidating—and he struggled to get the words out as his vision began to blur.

"I'm sick of people telling me what to do today, and I'm not going to let you endanger them. You got what you wanted, and you didn't keep up your end of the bargain. Off the plane." She waved the gun toward the exit. Al debated whether or not she really knew how to fire the gun, but he couldn't take his chances. He had to prolong the altercation as much as possible until he found a solution, but he had to think quickly. Standing on that tarmac was like walking out into an open season hunt with a bright red target on his head.

"You can fly this plane yourself. I heard you say it," she snapped. "You should have just let them go."

"You're right. I can. My goal is not to damage this plane, though, or endanger anyone around." Al began to move toward her in a calm, calculated saunter but with his hands raised in submission.

"Don't come any closer!" she yelled, pointing the gun shakily at his face. *Were there even bullets in the gun?* Al wondered. Perhaps she'd picked up some tricks from him along the way—a simple show of force and deception.

"What are you doing, Robin?" Tom asked. "We'll take him where he wants to go. Get out of here."

"Quiet. I'm saving your lives," she said to Wally and Tom under her breath. She then turned to Al and growled, "Slowly back off the plane." In his weakest state yet, Al succumbed to her demands. He had no choice in this tight, claustrophobic fuselage but to comply. Even an amateur could hit their target in a space like this.

Al couldn't be sure, but he was confident it was a .38. A bullet from a gun like that fired this close would put him down with ease no matter where it hit him. He would be spending the rest of his agonizing days of existence behind long steel bars with three shitty meals a day.

Surely they would expedite his trial to claim justice had been served before he'd died. That was *if* he survived the shot. That wasn't how he'd planned to go out.

Al rubbed his eyes with his free hand, struggling to see clearly. He couldn't reach for a pill at the moment for fear she would fire the gun. *You're nothing*, he heard a voice in his head say. It was a distant, spectral sort of echo, but he was sure it was the voice of his mother.

"I'm not going to say it again," Robin said angrily.

"Always the hero," Al said to her. He stared at her intensely for a moment, quickly weighing his options on how to deal with the situation. Right now, there were few if any that didn't end up bad.

"Okay," Al responded in his calmest voice. Wally and Tom remained behind her as he slowly stepped backward toward the ramp. As he found his footing on the steps, unaware of what awaited him on the runway, she continued to force him out at gunpoint, keeping the weapon trained directly on his face.

Al's feet found the asphalt. He felt as if he might collapse at any moment, but his heart was pounding, and now the adrenaline was flowing through him. It felt like a push and pull between his brain and his body to maintain consciousness. Robin was walking down the steps now too, forcing Al farther away from the tail section of the plane. If a sniper had him in their sights, they could surely take him out, which he imagined had been part of her plan all along. There wouldn't be much time for Al to act when they found him in their crosshairs.

"I'm in charge now," she said intensely.

"Control can change very quickly, Robin. You've demonstrated that," Al explained.

"Keep walking!" she shouted as he continued to retreat. Now it was just the two of them on the runway, locked a in a sort of dance as Al began to add a bit of side-step to his footwork.

"Don't forget, if you shoot me, this explosive goes off and all of us die. You didn't think your plan out fully," Al warned her. "The concussion will still take all of us out at this range. There's a lot of explosive here, more than is necessary." Wally and Tom remained at the top of the steps. Al sensed by their hesitation, that they did not want to be confused for the perpetrator. From a distance, their black suit jackets covering white shirts could easily be mistaken for his own.

"You'd better pray I'm not in the sight of a rifle scope right now," Al said. He stopped in his tracks, making one more attempt to change her mind. He had not anticipated Robin would be the one to test his mettle, and he was actually quite proud of her in some sick, demented way. Sure, she wasn't on his team, but her bravery was undeniable. He had to think fast.

"Ask yourself, do you really think this is what your husband would want?" Al began. "For you to become the hero? He would want you to return home safely. Don't you want to go home, Robin?" Al continued with his footwork and began to flank her, forcing her out on to the runway and trying to close the gap between himself and the staircase.

"Stop talking!" she screamed. Her eyes were quickly darting around the airport. The darkness had nearly swallowed the environment, and judging by the way she was searching her surroundings, she was waiting for someone to do *something*. Al was out of time. "*You're already dead,*" he said to himself.

"What?" Robin asked.

Before she could speak again, he darted toward her with as much an energy as he could muster, taking her by surprise. A faint crack rang out in the distance. There was too much happening at once to deduce its point of origin, but he knew it was a gunshot from a high-powered rifle.

A bullet whizzed by Al's head, ricocheting off of the fuselage of the aircraft with a ferocious *ping*. The high-caliber projectile had missed his skull by an inch. The commotion frightened Robin, and Al quickly disarmed her, placing the gun to her temple as he forced her into a headlock with lightning-like speed. Now he had her pressed against his body, her hands clenched tightly around his forearm, the briefcase dangling nearly inches from her panicking face.

The bomb had done its job, but it would not provide him with enough leverage in this situation anymore. He needed a better bargaining chip, and it was Robin. Al had not intended to murder anyone tonight, but he had to take a hostage forcefully to show that he meant business.

He needed to get back on the plane, and *fast*. If he didn't get out of that dreadful heat soon, he would surely faint on the runway and wake up in cuffs. Robin was nearly hyperventilating, her chest rising and falling rapidly as she clung to his arm. Her heroics had only made the situation worse, and from her whimpers he could tell she immediately regretted her choice.

"Slowly back up with me," Al commanded. He held her tightly as he retreated toward the steps. He scanned the area where all the authorities had gathered, trying desperately to make sure no one had drawn up the courage to storm the castle. When he passed by the wound on the plane, he was able to approximate that the bullet had originated from the sandy patch of land nearby.

Al waved the gun at Wally and Tom in an effort to force them back into the plane. He again surveyed the wall that had been formed by the agents, keeping an eye out for any other threats. "I told you I wasn't going to hurt you, Robin, but now I have to use you to protect myself. They're not going to fire on you."

He could tell she didn't believe him. Why should she? He had not fully disclosed his intention of keeping some staff on board the plane, even though he had not intended on her being one of the remaining crew. He had no choice now, though, and he used her body to shield himself as he successfully climbed back into the cabin of the plane.

The bomb that dangled in front of her face kept her in line, and he turned the gun on the flight crew to force them back down the aisle. They both retreated, their hands raised defensively, willing and ready to follow his orders once again.

"You two, get back in the cockpit," Al barked.

"Okay, but let her—" Wally began.

"Back in the cockpit!" Al demanded. He truly did not want to involve her anymore, but they had come too far, and Al knew that he could get them to comply by keeping Robin in danger. He was having trouble maintaining a calm demeanor. The situation had spiraled completely out of control, and he was forced to resort to more questionable methods. Al was now heavily off script, and improvisation was not synonymous with efficiency.

The tone of his voice was proof of his lack of control over the situation. Where he had once been calm and cool, he was now a screaming madman. Although he had planned extensively, the circumstances had derailed him a bit, and he needed to get back on track.

"Listen to me very carefully," Al said to them both. "We are going to depart again. When we reach an altitude of 10,000 feet, you are to maintain it. Landing gear stays down. When we are on a suitable airway for travel, reposition us to one that will direct us over Sedona. Keep the flaps at fifteen degrees after takeoff."

"It's dangerous," Wally argued. "To keep the cabin pressurized—"

"Please don't argue with me," Al said, pressing the gun firmly against Robin's cheek. He needed to get the air circulating in this plane again so he could keep his composure. Moisture had begun gathering inside his shirt, and if he didn't get this plane in motion, he'd be soaked soon enough. His anger was manifesting itself into sloppiness. He would need more pills as soon as possible to see himself through to the end.

Tom stepped forward defiantly, arguing, "At that altitude and flight speed, with the landing gear still deployed, we could suffer engine stall."

"I assure you this aircraft is capable, now get in the cockpit and fly the plane. Contact ATC and notify them that we will be taking off. Make sure they don't try anything stupid." Threatened by the gun, both of them headed toward the cabin. Al released Robin, feeling guilty that he had been forced to use violence with her. He *had* successfully turned fear into his ally, but who had he become? "Shut the staircase," he demanded. She pulled the lever, and the staircase began to rise. The faint glow of the spotlights that was flooding in from the exterior was sucked out when it closed, causing the plane to become eerily dark.

The twilight period had ended, and the light-swallowing darkness of night had now almost completely engulfed the plane. "Alright, get in your jump seat," Al said. Robin hustled toward the front of the plane without a word. They had nothing more to say to each other, and whatever relationship Al had managed to cultivate with her had been fractured. Right now he had to get this plane airborne again.

The engines began to howl again and he could feel the plane turning toward the end of the runway. They were taking off in a direction that was uncommon for commercial flights, but he had chosen this runway specifically because it would require very little reorientation of the jet to allow him an escape. He grabbed a pill from the bottle and choked it down. It was considerably harder to accomplish given how dry his throat was, but he managed. He was back on track, and it was time for the final part of the act.

25

The crack that sounded from Rex's knuckles connecting with JG's jaw was almost as loud as the gun shot only moments earlier. JG hit the asphalt hard, nearly breaking his wrist in the process. Before he could even regain his bearings, Rex was coming at him again to finish the job. Three agents immediately grabbed Rex, holding him back like a wild dog tethered to a leash. He was even snarling.

"What the fuck did you do?" Rex barked, struggling violently to break free of the men forming the chains around him.

"Easy, Rex," Otto pleaded.

"I gave Miss Kraft the upper hand," JG replied, massaging his jaw as he climbed to his feet. When he spoke, his mouth made a strange clicking sound, and he was sure Rex had knocked *something* out of place. Those old bones weren't what they used to be. JG had been an amateur fighter in his younger days, just for the sport of it, and he'd taken some hard hits in his life. Rex's punch was impressive.

"You *armed* her!" Rex yelled, still wriggling with all his might as the agents restrained him. "You armed a god-damned civilian!"

"It was a contingency," JG replied. "You didn't have a plan B."

"You crossed the line, Jim," Rex said, waving an accusing finger toward him. "They're gonna nail you to the wall—straight to the wall!"

"He was unarmed," JG said, defeated. "I had to try."

"He's armed now," Rex replied. He breathed deeply for a moment, relaxing himself in the custody of his subordinates, and held his hands up submissively to prompt them to release him.

"The manifest said thirty-seven people were on board," JG said. "Your people counted thirty-three walking off. That leaves four people still inside, and three are flight crew."

"We can count, Jim," Rex said snidely. "Thanks."

A crowd of people had begun to funnel through the wall of police cars nearby. Rex turned to Mitch. "Get four guys doing count over there. I want I.D.s. No one leaves until they are cleared. Check every single one of them against the manifest." Rex grabbed a walkie. "Owl 1, keep your sight on that plane."

Rex's energy was wasted though, as the plane's turbines had begun to spool. The exterior lights flickered for a moment, and then shined brightly to illuminate the runway ahead of it. Mr. Ader was going to get his wish, and the plane was going to leave the runway once again.

"You happy, Jim?" Rex said to JG. "Look! The plane's leaving again, and what am I going to do?"

"What was your plan?" JG asked. "To let him take off again?"

"To stall," Rex said, walking quickly toward JG. "We keep him on the ground as long as we can until we learn more. We search for a weakness. *That's* what we do."

"So you're clear that you were going to risk the lives of the flight crew on board?" JG asked.

"'**Flight Crew Dies with Crazed Lunatic**' is a lot better headline than '**Plane Explodes Over Phoenix, Flight Crew Still on Board, Hijacker Escapes**," Rex said. "I got the civilians out, and that's when I can make different calls. You had to go and screw that up. You have no authorization here, you're just a civilian like them. I should have never let you in on this."

"I'm sorry—" JG said.

Rex barely even let him get the words out before yelling, "Shut up!"

"I was going to move in on the plane," Rex said. "But we don't have that luxury anymore. I told you, if this goes bad, my hands are tied. Now you're going to see what ugly looks like." Rex began to walk away before stopping in his tracks, and turning back to JG. "Oh, that's right. You already know."

The plane's engines were nearly screaming now, signaling it would be ready to take off at any moment. The battle had turned into one between two men, right here on the tarmac, and they'd almost forgotten about the plane sitting on the runway and the *real* war that had been waged. Rex handed the walkie to Mitch. "Call USAF. Tell them to scramble two fighters," Rex said.

"Fighters?" JG cried.

"Yes," Rex said. "Fighters. It's protocol. You left me with no choice." Rex turned to Mitch again. "Inform air traffic not to let that plane out of their sight. Tell them to clear the air if they have to. I want as many units as you can find on ground pursuit. Call the national guard, the bureau, the stateys, whoever we can muster up. I want to know where the plane is headed. If the asshole does jump, we'll catch him."

Rex began to pace in wide circles. The thought of just filling the fuselage of the plane with bullets crossed his mind, but it would make for a terrible headline, and the bosses certainly wouldn't like that. It would *show* JG, that he was sure of, but it wasn't the right call. He wasn't here to teach JG a lesson, he was here to get his man. He'd been cradling a radio in his hand, and after a brief moment of deliberation, he whipped it at the side of the car nearby, shattering it into a thousand pieces of plastic.

JG stood watching, his head hanging low shamefully. He'd thought he'd made the right call, thought he could make a difference in how this one played out. The truth was, he might have done more damage than good. Flashes of the Flight 85 disaster plagued his mind yet again—a violent explosion followed by a plane spiraling into the Earth, only this time the number on the tail section was "197," and it wasn't his brother's face he saw screaming, it was *Robin's*.

The thought crossed his mind that he might even be put on trial for a move like that. If Rex or any of the other agents who'd been privy to what had happened spilled the beans, he could be sitting in front of a judge. It didn't matter. He had had good lawyers, and even if he lost, he wasn't sure he wanted to be in this game anymore anyway. The rules had changed, and he wasn't confident he was going to be able to deal with them.

"Get me to the tower," Rex said to Mitch. He trekked to the sedan waiting nearby, and Mitch hopped in the driver's seat. The car peeled off, leaving a thick trail of burnt rubber on the ground. JG tracked Rex through the window as the car sped away, and Rex just maintained his glowering stare while the distance between them grew. Rex was still chomping on that same old gum, his jaws flapping nervously. JG quickly lost sight of him. Soon, all the agents were packing up, a flurry of suits hopping into cars and tearing off into the night to pursue the plane reorienting itself on the runway.

Now, JG was alone. A cool gust of wind tore through the area, a welcome reprieve to the heat that had dissipated now that the sun had retired. He felt silly in his plaid jacket. His father had told him, "Always dress sharp when you go out into the world, that way if you fuck up you'll feel like an idiot, but you won't *look* like one."

The night brought quiet with it, save for roaring engines of the plane not too far away. It was quickly interrupted by radio chatter, and JG searched for the source. There, resting on the hood of one of the squad cars, was a radio that one of the agents had left behind.

26

F light 197 crawled down the runway. Circulating air helped to put Al at ease. He'd need to relax to prepare for what he was about to do, and sweaty fingers weren't going to help in any way.

"Al. Come in, Al," he heard a voice trickle in over the radio. He'd forgotten that the radio was still nearby resting on a seat cushion.

"Hello, Rex," Al said into the walkie.

"This isn't Rex," the voice replied. "It's JG Van Cortland."

"Mr. Van Cortland. It's great to meet you," Al said. "I'm assuming it was your bright idea to arm Robin. That backfired on you, though, didn't it?"

"It was, and I admit it was stupid," he replied somberly.

"Yeah, they're going to have your head for that one, but I admire your bravery and quick thinking. *They* certainly weren't coming up with any alternative options."

"Probably not, but they are now," he said in a subdued voice.

"Is that right?" Al asked. The plane was moving at a good speed, rolling down the tarmac as the pilots oriented the nose. Al could see the authorities had scrambled from the airport when he peered over his right side. They'd practically let him walk, and he was confident they wouldn't attempt to stop the plane now. It was too dangerous, especially if the media was watching, and he was sure they were. Al, who had now existed for only a handful of hours, had already gotten his fifteen minutes of fame.

"And what might that be?" Al questioned.

"They're going to scramble fighters," Van Cortland said. It was a response Al had considered, but he wasn't worried about them shooting the aircraft out of the sky. He still had innocent souls on board.

"They're just flexing their muscles," Al said to him.

"You think they won't shoot that plane down?" he replied. "Are you familiar with Flight 85?"

"I am," Al responded, "but I'm not going to let it get that far."

"Why don't you just rethink this?" he begged. "Ground the plane, and we can work something out, surely."

"Can't do that, Mr. Van Cortland," Al said. "There's no fun in that. Besides, you're just worried about your precious plane."

"No, I'm worried about the people currently on it. I've got plenty of money. I could have another aircraft ready to replace it in under a week," JG said. "Listen to me, Al, don't think they won't hesitate to make this worse. Quit while you can—those employees are still in danger."

"Of course they are, Mr. Van Cortland," Al said. "The element of danger is what makes it all worthwhile. However, if I really thought I'd be putting anyone in any real danger, then I wouldn't have taken this plan on in the first place. You don't worry about Robin, or any of the other crew on board. They'll be free of me very soon."

"That's because you plan to jump," JG said. "You might have fooled them, but I know what you're up to. Just promise me this, Al—promise me you're not going to force any of them to jump with you."

"How did they even let you on the radio?" Al asked. "You're certainly not authorized to negotiate with me, and after what you pulled, I'm surprised no one's thrown you in cuffs in the back of a paddy wagon."

"They took off to the tower and left a radio behind," JG said. "This is just one man trying to reason with another."

"We're going to be leaving now, Mr. Van Cortland," Al responded. "Do your best to let the boys on the ground know that it'd be best if they just let me go." The plane was picking up speed, and soon it would be nose up and in the air. This conversation was getting as stale as the one he'd had with Rex, and he'd be losing the radio signal soon shortly. "I'm sure it's in both of our interests that those jet fighters don't escalate the danger."

"You've already done that yourself," he replied.

"Well then I suggest you get your public relations team working," Al warned. "I'm sure they can put a wonderful spin on this for you."

"Listen to me, Al—" JG yelped.

Al turned the radio off before JG could finish his thought. He was just a distraction. Al was so close to the final part of the act he could taste it, and with very few people left on board, he was finally able to relax as he tended to the items around him, including the cash and the parachutes.

It was possible that the jets, if authorized, might attempt to take out the plane in an effort to facilitate damage control, but Al knew that if the flight confirmed he made the jump before they had their chance to mount an assault, there wouldn't be an issue. The jets would be moving far too fast to figure out his location once he leapt anyway, so he would need to make sure that ATC clearly understood what he was preparing to do. The crew's involvement was not over *yet*.

Al heard the engines scream as the plane barreled down the runway. The Arizona climate was not known for its turbulence, so he had not bothered to secure himself safely in the seat for takeoff. Preparing for the final steps was of the utmost importance. Outside, the silvery glow of the moon had emerged along the mountains that flanked the airport, and the plane would soon be approaching its next destination: the jump point.

For a moment, Al worried that they might be flying blind. If the Feds had hijacked the operation up in the tower, they might not be privy to the traffic in the air, and he hoped that Wally and Jack would keep a watchful eye on the sky if planes in the surrounding area had not been grounded. That was unlikely, but a midair collision would certainly make an ugly end to the operation, and worse, make Al look like a fool. It could get ugly now, so he would need to get out of this mess as soon as the opportunity presented itself. Light had been his ally on the tarmac, but darkness would aid in his disappearing act. Despite the minor setback with the fuel truck and Robin's attempt at a moment of glory, Al was still on schedule.

As the plane lifted into the sky, Al grabbed the seat next to him to brace himself. Although he had not predicted turbulence, their speed in the air coupled with his instructions to not retract the landing gear had made the plane less than aerodynamic, and it would remain that way as they continued through the short bit of travel. They would be flying directly toward the Navajo Nation Reservation, and Al imagined that it would be around that time when the jet fighters would come close enough to intercepting the plane. It was also near where he had planned to ditch. He was counting on the fact that they would have a hard time finding him, since radar and guidance systems—despite modern technology—were still very primitive when it came to finding a needle in a haystack like a man jumping into the night sky.

Now that Al couldn't see so much as a cloud from the plane's window, he wouldn't be able to look for any specific landmarks like he had before. His impetus to make the jump would be based purely on how much time had elapsed since takeoff. He had planned to exit the plane near Sedona. The town was characterized by a harsh red desert that sat among spectacular canyons and was a popular destination for tourists looking for useless trinkets in its quaint little shopping district.

From there, he would walk on foot to meet Sam at the pickup point they had predetermined near Flagstaff. The trip between the two locations would be treacherous, especially given his current condition, but he would be obscured and camouflaged by mountain ranges that would provide relatively good cover.

It was easily fourteen to sixteen miles to get from the planned landing area to the pickup spot, but the cover of night, Al hoped, would aid him. He had hiked the area a few times as a teenager when he had been forced on small trips with his aunt, and he knew that it could be done in the time he had allowed for the trek. Of course, he'd done it at a much younger, healthier age, but his blood was pumping something fierce, and he still felt more alive than he'd felt in a long time. Of all of the dangers he had courted in the last few hours, his most ambitious feat was still ahead.

27

The flight had been traveling for about thirty minutes now, and the sky was finally as black as ink. The plane rattled back and forth, turbulent tremors tearing at the fuselage in the rough air it had been fighting. Al placed the other parachute pack on the front of his body, fitting it to the "d" rings that resided up front. If one failed, then this trip would end with the agents scraping his remains off the side of a cliff, and he needed the backup just in case. He used a small pocket knife he'd stowed in the breast pocket of his jacket to cut a seatbelt apart, forming a makeshift strap to secure the duffel bag of money to his body. The parachute could hold a man twice his current weight, and the money wasn't particularly heavy despite the large amount he'd procured.

"You're not going to get away with this," a soft voice said. He had not even heard Robin approach, another sign that he had gotten too comfortably distracted. Now that he was armed, he'd taken the upper hand again, and he'd lost all fear that any of the flight crew might make an attempt on his life.

"I am. I have to—that's the point," Al said as he continued to prepare. Making it this far had reinvigorated him, and a second wind allowed him to tend to the tasks at hand while he spoke with her.

"Okay, last set of instructions," Al began. "I want the flight to remain no higher than 10,000 feet. I want the flaps locked in at fifteen degrees. The pilot may argue that those conditions are inadvisable, but assure him it's fine. I told them I wouldn't present them with any danger, and I'm still holding up my end of the bargain. Scary, maybe, but doable. Landing gear stays down, and air speed should be no higher than 100 knots."

"Any other requests?" she asked scornfully.

"Last thing, and this is *important*."

"As if any of the others weren't?" she snapped.

"This one *is*," Al said. Robin ran her hand through her hair nervously. Any other person might have cracked by now, but she had performed valiantly, and now he wanted her to understand that this was *really* going to be over.

"Where was your wedding going to be?" Al questioned.

"Why do you care?"

"Answer the question."

"Los Angeles," she said hesitantly. "That would have been our return flight if *you* hadn't shown up."

"Then that is where I want the plane landed," Al said. For the first time tonight, Robin looked at Al sympathetically. There was, after all, some kind of fragmented soul left in the dying man's body. Perhaps she now understood fully that this was never about her, or the passengers, or any of the other people Al had involved in this adventure. This was about Al, and only Al.

"I told you that I would get you home safely, Robin,

and I'm keeping up my end of the bargain." She stared at him blankly, and he understood why. He kept promising a woman he had threatened with a bomb and held at gun point that he was going to protect her, and the entire scenario was incredibly contradictory if he thought about it. "Congratulations, you've kept everyone on this flight out of danger. They'll call you a hero when this story is retold. You'll be a litmus by which the handling of a crisis like this is judged. That will be *your* legacy."

"I didn't ask to be a hero," she said somberly.

"People rarely do," Al replied. He cut another seatbelt up and further secured the duffel bag of money to his body. He was feeling the weight of the parachutes now. Their heft was making his knees feel weak, but soon he would be embarking on a date with gravity that would briefly put them at ease.

Robin clutched the seat in front of her as the plane shook violently yet again. The turbulence they were experiencing could knock a person off their feet without warning. This portion of the trip was quickly becoming treacherous, and it threatened Al's ability to keep the crew alive. The clock was ticking, and when he checked his watch one more, the time had almost come for the "voilà" moment of his master plan.

The plan had seemed anything but masterful in the last hour. Al had narrowly dodged a bullet and had taken a hostage at gunpoint. Despite the setbacks, his improvisation had worked out quite well, and though it hadn't gone as smoothly as he had anticipated, everything was still moving forward.

"Al, that's not your real name, is it?" Robin asked. Al simply shook his head back and forth in response. Robin seemed to stand by idly now. She was watching him prepare, and though she would have been safer in the cockpit, some strange feeling inside told her she was supposed to be there seeing him off.

"Even if your plan works, how will anyone ever know it was you?" she asked.

"I'll know," Al said confidently. He adjusted the parachute again to make sure it was comfortable, pulling the straps snugly as he stood tall. He was all set and ready to go. He looked like a paratrooper ready to drop into a business meeting.

"Now go to the cockpit, and don't open the door. Expect a slight bit of turbulence. It's going to get windy in here. Tell the pilot and flight engineer not to worry about it. All they need to do is maintain speed and altitude, one hundred knots, and 10,000 feet or lower—"

"Flaps at fifteen degrees," she interrupted. Al simply smiled. As Al made his way toward the back of the plane, Robin's eyes stayed fixed on the briefcase. There was a look of concern in her eyes that undoubtedly asked why he was leaving it behind.

"Why can't you take the case?" she yelled to Al.

Al turned slowly, dropping the dark shades lightly to the bridge of his nose like he was some sort of rock star. "Never tell the audience how good you are!" Al shouted back over the loud plane. "They'll soon find out for themselves!" With that, he turned and walked toward the aft staircase.

Robin considered the words as her eyes shifted between Al and the briefcase, and the "ah-ha" moment finally hit her. The bomb was a fake. It always had been, but the threat that the bomb was real was what he'd needed to harness the situation. Although he'd had to resort to brandishing the firearm for a brief period, the bomb had worked far better than Al had anticipated during the early stages. He assumed it would—it *was* a bomb, but it had performed admirably. Now, however, it was no longer necessary for Al to use fear as a weapon. He would thank Sam later for that.

Al pulled the red lever, opening the staircase door once again, and a gust of wind nearly knocked him off his feet. He had turned the interior of the plane into a violent hurricane—and it was inadvisable to maintain those conditions for long. Although much of the oxygen would escape the cabin, the plane was low enough in the atmosphere that proper pressurization was not a concern. Some of the money began to flow out of the open bag like confetti. Al used the knife to once again cut the bands that had been applied to the stacks to keep the bills together, and a slew of bills fluttered out of the open door, flapping off into the black abyss that lay ahead of him.

"Go, Robin," Al yelled back to her after realizing she hadn't left for safety yet.

"You'll die," she cried out sympathetically. She was right. It was very possible he would die. He'd known that when he came up with the idea in the first place.

"I'm already dead," Al assured her, and she retreated, back-stepping slowly toward the cockpit. She knew that her place in this story was finally over—hopefully—and that to risk staying inside the cabin would be foolish.

The moon was now the only source of illumination in the sky, barring the aircraft's lights near the tail section of the plane. They were painting the nearby clouds with an incandescent glow, and the night sky was less clear than the original weather report had predicted—but Al was going to proceed even if he was jumping out into a hailstorm. He was relying solely on the flight path he had anticipated. If the pilot tried to pull a fast one on him, the cloud cover blocking any visuals would leave him royally screwed. Al hoped they wouldn't dare—as far as they knew, the faux bomb was still a threat.

The plane sank violently, and the sudden movement almost sent him tumbling out of the rear. It would have been a silly way to end it all—falling clumsily into the Earth below—and luckily his leg had become caught on the seat nearby, trapping him inside. The oxygen masks deployed from the ceiling in response. Al was breathing just fine, so he deduced it must have been an automatic response from the plane. Inside the cockpit, they would be breathing plenty comfortably, and as Al turned once more to look toward the front, Robin's absence confirmed she had taken her place with the remaining flight crew.

This was it—the moment he had planned for. As he stared into the silky masses of clouds that trailed in front of him at incredible speed, he hoped that he had been at least *somewhat* close in his geographical calculations. If he was caught later, his face would be plastered all over the media worldwide, and the press would quickly leap at the chance to proclaim the news of the man who was insane enough to demand ransom money from the federal government via threat of a bomb and commandeer a jetliner before jumping through the night sky. Being caught wasn't the ending Al had hoped for, though. The disappearing act, well, that was what would make his act illustrious. When he thought about it, it really did sound as ridiculously mad as he had originally imagined, and yet here he was, making it real.

The view was strikingly magnificent. Most chances people got to see the Earth from that high were limited and obscured by windows and panels, but Al had a stunning view of the sea of dark clouds. If he had died at that moment, it would have been a romantic way to go, but he had a job to finish.

He grabbed a nearby handle, bracing his body as he mustered up the courage to hurl himself from the stairs. A howling grew loud nearby, different than the screeching of the plane. Sure enough, two jets had ascended nearby, slightly flanking the plane as they trailed behind. They were fighters, designed specifically for intercepting. They had found the plane quicker than Al had imagined. He realized they must have been scrambled from Luke Air Force Base, which was approximately fifteen miles outside of the Phoenix area. The fighters were surely armed, and although he didn't think they had been sanctioned to fire at will, the longer they followed, the more likely the situation could spiral out of control. This wasn't over yet.

28

"Yes, sir," Rex said gravely. "Understood." The damn gum that he'd been chewing on to calm his nerves was like chewing on a deflated balloon now, and he wondered how much longer he could stand it while his superior chewed *him* out over the phone. Rex's gaze did not break from the myriad of flickering lights and controls in the control tower. Flight 197 was still within range of communication, and Rex had become a bit of a hijacker himself when he'd stormed into the room and taken control from the personnel occupying the tower. "We will engage, sir." Rex returned the phone to the receiver and folded his arms tightly against his body as he tracked Flight 197.

"This is Eagle 1," a voice echoed through the room. "We've intercepted Flight 197 and are currently trailing at a heading of 90, speed 100 knots."

"We see you, Eagle 1," Rex replied through the radio.

"Copy that, Phoenix," the pilot of the fighter replied. "Please advise."

All eyes in the room were looking to Rex. To say the

tension in the room was high was an understatement. Most of the men in the room were relatively green. They'd barely caught any wanted thieves, let alone hijackers. None of them—Mitch, Ken, or even Otto—had ever witnessed a plane blown out of the sky voluntarily on their watch. Sure, Otto had put some time in during the war, and he'd seen his fair share of both explosions and death, but what was about to happen made them uneasy. No one had thought it would come to this, and the worst-case scenario was now upon them.

The control tower personnel had taken a back seat—a bunch of white shirts and black ties lined up against the rear wall of the tower and absolved of all sin. This was an FBI operation now, Rex had made that much clear to them when he'd arrived. If they didn't have any relevant information, he didn't want to hear them.

All Rex could think about was getting his man. He'd become obsessive, perhaps even blinded to Robin, Wally, and Tom's predicament. If that plane wound up scattered over a suburban neighborhood, there'd be hell to pay, and Rex would most likely be the one shelling out. Rex's teeth were starting to hurt, a pulsing sensation reaching deep within his jaws when he said, "Move to strike formation."

A creaking door in the rear of the room called his attention. A withered, now quite sickly-looking, old man crept in. Though he was obscured by the dimly lit room, Rex knew exactly who it was. Mitch moved to stop him, but Rex waved him off and allowed JG entry into the room against his better judgement. It was, after all, partially the old man's fault that they were all sitting in the tower.

"Hey, Phoenix," Wally's voice shook as it came through.

"This is Phoenix, 197," Rex replied.

"Hey, we're getting uh... a little nervous about these fighters you've got trailing us. Please tell me those are just for our safety."

"They're just tracking you," Rex lied. "In case the suspect jumps."

"You sure about that?" Wally asked. "Because I spent enough time flying to know when a fighter's ready to make a move, and well... well you've got us all sorts of worried about their positioning."

"Just maintain course, 197!" Rex commanded.

"Don't do this, Rex," JG chimed in.

"Jim, you shouldn't even be in this room," Rex said, his teeth clenched so hard together the words barely even came out audibly. "I made that mistake once, and I'm not going to make it again. You've got two options. You can either stand silently over in the back there where you belong, or you can turn and walk out that door and go back to wherever it is you go. I'm not going to warn you again. We're in the red now, and you have no authority here."

"But, Rex—"

"There are no buts," Rex replied. "I just got off the line with the big dogs and they want this taken care of now. They don't want to wake up tomorrow morning looking like fools, and if I don't handle this now, they're going to— and so will I."

"Looking like fools?" JG started. "Funny you say that, because the press is going to get a hold of this story, and they're going to have quite a few versions to sort through. One could say they might have different *sources* of information, and it will be hard to know which one to believe. Either way, it will be a shit show."

"Are you threatening a federal agent?" Rex asked.

"I didn't threaten you," JG said. "I'm merely pointing out how the facts can be misleading, twisted even."

"Where is that plane right now?" Rex asked the en route controller.

The young guy, a nerdy looking young man who fiddled nervously at the controls, scanned the display in front of him, before saying, "Right now? Roughly over Prescott National Forest."

"You hear that?" Rex asked JG. "Let me translate for you. The middle of fucking nowhere. In other words: damage control." Rex got close to JG, right up in his face as he had before, only this time he wasn't going to hit him, he was going to set him straight. "So you can threaten all you want. It won't make a difference. As far as the press knows, the idiot blew the bomb midair. He was crazy like that, lost his marbles. You understand? They might have run out of fuel from traveling at such a low altitude."

"How's it going to play when the press finds out you shot down a civilian aircraft?" JG asked. He didn't care if Rex socked him one now. What did he have to lose? "I've got a lot of money, Rex. I can buy the press. In fact, I often do."

"I'll be sure to tell them how the hijacker received the firearm," Rex replied with a 'don't fuck with me' smirk plastered across his face. "Then we both hang."

Hang he would. JG was moments away from reliving the nightmare he'd never truly forgotten. Now, he wouldn't hear about it second hand, or learn after the fact, but he'd have the wicked privilege of watching it unfold in real time.

"Phoenix," the pilot said over the radio, "this is Eagle 1. I can see the target standing in the tail cavity." JG's heart skipped a beat. If Rex was going to make a move, he was going to do it now. The target was right there, ripe for the picking. If he wanted Al Ader, he could have him right now, but what would it cost?

"You don't have to do this," JG pleaded.

"All right," Rex said. "Then what's your plan?" He'd give JG one more shot. Failure tasted like bad medicine, and though he would only have been following orders, he was well aware of the negative trickle-down aspect of these types of operations. That was the job he'd signed up for, and sometimes that was the way the chips fell.

"Let him jump," JG replied. "Get him on the ground. Those people don't have to die so we can catch one idiot."

All Rex could think about was the Bauer brothers. The axe had fallen on him that time, and if he let Al go, and he was never caught, there might be no coming back for Agent Rex Schulz. He'd done the right thing that time, and it had landed him in a hell-hole desert with a bullshit detail. He'd die here in Phoenix, just another schmuck, if this didn't go right.

"You never cared about them," JG replied. "Don't blame the men calling the shots. It was always about him. Don't worry, Rex. You go through with this, and you'll have your man, but you'll also get to live with what you did here tonight, and what it took to get it. I hope you get the badge pinned to your jacket you've been hoping for. I hope it's worth it, because I can tell you the nightmares won't stop. They *never* do."

29

A l became worried the screaming jets following the plane could not see him. The lights in the cabin had been dimmed. Not only did he need a way to signal to them that he wasn't going to be on the plane anymore, but he had to get them out of the way, or his jump could become even more dangerous than it already was. Given the speed at which both he and the fighters were traveling, he risked colliding with one, or worse, get sucked into one of their turbines and spit back out. That wouldn't be pretty, and his body would wind up scattered all across the southwest.

He opened the duffel bag and pulled out a wad of cash, slicing the bands that had kept them together. The cash quickly floated around the plane, flapping wildly, and eventually flying out of the cavity in the rear and toward the fighters in a glorious blaze of dead-president-branded confetti. If his message that this stunt was not about the cash had not been clear enough, it surely would be now. It was a distasteful slap in the face in the most magical way possible, and Al was miffed he hadn't thought of it beforehand.

It worked, and both jets screamed left and right, escaping the potentially hazardous projectiles that flapped toward them. Unlike his body, the turbines would make quick work of the cash, but the fighters dodged nonetheless. He let some more cash fly into the thick clouds to buy him some time once the jets had maneuvered away. There was no reason to leave any cash intact on the aircraft. Even if the flight crew wanted to keep it for their trouble, the bills were marked, and officials would flag the crew right away for potentially conspiring with him.

The phone on the wall faintly rang next to Al's ear. The sound of air rushing throughout the plane made it difficult to hear, but a blinking light saw to it that the call did not go unnoticed. He lifted it off of the receiver, covering his other ear to hear better.

"Hey, you alright out there?" Al heard Wally ask.

"All okay here, thanks. Just keep her level!" Al yelled in reply.

"He's going to do it. The crazy bastard is going to do it," he could hear Wally say to his companions in the distance. Al noted a tone of excitement in Wally's voice, and maybe even encouragement. He debated whether that had to do with his feat, or the notion that the flight crew just wanted to be rid of him now that the fighters were tracking them. Either way, there was no backing out now.

"Time for me to go," Al said loudly. "You've got company. Let them know I am no longer a threat. Thanks for all of your help. Godspeed." Al hung up the phone. The jets were approaching the plane again, rising up into the sky and cutting through clouds like knives. He could prolong this no further.

Al climbed to the edge of the steps. The dizzying view from over the edge was vertigo-inducing. He worried he might be plagued with one of his dizzy spells at that moment, but the rush he was feeling kept his senses heightened and his attention focused. The only light nearby was from the incandescent bulbs on the under-body of the plane hitting the sky below, and the falloff was aggressive. Below the well-exposed cloud line was a massive pit of black. He couldn't see much beyond that, and he wasn't exactly sure *where* he was, but he had to relieve the plane from danger.

Al's hair was whipping wildly around his face now. It was a miracle the sunglasses had even stayed on this long. He removed them, tucking them into the pocket of his slacks. The wind was strong outside the plane, and he couldn't risk another shift in elevation like the last one while on the stairs. He tightened the straps that held the duffel bag to him once more, placed his hands on the straps around his rear parachute, and closed his eyes.

For a moment, it was like Al could hear nothing. Time had almost seemed to stop, and the cool breeze was celestial at this height. He was second guessing his choices now. He had never even been on a plane, let alone been crazy enough to jump out of one. He had made it this far, but the reminder of his mortality felt stronger now than ever. *Jump in the fire*, he could hear his mother say. For once in his life, they sounded like words of encouragement. He opened his eyes, removed his loafers from his feet, and placed them inside his jacket. Any more procrastination was unwelcome. He had to do what he came to do.

"Abracadabra," Al said to himself, and dove into the night sky, free falling through the thick clouds. The cool and forceful breeze was a welcome departure from the heat that had kept attempting to ruin his day. As he plummeted through the air, turning his back to the ground and basking in the moment, he watched the plane continue into the distance, farther and farther away from him. He was slightly worried about getting caught in the thrust from the engines of the plane, which could easily have sent him tumbling and disoriented him beyond recovery, but he managed to get a clean dive.

The jets screeched by as they pursued the plane. Obscured by the cloud cover, he quickly lost sight of them and was now alone—falling through an isolated abyss. Whether or not they had called off the pursuit or had been directed to search for him, Al wasn't sure. He'd hoped that either the fighters had seen him jump or that the flight crew was aware of Al's jump and called them off. Either way, they wouldn't be able to locate his small body in the dark ocean of the sky through which he was rapidly descending.

Al fell at roughly one-hundred-thirty miles per hour, hurtling toward the Earth's surface. Now that EA 197 was in the clear, he began to survey his surroundings. He had chosen a night when the moon would be bright, but the clouds had complicated that a bit. Considering the diagnosis had made his death imminent no matter the outcome, he was quite enjoying the plunge and the freedom it offered.

The sky was quiet, save for the wind howling in his ears. It was incredibly divine, but Al didn't have much time to consider the true beauty of a moonlit dive. He needed to get his geography straight and figure out where he was going to touch down. The clock had already been ticking a considerable amount of time, and though he could have stayed in this euphoric state forever, it was ill-advised. He would need to deploy his parachute very soon, and there was no time for second guesses. A successful landing would be the icing on the cake of the fable.

As the Earth came closer and closer, Al was confused to find not the striking red cliffs of Sedona, but a sea of dark, patchy spots. The terrain below came into focus, and he recognized that he was surrounded by forest—the absolute worst-case scenario for a successful jump. He could break limbs, get stuck, or worse, be impaled if he attempted a landing in a thick canopy of trees at night. Every limb was like a sword-bearing soldier waiting to strike, and below, there was an army awaiting him.

He had to deploy the canopy—his time was running out. He pulled the rip cord, and abruptly slowed down as the olive parachute flowered above him. The military-grade design did not make for a smooth process slowing down, but he was just happy his selection had *worked*.

Now that Al was gliding, he would be able to buy himself more time to look for a safe place to land. He had grossly overestimated the time it would take for the plane to reach the jump zone, and he would now need to impro-vise. It was a cold, windy night, another factor the weather reports had not predicted. Was that because the weather had changed, or because his geography had been poorly mapped? As he'd anticipated, there were very few ways to control the parachute, but he'd been worried he would struggle with the unfamiliar Drop Zone-brand pack far more than he already was.

Al was gliding what he *thought* was westwardly at that

point, and as he continued to fall, he noticed a large break in the trees he thought he just might be able to reach with some tight maneuvering. The wind was adding an extra layer of difficulty while controlling his descent, but if he could just get *closer*, he knew that he might at least clear the trees and arrive in whatever the large space was. Power lines were another danger to consider, but out here in the desert they were few and far between. A cursory glance at his surroundings assured him that was not what he should have been worried about.

As he continued to rocket through the air, he thought he *just might* make it, but it would be *close*. As he continued toward the clearing, he lifted his feet up, gliding nearer and nearer to the trees, taking extra precaution that he didn't get caught on them. Now that he was up close and personal with the tall branches reaching up toward him, he realized how fast he had been moving. He'd picked up a considerable amount of speed, the wind at his back propelling him with far more force than was necessary.

The limbs were reaching up for him with their large, twisted and contorted fingers, seemingly grabbing for him. A violent impact on his foot nearly sent him spiraling. One of the trees had gotten a hold of him, and he pulled his feet up as high as was possible, tightening every muscle in his core as hard as he could. Every inch gained was a gift. Once he finally cleared them, the reflection of the moon rippling below made Al instantly aware of what it was he was plummeting toward: water.

Of course, he thought to himself. There was only one body of water this large for miles: Mormon Lake. Although a water landing was not what he'd planned for, he was prepared for it nonetheless, and it was safer than getting caught in the thick foliage now behind him. In fact, he'd been wary of making contact with the ground, and the water surely would see to it that it provided some cushion if the conditions were right. Mormon Lake was only about ten miles northwest of the Sedona area, and even though it wasn't his intended landing place, it was actually closer to the pickup point Al had determined with Sam.

The body of water was more a marsh than a lake, and Al hoped that the recent weather patterns had made it larger and deeper. In its dry state, it was more like a wide puddle than a proper body of water. It would still be hard to anticipate his footing during the landing without proper knowledge of the depth of the water, and the only landing experience he had was garnered from para-trooper instruction manuals written during the Second World War. Perhaps this might become more difficult than he imagined. Regardless, now that he was coming closer to it, he was glad the water had stuck out like a sore thumb, because he really didn't have any better options.

The wind was picking up even more strongly over the water, and as Al drew nearer and nearer, he struggled to control his landing. The wind had its own muscles, and they were in direct contrast with Al's. Before he knew it, the water was right in front of him. The reflections had been playing tricks with his depth perception, rippling and breaking in small waves of flickering light that destroyed all the details of depth perception. Al contorted his body to remain as dynamic as possible, hoping to avoid an impact that would be similar to hitting concrete. Al took a gigantic breath, forcing as much air into his lungs as was possible, and shut his mouth tightly.

Al plunged deep into the ice-cold water with a deafening crack that silenced all the sounds during his windy plummet. He assumed that desert water would be warm, but it was chilly at best, and at this time of night the absence of sun wasn't doing it any favors. Every cell of his skin screamed in agony as he sank deeper and deeper. He was sure that a healthy individual wouldn't have found it as painful, but after an eventful and nerve-wracking day, he was feeling flimsy at best.

Thankfully, the water was deep enough that he didn't break his legs skidding across the surface. A bad misjudgment would have halted his plans of walking *anywhere*. Now Al had a new problem; as he attempted to surface, the cords and ropes that had successfully guided him into the lake began to turn on him, wrapping him up in their tentacle-like threads as he made his way toward breathable air. Above him, the parachute was covering a wide area, and he risked getting caught in it and suffocating if he tried to surface where he currently was.

Al debated cutting the money loose, since the duffel bag had become involved in the entanglement, but it would be foolish to waste time trying to find it in the lake once he made it to safety. Just because he'd landed safely didn't mean he didn't have to get moving once he surfaced. If he didn't break free, he would surely die in a watery grave. He needed to release himself before trying to breach the surface. The knife he had used to cut the seat belts was still in his pocket, and after retrieving it, Al slashed feverishly at the ropes, hacking away as fast as he could.

One thread finally broke, and he continued to the others. He was running out of oxygen, and coupled with the panic he was experiencing, his blood was burning through it with record speed. He was pleased he'd selected a serrated knife, which helped him quickly tear through the material. Once the last piece was cut, he swam as quickly as he could to a lighter glow that rippled on the surface above him, aware that the moon was guiding him to a place where the parachute had not been floating above.

Al popped up from surface of the water, gasping for air and kicking his feet as hard as he could. For a moment, he was thankful that his mother had been so insistent with her unorthodox methods of teaching him how to swim. Al was even heavier now that his clothes were sopping wet, and he couldn't keep up this exertion for long. He had seen the beach line not too far north when he plummeted, and he knew that a short swim would get him to temporary safety.

Al grabbed the edge of the parachute, dragging it with him as he kicked as hard as he could toward the shore. His tank was only running on fumes. He still had a long way to go, but as soon as he hit land, most of the hard parts would be over. For starters, he was no longer trapped on Flight 197.

It was hard to see clearly, and he was focusing on swimming straight rather than checking his surroundings. The parachute was tough to drag. It seemed it was catching every drop of water in the lake like a giant pocket, but he kept at it. He knew he was close when he heard the sounds of tiny waves breaking against the shoreline, and after a handful of kicks, his feet celebrated when they found sandy ground.

He stepped forward, trudging through the water that was now only hitting his knees, and collapsed on the beach as soon as his shins cleared the water. It felt good to finally rest, and his heart was beating like a war drum. He yanked the parachute as hard as he could one final time, making sure it wouldn't get swallowed by the lake, and hoisted it over his body. If he was going to get away with this crime, he needed to be careful about leaving evidence. He wanted to be absolutely sure that if anyone came looking for him they would have a hard time picking up his trail.

He didn't have a lot of time to rest, but his body was screaming at him to take a break. Every muscle in his frame ached, and he worried that if he kept pushing himself without a reprieve, he might truly collapse. He flopped on to his back, his eyes wandering around the cloudy night sky, and wondered how Flight 197 was faring.

30

W here once laughter had been heard among the men chasing the crazed criminal in loafers, there was now silence. Those same men watched anxiously as Agent Rex Schulz monitored the jet-pursued Flight 197 and gnashed his teeth against what could barely be called gum any longer. The chewy cigarette alternative that he'd been gnawing on for half a day now felt like he'd taken a bite out of a tire. Rex Schulz had never needed a cigarette more in his life than he did at that moment, and still, he resisted.

"Command," the pilot chimed in over the radio.

"We're here," Rex replied.

"We had to pull away for a moment."

"Why?" Rex roared.

"The suspect opened the aft staircase," the pilot explained. "And he sent out some debris."

"What do you mean debris?" Rex asked.

The pilot hesitated for a moment. "Well, command, it's a bit dark, but I'm pretty convinced I saw Andrew Jackson's face for a second before it disappeared if you catch my drift."

"That motherfucker," Rex said to himself.

"He told you it wasn't about the money," JG interjected. "Now do you believe him?"

Rex paid him no attention, instead focusing on the displays ahead and cradling the radio tightly as if it would be stolen from him. "Did he jump?"

"He's no longer present," the pilot responded. "What about you Eagle 2? Did you see anything?"

"Negative," the other pilot responded. "I saw the cash too. He let a ton out of the back door."

"Sorry, command," the first pilot said. "We had to pull away. We didn't know what he was going to do."

"Are you back in a position to strike?" Rex asked.

"God damnit, Rex, he jumped!" JG said. "He's long gone!"

"We are back in position," the pilot responded. "Please advise."

"Prove it," Rex said. "Come on, old man. Since you're so sure, prove it."

"Don't patronize me," JG pleaded. "He jumped. I know it. He used the cash as a diversion. He got them out of the way, and that's when he took his chance. You know I don't give a shit about that plane. I'll buy another. I'll buy ten more. Bring those people home, Rex. You want to be a hero? You want to leave a legacy behind? Forget getting your man. Like I said, I can buy the story." JG dropped his voice to a near-whisper, his finger pointing to the men watching it all unfold. "Show the rest of these guys what a real hero looks like. Those guys on the top don't give a shit about you. I know what they did. I heard about how they gave you the boot, why you *really* came to Phoenix. You're just the fall guy, Rex. None of this is your fault, but best believe if this goes bad, if that's how this plays out, the axe falls on *you*. If you do get him, they'll take all the glory. You do have an opportunity to make this right, like you promised me. What's more important, Rex, putting this scumbag behind bars or bringing those people home safe?"

Rex looked at the men flanking every wall and crevice in the room after JG finished. Their eyes were wide and attentive. They might as well have had popcorn in their hands. JG was right. A new generation of young agents was watching, paying close attention to how someone who'd been around longer than them and had far more experience handled a situation like this. He could take that plane down right now if he wanted to, but what type of example would that set? And furthermore, what if Al *wasn't* on the plane any longer? If he came sneaking out of the woodwork one day, bragging to anyone who would listen about how he did the Feds dirty, Rex would look like the worst agent in history.

Regardless of how he felt on the inside, the orders had come from the top down. Kerry Ahern had given him specific instructions: "Take the fucking plane out. I want to scrape that bastard off the ground." That was a direct quote. Rex should have done it sooner, but he'd been hesitant. He felt guilty about following through with it himself. When he was *sure* Al was still present, he was confident in his actions, but the fighters had lost sight of him, and now he just wasn't very sure of *anything*. If Rex didn't follow through, the boys up top *would* have his head, and he could kiss his career goodbye for failing to follow orders when he should have.

The radio crackled. "Phoenix, are you seeing this?" It

was Wally, and his voice was cracking with fear. "Please tell us you're seeing this."

"What's wrong, 197?" Rex asked.

"We can't talk to your fighters," Wally advised. "We're trying to send them signals with our lights. We're convinced the suspect jumped. Can you please, for the love of all that is holy, confirm that you're reading me?"

"How can you be sure, 197?" Rex replied.

"We noticed the change in elevation," Wally replied. "We think he leaped out about thirty miles back."

"Hang tight, 197," Rex replied. Rex switched radios, now channeling the men piloting the fighters. "Eagles 1 and 2, are you sure you don't see our man back there?"

"Negative," the pilot responded. "In fact, it looks like 197 is having quite a bit of a light show out here. I broke it down in Morse, and they're definitely spelling the word 'jump,' please advise."

Rex dropped the radio to the desk in front of him, defeated. His face followed, hanging low as the realization that he'd fucked up set in. There was no point in doing any damage to Flight 197 now. He'd be the laughing stock of D.C. if he wasn't already. The only thing left he could do now was go after Al with the resources he currently had, and on a holiday weekend, they were limited. He was determined not to quit, and he grabbed the radio one final time before saying, "Alright, Eagles 1 and 2, pack it in and end the pursuit. Do not fire on the target, repeat, do not fire on the target. Circle back and see if you can find him. We'll meet him on the ground."

"Copy that, Phoenix," the pilots responded in unison.

The voices in the room erupted in a low rumble that was mixed with the tones of relief and sighs. Rex stared off into the night sky through the control tower, not sure if he was more angry with Al or himself. For now, the threat was over, but the *real* chase was just beginning.

"You did the right thing," JG said to Rex. The words didn't hold much weight. JG wasn't his boss, and he wasn't cutting his paycheck. He also didn't have the power to move him back into a position of authority, and though Rex too felt relief that the high-stakes portion was finished, he knew that the next seventy-two hours of narrowing the search field would be grueling.

Rex moved to the en route controller behind the controls in the tower. "What's 197's location right now?"

The en route controller checked the chart in front of him. "Looks like the latitude is roughly 34.9083543 degrees and the longitude is —111.4632051 degrees with a heading of 90."

Rex turned to the men standing idly by. They were eager and ready for their next command. They too knew their weekend was about to become anything but a holiday. But now that Flight 197 was safe, they were armed and ready to begin the hunt for Al Ader. "I want all data collected immediately," Rex yelled. "Current location, area maps, topography charts, air speed. If it helps us, I want it. Call every fucking cop and agent in the surrounding states and tell them to get to work. I don't care if they're on vacation. If they're sleeping, wake them up. We need every pair of eyes we can get. "

Mitch hustled over to Rex, always ready for the next task. "What can I do?"

"Get the cars ready. We're heading out," Rex replied. "And get us some damn coffee."

"Otto," Rex said, turning to the southerner whose cigar had burned down so far it looked like he was smoking a small stick of glowing ash. "I want you to get to

LA and meet the plane on the ground. Round up the flight crew and get as much information as you can. Search every fucking nook and cranny on that plane it until you're positive a fly couldn't hide in it."

"Yessir," Otto responded, and he was already on his way out before the word even left his mouth, a trail of cigar smoke following with him.

The men had rallied and left the room so quickly that the only two people left were JG and Rex. Rex had calmed down a bit, but he was still disappointed JG had involuntarily aided Al. He and JG had the same interests, he recognized that, but their approaches had been drastically different.

"I guess we're going on a manhunt," JG said.

Rex turned to JG, his eyes fierce. "You'd better hope he died in the jump."

31

"They're back," Wally warned Robin and Tom as the fighters returned near the tail of the plane. All the color in his face had nearly vanished. While he'd been a relatively handsome man for his age, he looked like he'd aged ten years over the course of the night.

"We are royally fucked," Tom replied.

"Not if we get them the message," Wally rebutted.

"Yea, sure," Tom said sarcastically. "It's been a real privilege flyin' with ya', Wal."

"Don't talk like that," Wally replied. Tom's antics were making him angry, and now the two of them were bickering badly. Their calm and cool nature that came with experience had fallen apart.

"Quiet!" Robin snapped. "The more you two argue the harder it is for me to concentrate." Robin was still anxiously clicking the switches that controlled the exterior lights on the plane, alternating them on and off to spell out the word "jump" in Morse code.

"J...U...M...P..." Robin said silently to herself, alternating the switches with a zen-like concentration. "Maybe they're telling the truth at ATC," Robin offered. "Maybe they're just staying with us until we return safely?"

"And why would they do that?" Tom argued. "Keep signaling!"

"I spent enough time in Annapolis to know what a strike formation looks like," Wally replied. "I signed up for this job to *stop* getting shot at by fighters."

"Maybe the bastard didn't jump," Tom offered. "He might still be back there tryin' to pull a fast one. It'd be a hell of a getaway if he stowed on the plane and they missed him when we landed."

"That's impossible, and you know it," Wally argued. "That'd be the stupidest idea anyone ever came up with."

"Is it working?" Robin asked.

"Yea." Wally craned his neck out the front windshield. "I can see it in the clouds. Just keep it going, same frequency. Keep repeating it." She was unsure if her attempts at salvaging the dire situation were in vain, but they had run out of options. Everyone in the cockpit was convinced that if they didn't get the note to the fighter pilots soon, they were going to fire.

"We can't be sure he jumped," Tom exclaimed. He was panicking. "We've been repeating the message for nearly five minutes and they're still trailing us for God's sake!"

"We all felt it," Wally asked. "The change in elevation even registered on the controls." Only moments earlier, Al's leap into the black void above Arizona had shifted the weight of the plane enough that it shook noticeably, and after that, Wally was convinced the crazy bastard had actually done it.

A loud scream emanated from the port side of the plane, and Wally peeked out of the windshield once more to get a look. The jets had joined each other and passed by Flight 197 before turning away. Wally's eyes lit up like bright bulbs, and he slapped Tom on the shoulder with a firm hand.

"They called them off!" Wally cheered. "They fucking called them off!" He clasped hands with Tom, and both erupted in a gleeful cheer like children who'd just won a big elementary basketball game. Tom turned and hugged Robin, nearly lifting her off her feet.

"You're a genius!" Tom exclaimed. "How the hell did you think of that?"

"I don't know!" Robin said, a smile stretching across her face that she couldn't have hidden if she wanted to. "I just considered how the hell anyone spoke before radios." She'd been beaten, broken, and scarred by the men surrounding her the better part of the day, and yet it was her quick thinking and resourcefulness that had passed the ultimate test. A quick flash of the plane tumbling into burning debris over the Arizona desert penetrated her thoughts, but it was easily assuaged by the reminder that she was still breathing, and the plane was now free and clear of all threats.

"I wouldn't have known the codes, though," Robin said, planting a hand on Wally's shoulder, "so I guess you're not old hat just yet." Wally turned momentarily, and placed his hand on top of hers.

"If today doesn't get you into a corporate office and behind a desk where you belong, I don't know what will," Wally assured her. "They put you to the test, and you passed."

"Hey," Tom began, "I'm sorry about...today. I got a little hot before, you know? Without you, we might not be having this conversation."

"Don't mention it," Robin replied. "I think we were all a little on edge."

"Yea, but you got bigger balls than I do," Tom replied. "I can't believe you a drew a gun on the moron. What the hell were you thinking?"

After a moment of pause, the group erupted in laughter. It was, Robin admitted, a bit aggressive, and had backfired in the end. What mattered was that they were here and safe, and Al Ader was long gone. Nothing else could go wrong.

A beeping sound interrupted their temporary reprieve, and before Robin could even find the source, she knew something was terribly wrong. The plane started to roll on its starboard side, and suddenly the flight became very choppy again. Every piece of aluminum on the plane began to rattle. The plane was sinking—Robin could feel it in the pit of her stomach.

"Shit!" Wally yelled, "We just lost engine two!"

Tom immediately turned to face the controls flanking him, and a blinking light indicated the same. "It's the landing gear. It's giving us too much god damn resistance."

"No," Wally said, "it's the staircase, we've got to get that staircase shut. Cut the fuel!" Tom was now assuming his position as copilot, and the reality of the situation smacked Robin hard—they weren't out of the woods yet. If the mental punch wasn't enough, the plane jerked slightly, nearly knocking her over as she braced herself in the tight quarters. The atmosphere was becoming unruly, and a plane not flying in its best shape, with its landing gear fully extended and a staircase flapping in the wind was just asking for trouble.

"I've got it," Robin said, and she flung the cockpit door

open and once again found herself in the guts of the plane. This time, the environment was ghostly and empty. Now that Al and the other passengers had vacated, she was alone. The only company she had was the cash that was still circulating around the interior of the plane like she was in some kind of monetary bingo machine. The gusts of air stemming from the rear of the plane were violent, and the plane had become icy cold in direct contrast to the unrelenting heat they had experienced on the ground in Phoenix.

Robin had assured the pilots she was capable of shutting the staircase, but she considered now that she may have spoken too soon. Climbing through the fuselage was akin to maneuvering an obstacle course. The masks that had deployed from above the seats were swaying like tendrils seeking to grab on to her and prevent her from getting the flight crew to safety. With every gust of wind, the air nearly knocked her back a few rows. Each time she lurched forward and gripped the headrest of a seat, she had to clench the fabric so tightly she was convinced the bones in her knuckles were going to tear directly through the skin.

The staircase was bouncing up and down on its hinges every time the plane had changed even the slightest amount in altitude. The staircase reoriented itself with gravity followed by deafening, screeching sounds. If all the variables working against Robin combined weren't enough, debris from the patrons on board not long ago seemed to attack her like rogue projectiles every time the pilots adjusted the plane.

She made a quick sprint for the rear, and after passing by several more rows, she felt the plane's nose aim downward behind her, and now she wasn't just fighting the havoc of the plane's contents, but also gravity itself. She pulled at one of the seats with all her might, gathering a strength she was unaware she even had in her, and now she was in the middle of the fuselage—halfway.

The plane dipped again, and Al's briefcase came careening toward her, nearly hitting every seat on its way as it bounced frantically toward her. She ducked her head with only a fraction of a second to spare, and the briefcase continued toward the front of the plane until it smacked the cockpit door with a thud. She turned to look at it. The clasps had broken free and the "bomb" was now exposed. Robin—for the first time—was thankful that Al had decided to dupe them with the phony mechanism, because if it had been real, she wondered if the impact might have blown them up midair. She didn't much know how bombs worked, but she didn't think any type of abrasive treatment of an explosive like it had just endured was in any way safe.

She hustled forward once again, every mask that had been waving to and fro now trying desperately to grab hold of her wrists. She fell to the ground, nearly smacking her chin against the hard floor below her. Down low, she found, there was far less resistance, and so she began to crawl as fast as she could. Remaining upright might make her body like a sail, and she continued to pull herself toward the staircase as the plane reoriented itself once again.

Now the nose of the plane was pointing upward, and she tumbled down the aisle and toward the gaping hole and the night sky behind it. She was struggling to brace herself before catching the last seat, the cavity before taunting her like a hungry mouth flapping its jaws and intent on swallowing her whole. She heard the sound of the starboard engine stuttering, and she was thankful that the men up front were trying hard to get it started. She wasn't sure how much more of this fun house she could take.

The engine would not come to life, though, and she heard the sound of the port-side engine roar loudly as it picked up the slack for the unresponsive one.

Luckily, the plane turned on its starboard side for a moment, and as she rose to her feet, Robin found herself face to face with the large lever she'd used to open the damn staircase in the first place. She grabbed it with both hands, pulling the level with all the force she had inside of her, but the lever didn't budge. She gripped tightly again, letting out a grunt so loud the flight crew might have heard it in the cockpit.

She paused for a moment, catching her breathe before she ruptured the blood vessels in her checks from the strenuous activity. "Always the hero," she heard the faint voice of Al say in her head. He was right, she'd always been the hero, and she wasn't going let some faulty lever stop her. She grabbed it once more, leaning all of her body weight into it and pulling with every fiber connecting every piece of muscle tissue in her body, and with a welcome screech, the staircase slammed shut.

The plane went nearly silent save for the scream of the port engine doing double duty. Every piece of debris inside the cabin went idle, and the only other movement she could see was the floating cash begin to settle to the ground in a flurry of falling, fluttering green paper. She paused for a moment, praying to herself that this would be absolutely the last curveball she was thrown today.

She made her way back to the cockpit, the calming silence welcome, and thought about giving corporate—

specifically that asshole Van Cortland—a piece of her mind regarding aft staircases and their usefulness in the field. She couldn't help but wonder just how, or even if, Al had survived that jump. But he'd been full of surprises, and she considered that if anyone was going to get away with it, it was probably *him*.

"Aft staircase is closed," Tom said to Wally.

"You're welcome," Robin said when she appeared. She wiped the sweat from her cheek with the back of her hand. If she was honest, she was looking forward to seeing Glenn, but she was looking forward even more to getting out of the uniform and taking a shower. She'd sweat in places she never knew possible over the course of the day, and her skin had a permanent sheen to it from the oils that had continually seeped from her pores. Her makeup was a mess, but at this point, it was the least of her concerns.

"Looks like I owe you one again, Robin," Wally turned and said.

"Just get the damn engine back up," Robin replied, slumping against the wall of the cockpit. Wally was fiddling with the controls for the flaps on the plane to compensate for the fact that the second engine was of no use currently, and constant adjustments needed to be made if they were to continue like this. Tom tried again to start the engine, but all it returned was a sputtering sound. Tom killed it once more, and Wally grabbed the control stick firmly with both hands.

"Hang on," Wally said and positioned the stick in such a way that the plane rapidly descended. "Try again!"

Tom took another stab at it, and after what seemed like a moment of choking, the engine received the welcome ram air it needed to finally become operational.

The plane leveled out, and as the aircraft cut through a thick swath of clouds, it came out into a clear, open sky peppered with stars.

On the horizon, a range of mountains could be seen clearly in the bright glow of the moon. It was picturesque, and Robin, Wally, and Tom stared silently at it for a moment as the plane traveled toward it.

Tom grabbed the transponder and positioned it near his face. "This is EA 197 requesting landing."

"Landing granted, 197," the man in the control tower replied. "How does Denver look to you?"

"No," Robin replied abruptly. Wally and Tom turned to her, surprised by her assertiveness in the cockpit. Flight attendants didn't get to make calls like that, but as far as she was concerned, she'd earned it. "The bomb is still on board. He made it clear we should land at LAX," she reasoned with the two men.

"How much fuel do we have?" Wally asked Tom. He didn't break his gaze with Robin as he waited for the report.

"Roughly 3,800 gallons," Tom replied.

Wally waited for a moment before responding, the transponder waiting idly in his hand as his eyes stayed locked with Robin's. The man named Al Ader was gone and they were still fulfilling his demands. He considered that she was bluffing, but who was he to argue? They could get to LA with relative ease, and though Wally wanted to be out of the damn plane, he saw no reason to fight her on it. "LAX it is," he said to Robin with a smile. "Negative, ATC. We're requesting touchdown at LAX for security reasons. We would like to climb to 34,000 feet for the duration of the flight. The drag on the craft has caused us to bleed out a bit more than usual."

"Copy that, 197. You are good to go for LAX, and you just sit where you are comfy. The airways are clear," the air traffic controller replied. "It's good have you back."

Robin fell into the seat that Jeff had occupied for the initial part of the flight and rested her eyes. For the first time since the plane had left Los Angeles, the journey was calm. They'd be home soon—hopefully.

32

Although Al would have loved nothing more than to continue resting, he had to work to finish. He was quite literally not out of the woods. He heard the faint shrieking of the jets high above him, and considered that they might still be in the area.

They would no doubt be on the hunt for him. Even in the dark, the bright red parachute was large enough that they might be able to spot it. He would need to spread it out first to fold it properly if he was going to fit it back in the bag. Now that the parachute didn't have the drag of the lake holding it back, the water-resistant nylon fabric was surprisingly light again.

Al folded the parachute neatly into small squares. He wouldn't need to make sure it could be redeployed, because he had no intention of making a jump like that ever again. He just needed it to be manageable enough to carry. After confirming it would fit, he crammed it back inside the bag.

Thick swaths of trees lay in front of him, and he waited until he got nearer to the tree line to remove his shoes from his jacket. He flicked the water-logged loafers, trying to rid them of any excess water he could. They were drenched, unfortunately, but at least he had something. He had no intentions of making this trek barefoot, and that would make it a totally different adventure all together.

When Al arrived at the tree line, he placed them on his feet. Footprints in the forest would be unavoidable, but he didn't want to leave perfectly shaped evidence of his shoes in the sand for anyone to find. That type of laziness would at the minimum tip anyone off as to the direction in which he had begun his journey. When he started, he felt the firearm digging into his back now that he was walking again and removed it, tossing it as far as he could into the lake. It hit the water with a heavy plunk, and he was confident that it sunk deep enough that it would be a long time before anyone found it. He had no use for a weapon at this point, and it was unlikely they would ever find it in the bottom of that lake.

After removing a small compass from his pocket, he guided it around, left and right, seeking a northern reading. North was directly through the forest in front of him. There was a road, the name of which escaped his mind, to the east of the lake, wedged in between the still unfinished I-17 and Highway 40. It was often closed in the winter, and Al thought it might be a good anchor to keep consistent in case something went wrong with his compass. Of course, it was foolish to think something would go wrong with something as primitive as a compass, but he could leave no room for error this far into the act. The road ahead, assuming he even found the damn thing, eventually led to both Lower and Upper Lake Mary. If he could just manage to follow that far enough, the landmark would help him calculate how far he had left until he reached Flagstaff. Mormon Lake had not been his intended landing zone, but as of now, it seemed it was turning out just fine.

The area was mostly empty—there was an effort to conserve the protected land that had become known as Coconino National Forest. Its obscurity would continue to afford him good cover, and there wasn't much out that deep in the wilderness in the way of residential pockets. It was going to be quiet for the rest of the night. All he would need to do was look for the lights of Flagstaff, and Al was confident they would eventually reveal themselves if he stayed on target. He still had a long road ahead, but during the final leg of the trip, he needed to find a place to dispose of some baggage.

As he continued north, ensuring a touch of easterly bearing every so often as he moved along, Al found a clearing in between the trees that would be a safe place to dispose of the cash. Uncontrollable fires were a serious risk this far out, and his goal was not to destroy precious land or endanger other people's property. He walked out to the clearing and removed the duffel bag from his body. Inside his breast pocket, Al had secured a small plastic pouch containing a book of matches. He had anticipated that inclement weather could play a factor, and although he hadn't considered a lake, the precaution had paid off nonetheless.

Al unzipped the bag and was impressed to find it had kept the cash remarkably dry. *Leave it to the feds to have good canvas material to protect their assets*, he thought to himself. Al removed the bills stack by stack and piled them up neatly, then arranged them into a pyre. He was glad they had not become as wet as *he* had.

He struck a match against the back of the booklet and held it under the small space in the pile he had created to ensure some flow of oxygen. The bills began to slowly catch fire, forming a small pile of ember as the cash disintegrated. As the fire continued to burn, the bills began to flake like fireworks against the black void of the night sky. This was the element of the heist that would transform his crime into something *more*. The pile was burning unevenly, which would leave a nice trace amount of evidence behind so they could witness his handiwork and, in turn, receive the *message*. He had made it loud and clear on more than one occasion, but why not throw in a visual aid for the feds and the papers?

A dog in the distance began to bark. Al worried that he had alerted it to his presence with his ceremony. He had thought it likely that he was alone, but surely he could use this to his advantage. If someone was aware of what was happening out in the clearing, they might come investigate a fire like this. Better yet, if they caught the news over the television and directed the local officials to look here for clues once they found the embers, they would surely be able to witness Al's tribute firsthand.

The television, Al said to himself, his eyes glowing a bright orange as the pile in front of him smoldered. He'd barely seen any press during his time on the ground in Phoenix, but he was sure they were present. What had they said about him? Were people tuned in? Had he captivated an audience as much as he had hoped? He wouldn't know until he got in front of a television or newspaper himself, and that was a still a ways off. For now, he could only dream.

There'd be plenty of time to revel in his success, but for now, it was time to go. Al couldn't risk anyone identifying him out here, and he once again set forward into another thick pocket of trees. The needle attached to the compass in his hand pointed steadily north with just a hair of eastern bearing. He had to get to Flagstaff as fast as he could, and in his most weakened—but inspired—state yet, it wouldn't be easy. The man who disappeared into the sky had now disappeared into the forest.

33

———

W hen Flight 197 finally touched down at LAX, Robin was more excited to kiss the ground than Glenn. Just as in Phoenix, authorities quickly swarmed the plane in transit before the brake dust had even dissipated. Robin didn't think it likely that Al was still on the plane. She'd all but seen him jump, but who could be sure?

Though she was relieved to be free of the madness, it was unlikely that she would be returning home anytime soon. She'd expected that there would be an onslaught of questioning before she was back in her bed where her day had started. There was no way the boys in blue were going to just let the flight crew go on about their business.

"Boys," Robin said to Wally and Tom, "it's been a privilege flying with you."

"And you," Wally replied.

"We might not be here without you," Tom added. "I half expect to be calling you boss soon enough, Miss Kraft."

"Well, for starters, when I get back you should be

calling me *Mrs.*," Robin said as she unbuckled her seat belt.

One of the agents outside tapped on the nose of the plane, and Wally climbed from his seat to take a look. The man standing below waved his arm toward the back door, and Wally took that to mean he wanted them to open the aft staircase. If Robin had anything to say about it, it would be the last time anyone opened an aft staircase on an airplane, and she was of half a mind to give Van Cortland hell about it when she finally had some time to cool down.

Robin led the two men behind her on their final trek down the corridor to the rear of the plane just as she had when trying to keep them safe. She grabbed the lever and opened the staircase. The motion was much easier than it had been at ten thousand feet, a minor relief that went a long way after the night she'd had. She wanted more than anything to get off the plane, but when the door opened, men flooded into the plane with guns drawn—and the stark realization set it in that they wouldn't be going *anywhere* just yet.

"On the ground!" One of the agents waved a pistol in Robin's face. The three remaining civilians quickly complied, and before Robin and the crew had a moment to speak, a handful of agents stepped over their bodies and moved immediately toward the cockpit. The sound of heavy boots clomping near the crew's faces was quickly followed by the firm grip of handcuffs around their wrists.

"Is this necessary?" Wally shouted. "We're the goddamn flight crew, you morons. Your man's gone!"

"Relax," Otto told the agent that had seen fit to cuff the flight crew. The cold metal was nearly locked around Robin's wrist, but the agent took them off before he could finish the job. Otto stretched a hand toward Robin, helping her up to her feet before he said, "Sorry. He's new. A little excited is all. Miss Kraft, I presume?"

"I am," Robin replied. Wally was busy muttering curses under his breath as the agents behind him tore the plane apart. They were practically ripping the seat cushions off of their chairs and breaking the overhead compartment doors off their hinges. "And you are?"

"You can call me Otto," he replied. "You know, Miss Kraft, I seen a lot o' shit in my life. I seen a lot of real dangerous situations go out of control real fast, and I gotta say, you did good."

Robin blushed for a moment. "I was just doing my job."

"Call it whatever you want," Otto replied, "but the papers already got a hold of your name, and well, they're gonna see it the way *they* do. Everybody on the flight sure did. Same with my people. That stunt with the gun?" Otto began to laugh. "Man, you got some balls. I knew the old man was up to somethin', but I didn't expect that. I can't believe you followed through."

"That didn't work so well," Robin responded.

"Maybe not," Otto said, "but you tried. Besides, it was real funny seein' the boss get so worked up."

"Funny?" Robin replied, a mixture of confusion and anger plastered from to cheek to cheek.

"Well," Otto said. "Ain't nothin' funny about all this. I catch your drift. Still, I think we were all of half a mind that Ader didn't plan on blowing up that plane. The boss's got a bit of a vendetta, and it was just a hoot to see him lose his marbles because *your* boss decided to try his hand." Robin chuckled for a moment. There *was* something kind funny about the whole ordeal now that she was so far removed from it all.

"Sir," the young, eager agent called out, the briefcase dangling from his hand.

"Careful with that, you knucklehead," Otto replied. He turned to Robin, shaking his head. "Kids."

"You know what you said about Ader," Robin began. "About not worrying that he wasn't going to blow up the plane?"

"Yea," Otto replied.

"Well," Robin said, "you'd be right."

Otto eyed her curiously for a moment, then turned to the young agent handling the briefcase. He snapped his fingers at the newby agent. "Hey, bring that over."

Wally and Tom were becoming restless, and before the briefcase arrived, Wally checked his watch. "My turkey's getting cold."

"Now just hang on," Otto answered. "I know you all want to go home, but you're going to need to be debriefed first. If you think this is going to be a holiday weekend, it's going to be anything *but*. I'm sorry, but that's the way this has to play. The next few weeks you're going to be seeing a lot of our faces, and when we catch the bastard—"

"If," Robin interrupted.

"If we catch him," Otto continued, "best believe that you three, among others, are going to be testifying at his trial."

"It's unlikely there will be a trial," Robin said.

"And what makes you say that?" Otto asked.

"Because he'll probably die before you catch him."

"As heartbreaking as that would be, I won't disagree with you," Otto replied. The agent laid the briefcase on the seat in front of Otto and grabbed both clasps with his fingers. He carefully opened it, still wary about what he might find, and inside was only the art project that Al Ader had crafted to *look* like a bomb.

"I'll be damned," Otto said with a snort. "Certainly looks the part." His hands traced a set of wires leading to and from the paper cylinders that resembled dynamite. He pressed down on them, and what he found didn't resist like tightly packed powder, but gave like paper. "Cardboard and a watch battery. At least your instincts were right," he said to Robin. "Now that we know what we know, it's safe to say you could have shot him when you had the chance."

"I'm not a murderer," Robin replied.

Otto turned to face her, his eyes dark and hollow. "It ain't murder if you're savin' lives." Otto turned to the agents at the front of the plane. "How are we looking up there?"

"Clear, sir," one of the agents in the cockpit called out.

"Well?" Tom asked impatiently.

"Alright," Otto started. "Unless he's hiding in the cargo hold, or underneath your uniforms—which I highly doubt—we're clear to get out of here. Follow me." Otto addressed the bevy of men currently turning the plane upside down. "I want every single thing that isn't bolted down in a collection bin, but not before we get photographs and dust for prints." Otto turned to the seat Al had been sitting in. "Especially that one."

"No," Robin said. Otto had pointed to seat 15B, and Robin redirected him toward 18C and 18B, where Al had spent the majority of his journey. "Those two."

"Ya know what?" Otto said to his team. "Just get prints from all of them. Dust *every* square inch of this plane for prints. We'll check them against the ones we pulled from the manifest. After y'all," Otto said, guiding Robin, Wally, and Tom down the staircase and off the plane.

As Robin walked across the tarmac, all she could think about was Al. She was curious whether he had ever even gotten where he was going. *She* had landed, but had he? She couldn't shake the strange feeling that she actually *wanted* him to succeed. It was uncharacteristic of her—the idea that she wanted the man who had recently held a gun to her temple to get away with it—but if she was being truthful, she'd been more angry with the way the Feds and Van Cortland had responded than what Al had done.

Al had forced her to play along with his game, but so had *they*. Al had kept her safe, but Van Cortland had endangered her, and Agent Schulz had likely sent the jets to follow them. Now that she was free and clear of the near-disaster, she wondered if Al had actually ever put her in any *real* danger. The bomb was a fake, and he'd certainly had no intention of shooting her. He certainly had the opportunity, and the only time she'd ever experienced any unwanted physical contact was the drunk man who got handsy. And after all, it was *Al* who set him straight. She quickly dismissed the thoughts when she started to feel sympathy. Al *was* a criminal, but fuck if he wasn't a good one.

After climbing the staircase and reaching the door that led inside the airport terminal, Otto stopped, his hand lingering on the handle. He combed his hair quickly with his free hand and took a deep breath before turning to Wally, Tom, and Robin before saying, "Are y'all ready for this?"

"For what?" Robin asked.

"Just... " Otto struggled to find the words, "keep your

head down and don't answer any questions. Stay close to me and don't make any eye contact. We're going to take you to a secure room where we can just ask some questions, and then you'll be free to go. I'm sure your significant others are waiting for y'all, and I don't want to keep you any longer than we have to. If I had it my way, y'all would head on home right now, but the boys on top gotta know what they gotta know, and right now y'all got more answers than anyone. There's a man on the run out there, and we got a very narrow window of findin' him. Right now, you're our best bet in figuring out the way he looked, or the way he thinks—anything that can help us narrow it down. Understand?"

"Yes," the flight crew said unison.

"Good," Otto said before twisting the door handle. "Smile, if you want. You're about to be famous."

Otto opened the door, and a roar of voices flooded the room as Robin, Wally, and Tom entered. Robin couldn't remember if she'd ever seen so many people in one place, and though there were no barricades or roped-off sections to keep the press at bay, the local police did their best to give the flight crew a clear path through which to navigate. The amount of flashes from the cameras that they experienced within a few short seconds was so dizzying that Wally thought he might have a seizure, and Tom started to see spots from the flurry of snapping lights. Robin, for the first time ever, was happy she had not had the money to hire a photographer for the wedding.

They were met with a barrage of questions and microphones thrust in their faces from the people standing by. Each fought for their attention and an opportunity for a photo or sound bite.

"Were you scared?" one of the news gatherers called out.

"What did he look like?" another screamed even louder.

"Can you confirm the hijacker's name?" a tall woman that stood out from the multitude of men vying for attention spoke even louder.

"Did you ever think you might die?" yet another photographer called out before flashing the bulb sitting above his camera. Robin was convinced that if she didn't get out of the room soon, she might just faint.

Though the number of bodies in the room barred any of the crew from getting a good look at the sea of people screaming their names, Robin was on the hunt for one person in particular: Glenn. Otto ushered them through the chaos. "Please, no questions right now. We'll have a press conference later. Right now we need to get these people to a debriefing. They've had a long night, and they're very tired."

"Miss Kraft," the tall woman yelled out, "people are calling you a hero. Would you agree?" Before Robin could even acknowledge the woman, she saw one particular man dead ahead that stood out from the crowd. He was handsome, with a sandy blonde mop of hair hanging from his head, and the look of concern in his eyes was undeniable. She never thought he looked so handsome in his life. She hustled toward him, her arms outstretched, and he pushed through the mob of people that had been blocking his view and ran to meet her.

When Robin and Glenn finally met, they embraced so hard that she thought he might actually injure her. For that moment, time seemed to stand still. She couldn't hear any of the questions and couldn't see any of the obnoxious flashes that had been flickering from all angles. She was back with Glenn, and the only thought crossing her mind in the moment was how guilty she had felt that she'd hadn't helped with the turkey as she had promised. She would make it a priority to show him how to cook his own damn turkey.

34

A l was caught in a dream-like state of euphoria as his legs kicked into autopilot. He wasn't at a full run, but his stride was more akin to a jog. He'd slammed down the last of his pills, which he prayed would get him to at least where he needed to go. How far had he gone so far? He'd lost track. If he was running ten or twelve minutes or so per mile—and that was still ambitious—he must have already covered at least five or six miles. He had roughly twenty to go.

An owl was hooting, watching him from a tall tree in hiding. He would be the only witness of Al's whereabouts, and since he couldn't communicate with the authorities, Al wasn't worried. What bothered Al was that at this point in his trip, anyone official looking would have a better chance of seeing him than he did of seeing them.

After a good fifty or sixty minutes, he felt an itchiness on his face. He had become so accustomed to the final element of his disguise—and had been so engrossed in the character of Al—that he had completely forgotten he had applied it. He paused for a moment and ran his fingers along his jawline. His nails found a small flaking near his chin where his skin met a material that felt less like his skin and more like latex—the prosthetics he had applied before his departure from the hotel.

He pulled at the prosthetics slowly in attempt to remove large pieces where the material had started to fail. He was sure they had seen their fair share of punishment throughout the stressful day, and as he scratched at the layer that covered his cheeks, it began to come off with ease. The cold water must have made them less pliable, Al thought, and he continued the process of detaching them. It was the element added to the character that he was most proud of. Whether or not anyone had a good idea of what Al Ader looked like was irrelevant. He'd never look like that again.

As a child, Al had collected tiny classic horror figurines, and when he came of age to read, he pored over books related to the making of the iconic pieces of cinema. Little did he know that one day, he too, would become a sort of mythical monster of his own making. Al had been very fond of the work of Jack Pierce—the mastermind that had transformed the handsome Boris Karloff into the terrifying Frankenstein's monster from the classic picture. Although Al did not require the level of detail that James Whale had perfected for the character, some simple lessons in prosthetic application had been sufficient to transform his appearance enough to not only hide his sickly nature, but more importantly, any recognition of his true identity.

Al tore the last piece from his cheek—a long piece of translucent elastic that had worked its way around his jaw and toward his eye—wiping his skin thoroughly to remove any debris remaining. At that moment, Al Ader died, and Jack would follow soon after. Although Al's time was short, and he hadn't received a proper funeral, the ceremonial fire seemed a fitting send-off. In the short time Al had existed, he had experienced more thrills than most people would in a life time.

"Godspeed, Al Ader," the returning Jack said to himself out loud. With the final element that made him like someone else entirely gone, it did not seem fitting to keep Al along for the ride any longer. He'd done his job, and he'd done it well.

Jack deposited the prosthetics inside his pocket, remembering to remove the ones he had coated his fingertips with as well. Gloves would have been too obvious, and potentially even hindered his actions when the going got tough. Simply applying the latex-like substance to the tips had sufficed to conceal his fingerprints—or so he hoped. The Feds would certainly find prints, but they'd never find anything in any record that would alert them to any information of value.

Jack—as he'd eased back in to thinking of himself as —looked down toward his pocket and noticed that the mother-of-pearl tie clip he had applied was missing. He must have lost it during the scuffle with Robin. He had been holding her tightly to his chest when he forced her into the hostage role, and it was likely that it had ripped from the fabric. While it did hurt a bit that Jack had lost the only item connecting him to his father, he too would forever be part of this fable if the clip became evidence. It, along with the fake bomb, would be the only clues left behind on the aircraft. Jack pictured the disgruntled faces of the bomb squad when Robin informed them that the explosive had been non-operational all along and chuckled as he continued deeper into the forest. He just hoped that she had made it to LAX, but he had no way of knowing that until he was in front of a television. She was resourceful, though, as he had learned, and he was confident she *had*.

With a third wind kicking in, an energy boost that gave him a resolve almost like meditation, he set off on a jog northwest toward Flagstaff. He spent most of the trip fantasizing about the stories that by now, he was sure, had captivated America—and potentially even the world. The idea that he had dominated even a holiday news cycle kept him going as the muscles in his legs begged and screamed for him to stop. He had never run a marathon in his life, but the amount of energy that flowed through him was like something out of one of those life-or-death situations he had heard of in which humans are capable of extraordinary feats. He'd read one of those stories once about a mother lifting a car to save her child. He never really believed them, but the night ahead was starting to change his mind.

There was a small gas station called Galaxy Oil and Tire near the historic Lowell Observatory. The Lowell Observatory's claim to fame was Clyde Tombaugh's discovery of Pluto via the Clark Telescope in 1930. The Perkins Telescope had moved nearby in 1961 after less-than-stellar results at its home in Ohio. It was the place Jack had designated for the rendezvous with his brother, Sam, and he chose it specifically because it was far away from prying eyes. The scientists had requested that the surrounding community keep the lighting at night to a minimum, which also kept the area dark. Darkness was quickly becoming his best friend—at least for the remainder of his quest.

Jack removed the pill bottle again from his pocket and

was disappointed to find he had an empty stock. He thought he had known that already when he rattled the empty bottle and yet now he was unsure. He was sure he had more, and then in a moment of confusion, he wondered whether the copious amounts of narcotics had begun to mess with his brain. It was either that or a lack of sleep combined with exhaustion, but it sent a tremor of fear rumbling through his body that he had thought he had harnessed finally.

No, not now, he muttered to himself. A war was waging within him, and now that he resembled Al less, he was returning to old habits. The ruse he had kept up was over, and his confidence was waning. Even *Harry Houdini* had died during one of his acts. He debated whether or not he would ever make it to the observatory as his heart pounded against his chest.

The observatory, he said to himself, and he thought of Sam again and the words he'd given him in the bar that day: "You need to make fear your ally. Harness it." Harry Houdini had died, but he certainly had not been *scared*. Jack just kept putting one foot in front of the other, his eyes laser-focused on the road ahead. The thought of his body decaying in the woods and being consumed by maggots was enough to keep him moving.

After trekking another hour or so, Jack checked his watch—he realized he was running unapologetically late; it was forty minutes after midnight. Still, he had traversed quite a bit of terrain in a short amount of time. He was amazed he had even made it as far as he did. The thought that there was a warm, cozy bed in his future coupled with the idea that he would be watching the news outlets report on his story was pushing him through the last leg at an accelerated speed—or maybe it was the drugs.

Either way, it was working. He just needed to stay out of his head.

Had he died on that trek, it might have been months before anyone even *found* his corpse. The wildlife surely would have picked him clean to the bone, and the authorities would be satisfied to find a lone skeleton with a parachute to successfully close their case. He was determined not to afford them that luxury.

Soon, Jack saw a noticeable change ahead: lights. There hadn't been an incandescent light source for miles. He'd been using the moon to navigate to the best of his ability, and now he was sure he'd hit his destination. He wasn't so sure where the time had gone—he didn't care. He prayed that it was indeed the lights of Flagstaff. He couldn't make another journey if he had detoured.

The dense trees quickly gave way to a break in the foliage, and when he came closer to it, it became clear that it was a *road*. He scanned the eastern and western route of the asphalt—he was convinced he was still facing north— and checked to make sure that no cars were present. It was so quiet he could hear the sound of his own heart. It was pounding at a rate of one hundred and seventy beats per minute. *How long can a heart even beat at that rate?* More importantly, *how long can an ill man's heart beat in that manner?*

Jack crept up to the guard rail that hugged the road so he could see what lay ahead. There, waiting in the shadows of the deserted Galaxy Oil and Tire gas station, was Sam's pickup truck.

He was flattered to know he could count on his brother—now an accomplice to the most wanted criminal on American soil—to wait, and Jack made his way toward the truck. He kept low to the ground, his heart finally slowing as he reduced his movement to a brisk walk. Sam saw him immediately, flashing his headlights three times to confirm it was indeed his brother. Jack stumbled as he neared the truck, and when he arrived at the fender, he finally collapsed from exhaustion. It was as if his body and brain had subconsciously reconciled the safe haven and hijacked *his* body, demanding it to give up. Sam ran out of the truck, helping Jack to his feet and into the passenger seat.

Jack's head was spinning. He felt a cool chill run up his spine now that his body had begun to cool down. He had been sweating most of the journey, and his lips were dry. He swallowed a dry, painful gulp and licked his lips to rehydrate, but all he tasted was blood.

"You crazy son of a bitch!" Sam started. "You did it! I don't know how the fuck you did it, but you did it!"

"Get me home first, then we can celebrate," Jack replied, exasperated.

Sam's face grew wary as he examined his brother in the dim light permeating from the dashboard. "You look like death."

"Fitting," Jack responded. "No more talk. I need a nap." He could barely get the words out. He heard the sound of the truck starting before everything went black.

35

The dead presidents on the faces of the smoldering pile of bills lying at Rex's feet were twisted and contorted in such a manner that he imagined they were laughing at him. The team that had arrived with Rex and JG—comprised mostly of federal officials, Arizona Police, and even fire officials—flooded the woods around the two defeated men, fanning out around the fire and cordoning the scene with yellow tape to indicate a crime scene. Groups of men quickly descended on to the available trail of footprints leading into the woods, the pile of cash, and the home nearby the site. A light rain had extinguished the fire, and had also begun to compromise the footprints in and around the scene—the only clue as to Al Ader's whereabouts. Despite the light rain that was quickly degrading the little evidence they had, Rex was thankful to have the light of day back on his side.

Mitch walked to the two men whose faces evidenced that they had not slept a lick during the night, pointing toward the house in the distance with his thumb. "Local called the fire department when he saw the fire. They're the 'L' series bills—definitely our man."

"And who is he?" Rex asked.

"Just a retiree—ex-lumberer," Mitch replied.

"Lock him down, too," Rex advised. "Everyone's a suspect."

One of the agents near the fire stepped through a series of footprints, and Rex nearly blew a gasket. "Don't walk through the fucking scene if you don't know how to do it properly!" The young man stopped dead in his tracks, struck with fear. Rex was on high alert. Perhaps the lack of sleep was getting to him, but it was more than likely the scene at his feet that was truly irking him.

The pyre at his feet confused him to no end. If he had been unclear about Al's motive the night before, his head was spinning now. Al had stuck a dagger in Rex's gut and poured salt in the wound to boot. Rex's eyes followed the trail of footprints leading from the pile of ash, eventually making his way to the thick sea of trees that seem to stretch almost infinitely. Where did it lead? He had no idea—at least not locally—but he knew that it was north.

JG had traded his fancy plaid jacket for one with FBI identifiers. He certainly, as far as Rex was concerned, had not earned it in any way. In fact, it felt like another slap in the face, but the sweltering heat the night before had been traded for a light chill deep in the woods, and the Fed jackets were warm. They weren't in the desert anymore. Where they stood seemed like an endless maze of possibilities for Al Ader to escape, and the realization that they might never find the mysterious Al Ader was becoming clearer to Rex and JG with every passing minute.

Despite the massive numbers of men that had come out to aid in the hunt, Rex had an uneasy feeling that the authorities would be chasing Al Ader for a very long time. Though JG felt the same, he was relieved to know that not a single soul had been killed, let alone injured. Still, the optics of the situation were not favorable, and JG was convinced that Eagle Airlines was going to have a very difficult road ahead. Worse, he had felt his age over the course of the last twenty-four hours more than ever.

"The APB was only in Arizona," Rex said to Mitch. "Expand it to California, Nevada, Utah, and New Mexico. Get some men down at the border as well. I want that sketch on every window and door in America."

"On it," Mitch said before hustling off. "Oh, sir." Rex tilted his head a bit, listening for Mitch's voice, but never removing his eyes from the pile before him. "Otto relayed a message from LAX."

"And?" Rex asked.

"The uh... " Mitch paused for a moment, "the device, well, it was a phony."

The silence between Rex and JG lingered for a moment. JG had compromised the mission, but ultimately Al Ader might have gotten away even if the entrepreneur hadn't intervened. Rex didn't have a plan. There just wasn't efficient protocol for situations like the one they'd just encountered. They could only handle it with compliance, and that was no way to deal with criminals like Al Ader—the tail was wagging the dog. When the dust settled, both Rex and JG would surely be tasked with making sure something like what happened to Eagle Airlines Flight 197 never happened again. They were at risk not only of people like Al, but copycats as well.

"I'll let that information absolve you of any sin," Rex said to JG. The two men didn't look at each other, but rather the scattered evidence at the crime scene. Rex didn't know if he had the courage in that moment to look JG in the eye, and JG didn't necessarily have it himself.

"Good," JG said sympathetically. "Because I didn't want to have to say I told you so." Rex's lip curled. If he wasn't so defeated, he would have released a laugh, but he just didn't have it in him. The axe was going to fall soon enough. He had a small window with which to catch Al, and even when he did, he was surely going to be chewed out for botching this job as the men above perceived he had the last. "I told you so," JG said. This time, Rex did laugh.

Rex turned to JG, a dispirited expression on his face. "He won."

"Did he?" JG asked, burying his hands in his pockets. The lack of movement was making him colder by the second, and the excitement he thought he might gain at the idea of finding the body of Al Ader twisted and broken in the woods did not warm him as he had hoped it would. "You saved those people's lives. Hell, you saved my company. We couldn't take another Flight 85. *I* couldn't take another Flight 85."

"It wasn't about them," Rex mumbled. The gum lodged between his teeth had become like chewing hard plastic. Rex was going to call it quits soon, but it was the only thing providing him comfort at the moment.

"It was about *him*," JG offered.

"My people don't like to lose, Jim," Rex began. "It's why we do what we do."

"You didn't lose yet," JG replied, his eyes wandering around the trees flanking him on nearly all sides. "Dead or alive, he's still out there."

"We lost," Rex corrected. JG knew he was right, but he didn't think it was the right moment to tell him that. The poor bastard had enough to deal with, and come Monday when the holiday weekend was over, the shit was probably going to be piled on so high there wasn't enough disinfectant in the world to keep Rex from being buried. JG had a shield of public relations people and a sword of attorneys—Rex did not.

"He's good," JG said. "You've got to hand it to him." JG knew it was the last thing Rex wanted to hear, but he couldn't help but say it. He was impressed in some sardonic way—he could admit that. If it hadn't happened to him, he might have even rooted for the criminal. Anyone with the balls to attempt a stunt like that deserved a pat on the back before they spent the rest of their life in jail.

"Maybe a genius," Rex said.

"Genius is a lofty word. He could have injured himself in the landing, in which case he's still somewhere out there, maybe even dead."

"Well then either he's a genius," Rex replied, "or this is the most expensive suicide in history." Just as Rex finished his thought, something in the pile caught his attention. The object was a piece of paper not quite like the cash that had been lit on fire. Instead it was white at the edges and decorated with an amalgamation of the colors blue, red, gold, and black. Rex leaned down toward the pile, scattering some of the charred bills out of the way. He knew better than to tamper with evidence, but he *had* to know what it was.

When he cleared enough debris away, he grabbed for the object and lifted it from the rest, pinching the corner with his fingers and fanning it out a bit before scrutinizing it. Now that he could see it clearly, he knew *exactly* what it was. It was a playing card.

He wiped the soot off of it with his jacket, clearing it away until it revealed itself clearly as a face card. It was a king, but not just any king, specifically the king of hearts, also known as the suicide king. The king stared back at Rex, the sword in its hand embedded nearly to the hilt in the king's head.

Rex twirled the burnt card in his hand for a moment, touching only the edges and taking care not to put his own fingerprints on it. If it was evidence, and if Al had left any of his own prints on it, then it might be important to the case. Surely, Al had left prints in and around the plane. The airport terminal was as good a place as any to start, but if he'd been careful not to touch anything, well then at least Rex had the card in front of him. He handed it to the agent who had begun inserting the cash from the fire into an evidence bag. "Bag that too."

Rex couldn't look at the fire any longer. The gum inside his mouth couldn't even be called gum any longer, and he removed it from his mouth and tossed it into a section of the woods that was free and clear of evidence. All Rex could think about was sleeping, but he had a long road ahead of him, and he knew for the better part of the weekend, if he was going to get any naps they would be in the back of federal vehicles and police cruisers. Rex didn't see much sleep in his future whatsoever.

The agents nearby had begun to fan out in even larger distances, now covering at least a one-hundred-yard radius in every direction, the center point of which was located where the money had been found. They'd brought German Shepherds with them to try to narrow down the whereabouts of the man who had leapt from the plane earlier the night before, but they didn't yet have a scent for them to track. They were likely wasting their time, but they had plenty of manpower, and they had to be sure there wasn't anything else to be found in the area.

One of the agents helping to bag the evidence crossed Rex's path, and as he did so, Rex got a whiff of the cigarette dangling between his lips. A cigarette had never smelled so good. He thought of his wife, Sandy, and what she might say if she knew he snuck one, but he felt he was owed a relief from the debacle.

"You got an extra smoke?" Rex asked the man.

"Of course, sir," the man replied, reaching into his pocket and pulling the pack out. Rex took one and used the man's still-burning cigarette to light his own.

"Thanks," Rex said. The man nodded, and Rex pulled on the cigarette so hard every square inch of his lungs felt it. They were filterless—raw and powerful. He coughed as he exhaled. It was the only moment of satisfaction he'd felt since he'd received the phone call the afternoon before.

"You know what I regret most?" Rex questioned JG.

"What?" JG asked.

"Picking up that phone yesterday."

"And why's that?"

"Because I never got any of that cranberry sauce my wife slaved over," Rex replied. "I love that damn sauce."

JG smiled at him, reminded for a moment that the man he'd come to blows with only hours earlier was not just a pawn or a machine in this game, but a man with feelings, opinions, and a family. There were no hard feelings, and they'd probably be seeing a bit more of each other over the course of the next year. "Happy Thanksgiving, Rex."

"Happy Thanksgiving, Jim," Rex replied.

36

Inside of Jack's eyelids, caught somewhere between sleep and a dream, an orange glow began to bleed into his psyche. When his eyes finally opened, they were met with the brightness of a clear blue sky. As Jack slowly became conscious and aware of his location, he realized he was still traveling in Sam's truck, but they were no longer on the interstate highways—they were driving through a quaint little mountain town. Nothing was open, of course, because it was a holiday. Despite his disorientation, Jack hadn't forgotten that so quickly.

Jack had slept the majority of the time—roughly eight hours. He had dozed off quickly every time he had intermittently woken up, and he never opened his eyes enough to initiate a conversation with Sam. He had warned Sam to observe the speed limit since he had hidden the parachute among tools in the bed of the truck. Though the prosthetics Jack had applied had concealed his *true* appearance, he was still wearing the same clothing. He was a wanted fugitive, and surely an alert with his description had been put out nationally to law enforcement. Still,

Sam had made good time, condensing the trip as much as possible.

Unfortunately, the time Jack spent in deep slumber had caused him to miss the scenic views of I-70 that lead through Utah, and through the Great Divide. Sam had constructed a small log cabin near Boulder that had given him a cozy life outside the sprawling cities of the country. Like Jack, Sam had cut ties with their mother, but he had done so at a much younger age. Jack had only fragmented memories of the three of them together during his infancy.

The two brothers had never discussed it, but Jack assumed that their mother harbored some resentment toward his brother as well. He had a different father than Jack, and he had been privy to stories that his father, too, had left his mother when she was young. Jack felt a tinge of remorse for his mother when he thought about it. Had she truly been an awful person, or had the blows that life had dealt her jaded her beyond recovery? His sympathy faded quickly when he recalled a memory of her splitting his head open with a whiskey tumbler she had hurled across the room one night, only to force him to tend to the wound himself. A friendly neighbor had taken Jack to the hospital the next day, and he was too young to place the blame on her, so he produced a fake story about a clumsy fall to the doctor and never spoke of it again. It was one of the first times Jack could remember her behavior, but not the last.

Jack didn't alert his brother when he woke, happy to have the moment of respite that he had earned. The truck rolled down a dirt road, and as a sea of trees parted, there Sam's cabin stood. Smoke funneled out of the chimney on top of the house, and two rocking chairs on the front porch finalized the model picture of coziness. Jack's theory was correct that this would be an excellent location to escape while the authorities' search commenced.

There were virtually no other homes nearby. They would surely be looking for Al Ader in the greater Arizona area, and perhaps, given the plane's eastward course, even New Mexico. Knowing what he knew about how badly the Feds would want to catch their man, Jack assumed that nowhere in the country was safe, but the least he could do was isolate himself as much as possible.

"Happy Thanksgiving," Sam said as the truck came to a stop.

"You as well," Jack replied. Sam had successfully escorted them far away from the search area, and Jack felt an overwhelming feeling of relaxation as he hopped out of the truck, grabbed the parachutes from the bed, and walked toward the front door to the house.

As Sam opened the door, Emmy ran out of the house toward Jack, screaming, "Uncle Jack!"

"Emmy," he said in his best Lugosi impression. "I want to suck your blood!" Jack blew a raspberry on her cheek, causing her to giggle uncontrollably.

"Why are you so dirty?" she asked, a bit repulsed. Jack had not considered that between his sallow cheeks and dirt-ridden body, he probably looked more like a home- less person than a master criminal.

"Come on, let's go inside," Jack said, and she ran in front of him, grabbing on to Sam's leg as she entered and giving him a limp that reminded Jack of Van Cortland's. Al Ader had certainly put the old man through the ringer, but he'd come out of this one—unlike the last—looking more like a rock star.

Immediately, Jack stripped his suit off. Although he

had dried off considerably during the long truck ride, he still felt an uncomfortable bit of grime and residue on his skin, a concoction of glue, sweat, and the water of Lake Mormon. After removing some of the tools from his clothing, but keeping the prosthetics in the pockets, Jack tossed the clothes and sunglasses in the fireplace, and the flames roared upon impact. With his clothing removed, the frail state of his body was visible, and Jack noticed Sam gawking at his torso while he set out to destroy the final bit of evidence: the parachutes.

Sam didn't say anything, but the look on his face was one of clear shock. There his bother stood before him, looking like the grim reaper would swing his scythe at any moment. Now almost nude, Jack himself thought he looked worse than he ever had, and he felt it too.

Jack grabbed the pack, looking one last time at the simple device that had carried him to safety, and placed it on top of the backup chute he had not used. After tossing them into the fire, he turned to Sam. "You might want to get some more wood. It will take a little while to burn if it's still wet."

Watching the parachute ignite was a liberating moment of hypnosis. Jack had officially tied up the last loose end, and it was unlikely any clues would be left along the way to connect him to the crime. A voice on the TV caught his attention as Emmy watched it intently.

"Breathtaking news out of Phoenix this morning as we listen to the testimonials firsthand from the flight crew aboard the hijacked Seattle-bound EA Flight 197," the anchor said in a desperate voice. Images of the crew being photographed by the press were presented on the screen, and Jack caught a glimpse of Robin—reunited with the person he could only assume was Glenn—as she was escorted away from the gate by the authorities. Jack hoped that they wouldn't question her, or the other flight crew, too vigorously. They had dealt with enough in the last twenty-four hours, and considering how admirably they had performed, they deserved some peace. It was unlikely they'd get it anytime soon.

"All crew and passengers were allowed safely off of the airplane after tense negotiations with the criminal conducted by the FAA and FBI," the anchor began again, and a poorly drawn sketch of Al in his sunglasses, with the mother of pearl clip secured neatly to his black tie, appeared on the screen.

"He looks a little like you, Uncle Jack!" Emmy said excitedly.

Christ, Jack thought to himself. One minute into the news program and a six-year-old had already correctly identified him.

"Okay, Emmy, time to go play," Sam said, lifting her off of the ground.

"Head Flight Attendant Robin Kraft is said to have successfully complied with the demands of the hijacker, effectively saving the lives of the thirty-six innocent people on board the aircraft," the anchor explained.

Sam shut the TV off before the anchor could continue. Although Jack was still interested in hearing how the media had reacted to the event, he needed a shower and a bed more than anything else in the world. The sleep he had enjoyed in the truck had not fully recharged his batteries enough to keep focus, and hopefully, although his body was still rapidly deteriorating, he would have time to hear more later. Jack didn't know *how much* time he had left.

He woke up after another nap to the warming glow of the setting sun winking at him from above the mountain outside his window. He thought he must have fallen asleep after lying down in the guest bedroom—though he didn't recall it. Sam had covered him with a blanket that now rested below his chin. He crawled out of bed, the ache in his body reminiscent of flu-like symptoms, and turned the dial on the television. Regardless of how poorly he felt physically, his brain was on a high of sorts. When the TV finally fired up, a different anchor than the one who had previously appeared was on the local evening news brief, and Jack caught the story detailing the events mid-story.

"The man, with only the given alias A.V. Ader, is believed to have jumped from the plane somewhere near the Coconino National Forest," the anchor said.

A.V. Ader? Jack thought to himself. What kind of *nonsense* is that? The note Jack had written was displayed on the screen. Jack realized he must have forgotten to retrieve it from Robin. He was sloppier than he thought. Jack remembered asking her to return it to him, but the excitement surely caused him to forget to retrieve it. On the note, a smear of ink had appeared next to the "L" in "Al," and he considered that perhaps either his own or Robin's sweaty fingers had vandalized the original penmanship. As silly as the mistake was, saying the name out loud phonetically gave Jack the biggest laugh yet, and he slapped his knee as he stared at the screen.

"Law enforcement is still on the hunt for Mr. Ader, and authorities believe he may have distributed the cash from the plane at an altitude of ten thousand feet before leaping. Although equipped with a parachute, it's likely that Mr. Ader, which the FBI doubts is his real name, died in the fall," the anchor said.

There it was. The FBI had to spin the story in their favor. They couldn't sleep with the fact that a man could pull off a stunt like that, and their embarrassment had coerced them into fudging the details for the press. *Good luck finding that body, though*, Jack thought.

The anchor resumed, "The FBI, along with California, New Mexico, and Utah law enforcement are asking for help in the search. Whether he is alive or dead, we're told there is a reward available for any information that leads to his discovery, or capture and conviction."

Sam entered the room rolling an IV drip on a stand. He planted it near Jack's bedside and began prepping a small needle with an alcohol swab as he continued to be glued to the television. The program was just starting to get *good*.

"The conditions in which Mr. Ader jumped were treacherous. His survival is strongly doubted. Nevertheless, the government will still be searching for his whereabouts, as well as for the money he may have kept, if any. It was certainly a large sum of money. The authorities met Mr. Ader's demand of $200,000 in cash, most of which the crazed criminal is believed to have jumped with. A list of the serial numbers printed on the money involved with the crime will be presented later in the program."

"All that money and you couldn't even save a buck? Not one measly buck?" Sam joked. "I drove across state lines in the middle of the night. What's that worth?"

"That wasn't the point," Jack responded. "And it would have put you in danger."

"I'm harboring a terrorist, Jack. I think you've done that yourself."

"Not for long," Jack said, turning away from him and gazing at the magnificent sun-washed mountainside. Sam opened a medical case, then tapped a vein on Jack's arm, searching for a place to insert the syringe. Having a brother who had spent a considerable amount of time in medical school had its benefits. Jack swatted him away and pulled his arm back under the covers.

"Come on. It's time for your medicine," Sam said.

"Not this time, Sam," Jack replied confidently, but his brother returned a frown.

"Jack—"

"I'm ready, and I'm tired of fighting," Jack assured him, echoing the final words of the icon who had inspired his stunt.

Sam gave up. "Can I get you anything?"

"How about a pen and some paper?" Jack asked before he left the room.

The anchor said finally, "Mr. Ader has already been labeled 'The Harry Houdini of modern-day hijacking.'" Jack's lips pursed a bit, producing a smile that grew from ear to ear and which he couldn't have hidden if he tried. "We'll be back shortly with more on this story."

"Try to rest," Sam said before leaving the room.

The news program quickly changed to a commercial for soda pop and Jack was left alone with his thoughts. He could barely remember the journey on foot after his fall from the plane. It was a blur of darkness and pain—the part of the stunt he didn't care to recall. Many of the events on the airliner were slipping from his memory as well. He could see Robin's face, but it was fading, and he had to concentrate particularly hard to try to visualize it.

The entire event felt like a fever dream that he had never really lived, but the information dominating the news cycle saw to it that no one would forget.

Surely the Feds would desperately try to convince the world he had died in the jump, but they would never find Jack—or Al for that matter—and as time elapsed, the case would only grow more intriguing. They also might lie that they had recovered the money, but with any luck, bills would sporadically pop up in time, whether from their release on the plane or in fragments from the ones that had not entirely burned.

They didn't like to lose, and it would certainly be an embarrassment as people all over the world wondered, "How did this happen?" Jack felt sorry for anyone who dared attempt to mimic his actions. Amateur copycats would surely claim to be him, or perhaps try it themselves using his alias. The Bureau would know if they found their man, and why anyone would want to incriminate themselves was beyond Jack, but he was sure that people might try to take the credit on their deathbeds if given the opportunity. After all, he was currently lying in his own, and he had considered leaving some teasing form of proof behind to be revealed when he was deceased.

Jack's life had been full of regrets and failures. It has been said every waking breath a person has is a gift, and as someone who had failed at taking advantage of that gift, Jack could say for sure it was sound advice. Everyone was going to die. It's the only thing a person can truly count on.

Jack had been dying since the day he was born, but when the doctor had given him a countdown designating his fate, he'd suddenly realized how much time he had squandered. Oddly enough, it was that severe diagnosis that had awarded Jack a new lease on the remaining time he had, and what propelled him forward. That realization had hypnotized him into taking the most daring display of defiance he could dream up. For the last twenty-four hours, he had *truly* been living.

As he watched the sun dip beneath the clouds, a poetic reminder of the previous night's events, he felt calm and fulfilled. Even though his demise was closer than ever, he no longer felt that same fear. He was scared, of course, but he also found a catharsis in the fact that his tale would outlive him. No one remembered Erik Weisz when he died, but they surely did remember Harry Houdini.

"No one will ever know your name," Jack's mother would always say. She was right. They wouldn't know his name, but Al, well they would sure know *his*.

THANKS

Thank you for reading *Incendiary*. I truly hope you enjoyed reading it as much as I enjoyed writing it. This book started as a screenplay, then became a first person novella, then reverted back to its third person roots and became a full novel. I'd like to thank Dale DeVino (and I truly recommend you check out *The Harbor Point Crime Series*) for supporting me through the learning experience of taking a manuscript to ebook and print. I already thanked my parents up front, but there's nothing wrong with saying "thank you" twice. I love you guys.

This is the first of many books I have planned for release. I'll be offering both stand-alone novels for those like me who like contained reads, but I'll also be releasing my first series very shortly. If you're enjoying my books, feel free to leave a review whoever you review books.

My next book up is the first of a World War II spy/thriller series. The first book is called *A Whisper in the Oaks*, a short read, and will be followed up by the first novel proper, *The Shadows of Might*. You can look for updates regarding its release in Winter of 2022 (and join my mailing list) at www.clarkemayer.com

ABOUT THE AUTHOR

Clarke Mayer is a filmmaker, photographer, and writer from New Jersey. Most of his day is dominated by a Black Mouth Cur named Pam who doesn't ever run out of energy. He likes to write, hike, and run, but most of all he likes to read and watch crime, spy, horror, and thriller stories.

CPSIA information can be obtained
at www.ICGtesting.com
Printed in the USA
LVHW030007091121
702796LV00005B/62

9 781735 547312